Dear Reader,

I can't tell you how much fun it was creating Callie, Julian and their very assorted mix of family and friends. I hope you have enjoyed meeting them, as well.

The character of Callie has been with me for some time, but my original idea was much different. Fortunately for me, Pooky just showed up one day insisting on being part of the show, and I am so glad he did.

On that note, I hope I have not inadvertently insulted anyone with my depiction of cross-dressers, and would like to take the time to apologize if I have. I have nothing but the utmost respect for anyone with the ability to walk their own road, despite whatever obstacles lie in their way. May God bless you, and keep you!

Please feel free to contact me. I would love to hear from you. You can reach me by visiting my Web site at www.elaineoverton.com, or write me at: P.O. Box 930756 Wixom, MI 48393.

PROMISES
OF THE *Heart*

ELAINE OVERTON

Overton

PROMISES OF THE HEART

An Arabesque novel

ISBN 1-58314-701-2

© 2006 by Elaine Overton.

www.kimanipress.com

Printed in U.S.A.

5.99

9.17/06
NRN

Dedicated with love to my sister and friend,
Sussie Chenault

Acknowledgments

Always first in my life, my Lord and Savior
Jesus Christ, in all things I give praise!!
To my family and friends for your endless
support, and encouragement.

A special thanks to Charlie of Charlie's Custom
Creations in Novi, Michigan, for your expertise
and technical help in creating a believable
mechanic. You gave me so much more material
than I would ever use. Thank you soo much!!!

To the staff of Arabesque books,
for all the behind-the-scenes work to create
well-written, entertaining stories, and giving
aspiring authors windows of opportunity.

Prologue

Bethel Baptist Church
April 19, 1986

"Max, we're ready." Paul DeLeroy stuck his head around the heavy wood door. He spoke to the groom-to-be who was currently straightening his tie in the mirror.

"All right," Max Tyler answered. He continued to position his tie, but he also watched his soon-to-be stepson in the mirror.

Paul was glaring at the little girl seated to his right. Max twisted his mouth the way he always did when he was deep in thought. Callie had told him just that morning that she thought her new brother didn't like her. Max had quickly dismissed it as part of Callie's difficulty in accepting her new family. After all, Paul was almost twenty years old and at college most of the time. What could he possibly have against a little girl? Especially one he barely ever came in contact with.

Max was certain Callie's fears were groundless. She'd protested from the moment Sarah DeLeroy answered the advertisement for a caregiver six months earlier. Max could still hear his little angel declaring that they didn't need "nobody," certain that she was big enough to not only care for herself but her beloved daddy as well. Bless her heart, Max thought, she had tried for the nearly four months since his wife, Theresa, had passed.

Luckily, Callie and Sarah had hit it off. That was until Callie began to notice just how well Sarah and her daddy had hit it off.

Max stifled a smile, remembering the indignant expression on the face of the nine-year-old as she explained that Sarah was nothing less than a succubus and that Paul was the son of Hades. Proving not only that his little girl was paying close attention in her ancient histories class, but that she had developed quite a vocabulary as well.

Now, watching Paul watch Callie, Max was forced to reconsider what she'd told him. Just then, Paul's eyes swung back around and met his in the mirror.

"Should we start the music?" Paul made an effort to explain his continued presence in the doorway.

"Give me another five minutes, and then start." Max silently studied the younger man until he closed the door and disappeared.

Maxwell Tyler did not get to be the successful businessman he was by misjudging people. He made a mental note to speak to Sarah after the ceremony. He needed to find out if there was anything to his daughter's accusations. The man known as a maverick in the business world was ultraconservative when it came to his baby girl. He wasn't about to take any chances with her welfare.

Max double-checked his cuff links before turning to face his daughter. His heart melted at the look of pure love and adoration in the bright eyes staring up at him. Clear brown eyes, so much like her mother's. Every night when he bowed on his knees to pray, he always remembered to thank God for his wonderful, but brief, years with Theresa. And most especially for the miracle she left behind.

He squatted down to her eye level, careless of the perfectly tailored tuxedo pants. "Callie, come here, sweetheart." He held out his large hand.

Callie had to scoot all the way to the edge of the stool before her feet touched the ground. Even at nine and three-quarters, Callie Tyler realized she was extremely small for her age. She secretly resented the fact that most of her friends were already wearing training bras, and she was still stuck wearing plain T-shirts. Not to mention, she didn't get to buy clothes as often because she didn't grow out of them nearly as fast as everyone else.

She placed her tiny hand in the much larger one, and looking up at him, she secretly thought her daddy had to be the most handsome man in the world. Callie twisted her mouth in an exact imitation of her father's thoughtful expression. She completely understood why that Jezebel wanted to marry him. What woman wouldn't?

Max turned her tiny hand over, palm up, and was not surprised to see the deeply embedded grease in the grooves of her fingers. Of course his little grease monkey would've checked on their pet project before getting dressed for the wedding. But even then, wouldn't the grease have come off during her bath? He frowned. "Callie, you did take a bath this morning, didn't you?"

Callie bit her bottom lip and dropped her eyes. "There was no time, Daddy. I went out to check on the Belaire, and it looked like it was leaking oil, so I had to climb up under it to get a closer look."

"Was it?" Max asked in concern before he realized he was losing the thread of the conversation. "Whether it was or not, you should've taken a bath." This was a painful reminder for Max as to exactly why he was marrying Sarah DeLeroy after knowing her so short a time.

Max was basically a small-time mechanic who'd made good. He'd taken his unique gift for auto repair and turned it into a dynasty of garages throughout the country. Max could repair almost any car, and at nine Callie was already showing signs of the same talent. But Max soon discovered that that was the extent of his ability in raising children. He needed a woman, someone to care for Callie during his many business trips. Someone who would not only care for her, but who would also give her a mother's love.

Theresa had been the love of his life and the only woman he thought he would ever love. That was until he looked into Sarah's eyes and found a much-needed warmth and compassion.

Before she caught them in bed together, Callie had adored Sarah, and Max was certain that once she got past her animosity she would again. But what about Sarah's unusually quiet son? Max knew little of the man, primarily because he was never around. He needed information.

Callie frowned at the expression in her father's eyes. "But good news, Daddy. The Belaire wasn't leaking. The stain was old."

Max felt his bearded face spread into a slow smile. How could he stay angry at this child of his heart? This one who looked so much like her mother but who was so much more like himself. He'd instilled in her the obsession with broken-down vehicles. He couldn't scowl at her now because that obsession was displaying itself in the form of greasy hands on his wedding day.

He wondered what Theresa would think of the job he was doing as a father. Before the accident, the three of them had been inseparable.

"Callie, do you remember what a heart promise is?" He gently rubbed the back of her tiny hand with his thumb.

Callie smiled, remembering the many times her mother had made her heart promises. "Yes, Mama used to say a heart promise was stronger than other promises."

"That's right. Do you know why?"

She tilted her head to the side and thought about the soft voice she still heard in her dreams sometimes. She conjured a picture in her mind, sitting between her mother's legs while she braided her hair.

A lot of people make promises they don't mean. They say things with good intentions, maybe, but for some reason they cannot follow through. But a heart promise is a promise made to the heart. And the heart won't accept anything less than the absolute truth…

"Mama said that you must be true to your heart always, so if you make a heart promise, you have no choice but to keep the promise. Your heart won't allow you to do anything less." Callie beamed, proud that she had remembered so much of what her mother told her.

Max felt something clinch inside his chest and pulled his daughter into his arms. "Oh, my sweet little girl. That is one hundred percent correct."

Another knock came on the door. "We're ready, Max," a muffled voice called.

"All right," Max called over his shoulder before catching both Callie's hands in his. "Callie, on this day I give you my heart promise that no one or nothing can ever come between us. Do you believe me?"

Callie smiled. "Of course, Daddy."

He hugged her tight against him once more. "Never forget that promise, Callie, no matter what happens after today. Your daddy will always love you."

"I know," she said with complete assurance, turning to retrieve her small bouquet.

It was an intimate ceremony for a mature couple marrying for the second time. They'd only invited family and their closest friends. Sarah had asked Callie to be her maid of honor. One stern look from her father had forced Callie to accept. And in truth, she had nothing against Sarah. She was actually very nice and really good with board games. Only Paul gave her the willies.

But still in all, on a perfect spring day she would much rather be making repairs on the Belaire. She and her daddy had been working on it for months now, but there was still so much to do. As she followed him out into the hallway, she wondered if he would be willing to work on it with her after the wedding reception.

Chapter 1

An industrial park near downtown Detroit
2:04 A.M. on a Friday night...

"Pooky! Watch out!"

Callie watched in horror as her cousin stood in the middle of the seemingly deserted street in a zombielike trance. So captivated by something in a store window, he never noticed the speeding car heading in his direction.

Callie vaulted over the workhorse, through the construction area, and dashed out into the street. The bright headlights of the red sports car shone on her face, right before the sound of tires screeching led her to believe the driver had finally noticed the pedestrians in his path.

The smell of burning rubber was strong and ominously

close, but Callie had no time to think about that. Her complete attention was focused on reaching Pooky before the car did.

Although Pooky was a solid hundred pounds heavier and several inches taller than she, Callie threw her full weight of 102 pounds into her cousin. She felt a slight breeze and saw a flash of red out of the corner of her eye just as the two entangled bodies went tumbling across the grassy knoll.

"My shoe! I just bought those yesterday!"

"Forget your shoe. Are you okay?" Callie did a quick inspection of her cousin, giving him the once-over. Her heart was still pounding at top speed, and she felt short of breath when she allowed herself to think about how close she'd come to losing the only family member she acknowledged.

Pooky attempted to sit up and felt the slight weight bearing down on him. "Callie."

"Yes."

"Will you please get off my back?"

"Oh." Callie sat back on her knees, still studying every inch of her cousin for injury. The bright fuchsia skirt was stained with oil from the pavement, and there was a gaping hole in the fishnet stocking, but beyond that everything else appeared to be normal. Or as close to normal as Pooky ever came.

Pooky held up the surviving shoe. "Damn. These were originally priced at one hundred and twenty-five dollars. I got them on sale at sixty percent off. Do you know how hard it is to find quality designer shoes—in a size thirteen—at sixty percent off?!"

Callie felt her bottom lip tremble with laughter, even as the water filled her eyes. She couldn't imagine what she would do without Pooky. This odd creature, despite all the flamboyant looks, was the only thing standing between her and complete devastation. No one could guess with a look the type of bravery and strength of will that was hidden beneath that burgundy wig. Unable to stop it, Callie felt a single tear slide down her face.

Pooky stood. "What are you crying about? I'm the one out seventy bucks, not to mention the cost of this outfit." Pooky reached down and lifted Callie to her feet as if she weighed little more than a child, which in truth she did.

Callie dusted off her worn green coveralls and haphazardly swiped at her eyes. "We both know that dress only cost you the price of the fabric, since you make all your clothes yourself."

Pooky reached up and carefully adjusted the wig that amazingly enough had survived the fall. "That's not the point. I still—" Pooky stopped in midsentence, noticing Callie's trembling body for the first time. "Hey now, sugar bear. I'm fine, really." Pooky twirled in a circle with arms outstretched. "See?"

Callie grabbed her much taller cousin around the waist. "I almost lost you."

"Girlfriend, please," Pooky called over a shoulder, limping back out into the middle of the street to collect the other shoe. "God's not ready for me yet, and the devil knows better than to mess with this."

Callie shook her head and swiped at her eyes again, feeling closer to calm. When would she learn that nothing, not even a near-death experience, could rattle this menace to society she lovingly called Pooky.

"Well, until God's ready or the devil gets braver, I guess I'm stuck with you."

"Guess so," Pooky answered distractedly, too busy inspecting the damaged shoe.

Only then did Callie remember that they were not alone on the empty street. She turned her head in the direction where she'd seen the flash of red. The car had finally come to a stop several yards away. It had crashed up against the side of a Dumpster.

Callie covered her mouth with both hands. "Oh my God," she whispered, breaking into a dead run. She heard the clippity-clap of Pooky's one-shoe gait and realized her cousin was right beside her.

Ten feet from the car they both stopped in their tracks as the passenger side door slowly creaked open. One long leg emerged and clumsily flopped to the ground, soon another joined it. They waited, frozen in time, for the body attached to the legs to make an appearance, but it never did.

Julian Cruise attempted to sit up. He willed his considerable strength to move his aching body but nothing happened. It seemed that getting the far side door open had zapped him of what little reserve he had remaining after the traumatic impact. His driver's side door was jammed, and he vaguely remembered slamming against something large and metal.

His vision was blurred, and when he lifted his arm to his face, he discovered there was no pain in his upper portion. He did a quick mental inventory and realized his lower body took the brunt of the blow, but as far as he could tell, nothing was broken.

A vision came into his blurred sights, and he recognized the outline of the woman he'd swerved to avoid hitting. He took comfort in the fact that she was apparently all right. He casually noted that she was much larger than he first assumed, not more than an inch or two shorter than his six feet. She was a big-boned girl. *Really* big boned. His analytical mind quickly took in what he could discern of the image in front of him.

Her bright fuchsia dress was the definition of tacky, and the fact that it almost matched the burgundy wig exactly only added to the overall tastelessness. He promptly concluded that she was a streetwalker, but as she bent over him, he gave up that hypothesis. Julian decided that this had to be the ugliest woman he'd ever seen. If she had to make her living seducing men, he was pretty certain she'd starve to death. And that darkening around the chin area that suspiciously resembled a five o'clock shadow certainly did not help matters.

"Mister? Are you okay?" Her soft, husky voice sounded like a siren alarm to his pounding head. He tried to nod but was unsure if he was successful.

"Is he okay?" A head popped out from under the large woman's arm. An adorable little face that was twisted in concern.

"I don't know," the woman answered. "He seems disoriented."

"Mister, we're going to get some help for you, okay? You just stay right there."

"Where is he going, Callie?" came the woman's sardonic reply.

"Maybe we should try to get him out of the car."

"I don't think we should move the body."

"He's not dead, Pook! Just hurt."

Julian silently listened to the strange conversation. He rubbed at his face again, trying to make sense of the image. The second figure was as confusing as the first. The coveralls and twisted baseball cap gave the appearance of a workman, but the size of the person clearly suggested a child. And there was something about the face, that rich golden skin and soft mouth. He surmised that this must be the amazon's child, a preadolescent boy.

"You know first aid, right?" The boy looked up at his mother in frustration.

"The Heimlich maneuver, but I don't think that's going to help us now, Callie."

"Well, hell! At least I'm trying to think of something! Stop being your typically sarcastic self and help me out here."

Julian frowned, thinking that if this was his disrespectful child, the boy would be quickly brought to task for speaking to him in such a manner.

"Look, I'll go find a phone. You stay with him." The mother turned to leave; her son grabbed her arm.

"Be careful, Pooky."

Julian thought that was a strange nickname for one's mother. He saw the mother's faint wink of an eye.

"I told you the devil knows better than to mess with this."

The mother disappeared from his line of vision, and he was left with the child.

"Hang in there, mister. Help is on the way."

The boy leaned over him, and Julian caught his first clear image of soft brown eyes framed in the longest lashes he'd ever seen. He thought it odd that a woman that ugly could produce such an attractive child.

Julian fell back on the seat in exhaustion, thinking that for the kid's sake, he hoped the boy developed some more manly features soon or else high school was going to be a really tough four years. With that thought, he fainted.

Chapter 2

Callie leaned over the unconscious man, looking for signs of life. The slight lift and fall of his chest gave her some small comfort. Amazingly enough, the man seemed essentially uninjured. Other than the slight disorientation he displayed, the fact that he was semilucid was a very good indication. He might come out of this practically unscathed, which was more than could be said for his classic car. She leaned forward a little more to get a better look at his face.

Callie Tyler had two distinctly unique abilities at her disposal. Her phenomenal gift for fixing anything on wheels and her uncanny ability of reading people. With one look, she knew without a doubt that this well-dressed, overly handsome man was gonna be trouble. He was unconscious now, she thought, but eventually he would wake up, and when he did, he would have retaliation on his mind.

She studied the milk-chocolate man laid out like dessert.

He had a finely featured face that did not seem to jive with the brawny body that came with it. His build gave the impression of a man who used his physical strength often. Even in a relaxed position, the bulging biceps were pressing against the light blue dress shirt. But his face was...Callie twisted her mouth in thought and decided *scholarly* was the only word that fit. Yes, he looked scholarly. A thinker, not a builder.

She tilted her head to the side to study his profile and realized that at his temples, short-cropped curls were just starting to show signs of a little salt being added to the pepper. What a lovely profile it was, accentuating full sensual lips that begged for attention. Callie found herself mystified by the perfect heart-shaped mouth outlined by a thick black mustache. She felt something like a compulsion to reach out and gently run her finger across his full bottom lip. So she did. That's when she noticed the cleft in his chin and found herself cooing like an idiot. How could something so small add so much to a face?

She felt the urge to follow her finger with her tongue, tracing those beautiful lips and then moving down to the little cleft. Only with the shake of her head was she able to break the spell. Something about this unconscious stranger was pulling her in like quicksand. She stood straight and stretched. It was really no great mystery when she thought about it. It had been almost two years since she'd been in anything resembling a relationship. *Face it, Callie, your horny hormones are on overload.* In fact, this was probably the closest she'd been to a true member of the opposite sex in months. Callie smiled to herself. Sad as it was, an unconscious man was turning her on like crazy. It was understandable—in his sleeping state he seemed close to perfect, but Callie knew that wide-awake he would be anything but.

"And it doesn't take a scholar to figure that out," she whispered to her sleeping ward.

Left with nothing better to do until Pooky returned with help, she turned her attention to the banged-up vehicle. She stepped back several feet and surveyed the damage from all angles. A 1965 Corvette Stingray in cherry apple-red with a soft white drop-top. Now *this* was the ideal male.

She ran her hand along the smooth body, simply in awe of the craftsmanship that went into each and every curve. Callie didn't doubt for a minute that this car was built with loving hands. She finally came to the driver's side, and her lust turned to sorrow.

She could not see the extent of the damage because of its position against the Dumpster. From what she could see, most of the damage looked superficial, but she would have to see the driver's side door to be certain. It was a small car, and Callie knew she was strong despite her size. She braced her body against the car and her feet against the Dumpster and tried to pry the two apart. It didn't work. She needed a crowbar or something similar. She went back around the car to get the keys out of the ignition, hoping there would be some type of tools in the trunk.

Unfortunately, the man's large body was stretched fully across the front seat, she would have to crawl over him to reach the ignition switch where the keys were. She bit her bottom lip in consternation; even Callie had to admit her actions bordered on improper. Here she was considering climbing all over an injured man to get his keys so she could go into his private things. She bent her knee and clambered onto the man, deciding it was for the greater good. The car needed her help.

She shimmied left and right trying to keep her movements

to a minimum. Problem was, he was much larger than he looked, and Callie realized too late that she would have to somehow reach over his head to get to the steering column and the keys.

She scooted and scooted until she found herself at his waist. The man shifted. Callie paused, holding her breath. She looked down at him, but he was still asleep. She let out a large breath and stretched out flat across his chest. Stretching her short arm toward the steering wheel, she was still falling several inches short of the target. Callie scooted forward a little more and froze. Something was firmly cupping her bottom. She swallowed hard, realizing the *something* was a large hand. She twisted her face to look at the injured man. His eyes were still closed, his breathing pattern was still faint, but now there was just the tiniest bit of a smirk to those luscious lips.

Julian thought he was dreaming. What else could it be? He remembered the accident, the woman in the middle of the street whom he swerved to avoid hitting. He remembered his pride and joy, his *baby* smashing into a tree. He remembered trying to get out of the car and the ugly woman and the boy who came to help him. His aching body told him not much had changed since then. So when he felt a soft, feminine body wiggling all over him, he realized it must be a dream.

He started to open his eyes but paused, wondering whose face he would see hovering over him. One of the few women of his past or a completely fictional character. He decided not to. Why ruin a perfectly good wet dream?

He reached out and cupped a firm little bottom that fit perfectly in the palm of his hand. He squeezed tentatively, amazed at how real it felt. He ran his other hand along a cotton-clad thigh. That was strange. He frowned. You would think a dream woman would be naked. No matter, he decided; undressing her would be part of the fun.

He ran his hands up her back, marveling at the compact little body. Undeniably female but much smaller than Julian's typical taste. His open hands curved around her ribs and cupped two small but well-defined breasts. Once again, he was amazed at the perfect fit. Running his thumb over the hard little nipples that were already pushing up against the thick cotton material, he wondered at how this body seemed to be custom-made for him. Of course, a dream woman was just that—made for him. Even the legs around his waist fit. They were wonderfully strong, muscular legs but in perfect proportion to the rest of the petite frame. Maybe his subconscious was telling him something.

Typically Julian was attracted to the long-legged model type. Being a tall man himself, he consciously avoided the shorter members of the opposite sex. Unfortunately, most of his relationships had been for the sake of convenience, not romance. Given his business, he attended a lot of dinner parties and social events that required a companion.

So, he ordinarily dated women who, well, for the lack of better words, complemented his tuxedo. Elegance, sophistication, refinement, those were the only criteria he required they meet. Granted, he'd never had the earth-moving sex his married friends often spoke of, but he didn't really think he was missing much. Until now. The lush little body sprawled across his chest was doing things to his libido that had never been done.

They both heard it at the same time. Loud, harsh laughter that was in no way related to humor.

"That's funny, man," came a coarse voice from several feet away. "I almost believed you. He almost had me." This time a chorus of voices joined in. But something in the sound was more jeer than jocular.

"Silver, I swear, man. I'll have it by Friday. I swear."

"Friday?"

"Yeah, man, I swear I'll have all your money by Friday."

"Do you hear this punk?"

The laughter started again.

"Please, Silver. Just three more days, man. That's all I need."

Both Callie and Julian could hear the building panic in the man's voice. There was sudden silence. They heard a soft whimper that quickly became a full-fledged wail.

"Oh, God! Please, Silver! Please, man, don't do this. I'll get you your money, I swear! I'll borrow—"

The two loud pops silenced the pathetic plea. Julian had paused in the exploration of his dream woman, wondering if the conversation he heard was all part of the same dream. But the sound of a gun being fired at close range was enough to convince him that what he was hearing was real enough. At the sound of the weapon firing, Julian heard his dream woman gasp. She *gasped!* Dreams don't gasp at things happening in the real world.

He opened his eyes and found himself staring into clear brown eyes. A small hand was quickly pressed to his lips to silence him. There was something very familiar about those eyes. Julian frowned thoughtfully. *The boy!* He was fondling the boy! But no—no, that couldn't be right. The body he felt was undeniably female. But the more he looked at the face, the surer he was that this was the ugly woman's little boy. But she wasn't a boy; she wasn't even a child. She was a woman. A fully developed woman!

The sound of feet shuffling brought his attention back to the scene happening outside the vehicle. His mind did a quick assessment as he realized the sound was getting closer, not farther. He knew that if the gang spotted his car, they would approach it.

Unfortunately, his flashy but wounded vehicle would glow like a beacon to the criminally inclined. And given that they had just committed murder, he was certain they would have no problem with killing him for his vehicle, especially if they knew he heard what had just happened. And what about the woman sprawled across his chest? They would kill her, too. And he was in no condition to protect either one of them.

"Hey, man, check this out!" He heard a voice calling to the group.

Julian felt his heart drop, realizing they had been spotted. His mind was racing. He had a knife in the glove compartment that he used for emergencies; maybe the woman could reach it before the gang reached them.

"Sweet!" another voice called. This one was much closer.

Julian opened his mouth to whisper his plan to his companion but stopped when he heard a siren. It was loud and blessedly close.

"Damn! Let's get out of here," the leader called, followed by the sound of feet running.

Julian realized that for the second time in one night, he'd come extremely close to dying. The sirens got louder and louder, and he felt himself fading. His last conscious thought was of the soft breast still pressed again his chest and the sweet scent of a woman's arousal that faintly permeated the air. How could he not have noticed that? Of course, she had to be a woman. Nothing else fit a man's body so well.

Chapter 3

At the sound of the sirens, Callie slumped forward; then remembering where she was, she sat bolt upright. *Never* in a million years did she expect that to happen. She wasn't even really sure what had happened. All she knew for certain was that her whole body was still tingling with need. Some small part of her mind was frustrated that he couldn't stay awake long enough to finish what he'd started. Never had she reacted that way to anyone's touch, certainly not some semiconscious stranger. Who was this man? Callie knew she would remember the feel of those gentle hands on her body for the rest of her life.

She began to scoot back the way she came in, consciously willing her mind to ignore the obvious and extremely prominent bump in the road. She pushed herself up off his body, but strong arms came up and locked her in place. Just as quickly, his body relaxed again, and his arms fell to his side. With three jumps she was out of the vehicle.

She squatted down to catch her breath and crawled to the end of the car to peek around it. She had heard the killers running but still wanted to see for herself that no one was waiting. She half-expected to see a dead body lying in the street, but apparently the shooting had taken place in one of the shadowy alleyways she saw in the distance.

The industrial neighborhood was abandoned this time of night. All except for a couple of warehouses that had been renovated into nightclubs. One of which favored those with alternative lifestyles, like Pooky.

Pooky had partied most of the night, as he always did on Friday night, and in doing so somehow got separated from the group he came to the club with. When he discovered he had no ride home, he'd called his cousin, who also happened to be his best friend.

Callie was no stranger to the area; she'd picked Pooky and friends up from the location often, when the liquor had flowed and the bartender seized keys. She knew the neighborhood could be dangerous, but until tonight she had no idea just how dangerous. The thought of Pooky roaming the streets freely this time of the night was not comforting. People weren't always kind to six-foot-two-inch drag queens.

In the distance, she could see the ambulance turning the corner and heading in her direction. Almost simultaneously she heard the clip-clop of Pooky's return.

"Girl—" breathing hard, Pooky fell against the trunk of the car "—you wouldn't believe how far I had to go to find a pay phone."

Callie subconsciously rubbed her trembling arms. "Pooky, there's a pay phone four blocks from here. I saw it coming to pick you up."

"Yes," Pooky drawled, "I called from that one first. But I

also had to find two others. You know in this neighborhood they won't respond to anything under three calls."

Callie shook her head and watched the emergency technicians unload a stretcher.

"Excuse me—" she touched a paramedic's arm "—while we were waiting, I heard shots fired over there." Callie pointed toward the direction she thought the sound came from, hoping it was right, praying the man was still alive.

The tech nodded as casually as if she'd said he needed an umbrella because it was about to rain. But then he quickly returned to the cab of his truck, and she watched him reaching for the radio.

"What's wrong?" Pooky had come up beside her.

Callie turned her head to find Pooky watching her with raptorlike attention.

"A man was shot."

"What?!" Pooky's hands fluttered in the wind. "When? Where? Are you okay?"

"Yes, I'm okay." Callie fought the urge to look back at the long legs hanging out of the car. "They didn't see me." Callie allowed herself to be pushed aside as the techs went to work. "I think the sound of the sirens scared them off."

"Were you hiding behind the car?"

"Uh, no. I was inside the car."

"Inside the car? What were you doing inside the car?"

"Um…" Callie's mind was far too frazzled to try to think fast. "I, uh…"

Pooky grabbed Callie by her upper arm and led her several feet from the men working to unravel Julian from the vehicle. "I know you like I know my own skin. What happened while I was gone?"

"I told you, a gang shot a man in one of those alleys."

Unable to stop herself, Callie's eyes wandered back to the open doorway of the car. The techs were carefully lifting their unconscious patient onto the stretcher.

Pooky's eyes widened in horror. "He died, didn't he?" Pooky quickly hobbled over to the stretcher.

"Pooky, wait!" Callie called, but was drowned out by the sound of Pooky's one heel clicking loudly against the pavement.

Pooky leaned over the handsome man. "Oh, you poor dear, sacrificing your life for mine."

"Ma'am. I mean sir…I mean. Look! We need you to move back so we can get this man to a hospital."

Unfazed by the voice of authority or the mystification his appearance always incited, Pooky leaned over the prostrate body. "God go with you as you journey into the next life, my darling hero." Pooky bent to place a brief kiss on the forehead of the body and was shocked to feel strong arms snaking around his neck. Soft lips met his as the head lifted off the cot.

Julian opened his eyes with the slightest frown. Then they opened wider and wider until they appeared ready to pop out of their sockets.

Pooky smiled down into the mortified face. "Oh my, you are not dead at all. In fact, I'd say you are very much alive."

The man on the stretcher opened his mouth to speak, but no words emerged. He stuttered painfully, finally managing three coherent words: "You're a man!"

"I'm suing!" Julian was forced to unbutton and rebutton his shirt several times. His mind raced every time he thought about what he almost did. What he *did* do. It was enough to make a man homicidal. They should consider themselves lucky that all he was doing was suing for the damages to his car and not the psychological trauma of the experience.

"Now, Julian, calm down." His mother was on the other side of the room, packing his overnight bag. Although he had no serious injuries, due to the nature of the accident, the hospital had kept him overnight for observation. "It's over; just let it go."

"Oh, no, that Frankenstein and his little Egor are going to pay—big time!"

"Why? Because in your haze of lust you mistakenly kissed a man?" Pamela Cruise turned her back on her son, not wanting him to see the humorous smirk she was unable to hide.

Julian spun around to glare at his mother's back. "I told you a thousand times, I thought I was kissing the other one, the little one."

"You mean the one you thought was a boy?"

"Yes. No! I thought I was kissing a woman."

Pam Cruise wisely held her peace, but the humor lighting her eyes told her son everything she was thinking.

"A real woman, not that…that thing!"

Pam's face sobered instantly. "That 'thing' is a human being, Julian."

Julian dropped his head like a guilty child, feeling humbled as only a mother could make him feel. "You're right, Mom. I apologize." He slumped against the bed. "The past twenty-four hours have been like something out of the *Twilight Zone*. I'm just ready to get back to the real world."

Pam zipped the bag closed and came up behind her son. She rubbed his tense shoulders, feeling a little guilt of her own. In some ways her middle son was such a prude, so different from the rest of the carefree members of his family. She couldn't help teasing him on those rare occasions when life caught him by surprise. "I'll go see if your paperwork is ready, and then we can get out of here."

"Mom."

"Yes?"

"Does Olivia know what happened?"

"Your dad and I explained to her last night."

"What did you tell her?"

"Just that you were in an accident."

Julian looked over his shoulder to meet his mother's eyes. "Does she know where I was coming from?"

Pam took a deep breath. "No. We told her you were coming home from work."

He nodded once. "Thank you."

Julian watched his mother quietly walk out, noticing her slumped shoulders for the first time. For his sweet, church-bred mother, lying was as natural as a fish on land. Especially when those lies were being told to her own granddaughter. His father, even his two brothers, had all expressed their displeasure in the way he was handling this predicament. He knew the stress of the situation was wearing on all of them.

Rachel had told him herself that she felt Olivia needed to know the truth, and she had asked Julian to explain to their daughter when he had the right words. But how did one explain to a fourteen-year-old that her mother is in rehab for cocaine addiction? Especially when that mother was trying so desperately to get better.

Julian's relationship with his high school sweetheart had been traumatic at best. A handful of memories and few of them good. Two stumbling virgins trying to find out how the pieces of God's greatest puzzle fit together. The tearful announcement nine months later that Rachel was pregnant. The even more tearful announcement to their parents that they were getting married. Julian's loud and near-violent argument with Rachel's father, who refused to have his daughter's life "ruined," as he called it, by a forced marriage to a boy with no future. Arriving at Rachel's house that fateful morning two weeks later to discover the whole family gone and the house empty.

Thirteen years later, a crack-addicted Rachel showed up at his door with a little girl and introduced him to his daughter for the first time. He watched his daughter Olivia's yearlong battle to understand how her once-ideal life had changed so drastically. How could the woman who dropped her off with these strangers be the same woman who'd raised her? According to Olivia's brief accounts, for the first eleven years of her life, she and her mother had shared a small house on the West side and lived a quiet but pleasant life. Then one day without warning, her sweet, gentle mother began to change, and eventually her behavior spiraled out of control. One month later, they were standing on Julian's step, and her mother was announcing that the man towering over her was her long-lost father.

Everyone's life had changed that day. Julian visited Rachel regularly, and to the people at the rehab, he was the outside contact, not her overbearing parents. He'd helped her in every way he could, paying for her treatment, providing her with the little necessities of womanhood, and caring for their daughter.

In the few months she'd been in treatment, Julian had seen some improvements. Rachel had a desperate desire to get well enough to care for her daughter again. Some part of Julian hoped that if Rachel recovered completely, maybe Olivia would never have to know about her mother's dark struggle with her inner demons.

He stood and walked to the window. His weekly trip to the rehabilitation center had definitely taken a unique turn last night. Staring out on the busy avenue, Julian wondered what had possessed him to try to kiss a total stranger. Something that was so out of character for him. His mouth turned down in disgust as he remembered what had happened. He knew something was wrong the moment his mouth touched the other's. Although he had never kissed *her,* he was certain what she would taste like. Visions of warm honey danced in his brain, but instead he'd tasted stale beer. After everything that had happened, he was still left wondering what she would taste like.

Why was he still obsessing over her? It wasn't like she would ever meet his criteria for a woman; not unless she suddenly grew ten inches overnight. She was cute, in a boyish way. He closed his eyes. Who was he kidding? There was nothing boyish about her. Small maybe, but every bit feminine. Even now, he could close his eyes and remember every curve and contour. Her scent, the sound of her breathing, the smell of her…want. Yes, definitely woman—just in no way his kind of woman.

"Julian?" Pam spoke from behind him. "They're here with the wheelchair."

Julian turned and grabbed his jacket off a nearby chair. "I don't need a wheelchair."

"Hospital policy, sir," the orderly spoke from the doorway.

"Fine. Fine, whatever it takes to get out of this place." And back into his nice, calm, sedate life. *That's what I need,* Julian thought, flopping down into the chair. The comfort of his ordinariness. And he would have that. Once he sued the pants off the pair who wrecked his precious baby.

Chapter 4

"Why..." Pooky stood with the summons pressed to his false breast. "That lousy rat! We save his life and this is how he repays us?!"

Callie, lying beneath a Ford Escort that belonged to the man who ran the small grocery store next door, was silent.

Pooky frowned, knowing that a silent Callie was far more dangerous than an enraged Callie. He'd seen firsthand, on more than one occasion, what happened when that particular volcano exploded. "Callie? What are we going to do?" He bent low, trying to see her face and draw her into conversation. He needed to hear her voice. It would at least give an indication of just how much time he had to run for cover.

Still she refused to answer.

"Well, personally, I don't think he stands a chance," Pooky continued; at the same time, he began edging toward the large bay doors leading to the outside—and safety. "I mean, we were just innocent pedestrians, for goodness sakes. And we got him medical attention, didn't we?" Pooky's eyes batted rapidly in nervousness. "We saved his life!"

"We didn't save his life, Pooky." The soft, muffled voice filtered from beneath the car. "His injuries were minimal at best. But we did almost kill his 'Vette." Suddenly, the rack she was lying on came sliding out from under the Escort. "And, yes, he could win if he can prove reckless endangerment." Callie stood and dusted the excess rust and debris from her coveralls.

Pooky stood poised in the door. "Callie, you don't blame me, do you?"

Callie's head swung around. Shards of amber fire darted across the small space, right into his heart, and pinned him to the ground where he stood.

"Blame you? Why would I blame you, Pooky?" She tossed her wrench onto her workbench and stuck her hands in her oversized pockets. "Feeling guilty?" she drawled with heavy sarcasm.

Pooky's ringed fingers fluttered nervously around his neck. "Why would I feel guilty? It was his reckless driving that got his car wrecked, not me." Pooky knew he was walking a thin rope, but what else was there to do until Callie finally got around to speaking her mind? And from the look in her eyes, it wouldn't be long now.

"Of course," Callie began, slowly sauntering in his direction, "if you'd stayed where you were supposed to, instead of crossing the street in those ridiculously high heels to look in that store window at a purse of all things!" She took a deep breath to regain her composure. "Of course, if you'd respected the caution signs and cones put in place to keep people *out*— instead of going around them to get to the boutique—then maybe, just maybe none of this would've happened. But blame you?" She frowned in confusion. "What would make you think that?" Callie finally came to a stop directly in front of her cousin, who towered over her by a foot. "Huh?"

Pooky swallowed hard, realizing this was the angriest he'd ever seen his tiny cousin. "I don't know." He hunched his broad shoulders, made even more pronounced by the shoulder pads in his latest creation. "It could be the way the veins are standing up in your neck."

Callie shook her head and balled her small fist at her side. "That's not blame, Pooky. That's restraint."

Pooky bit his bottom lip, knowing he shouldn't ask the question, but he was finally unable to resist. "What are you restraining yourself from?"

"Wringing your thick neck!"

Pooky sucked in his cheeks in indignation. "That's a low blow!" Callie knew how sensitive he was about his thick neck.

"We can barely keep this place open as it is!" Callie's arms flailed wildly through the air. "How in the world are we supposed to fight a lawsuit with someone like this Julian Cruise?"

"Maybe after a few days to cool off he'll be more reasonable and drop the suit."

Callie looked up at her cousin like he'd lost his mind. "You're kidding, right? Do you know who this man is?" Callie returned to her workbench and pulled a *Crain's Detroit Business Magazine*, dated from two months prior, from beneath the pile of magazines and newspapers she'd collected over the past several months. She shoved it in Pooky's face, practically pressing the cover up against his nose. "This! This is the man we're up against."

Pooky backed up and took the magazine. First he noted the picture of the familiar handsome man featured in the cover story. Then quickly he scanned the first few paragraphs of the article. "Okay, so he's some hotshot money man, big deal. I still say we saved his life. Who knows what would've happened to him if we hadn't called for help. That gang might have gotten him and his car. He should be grateful. And maybe after he cools off he will be."

Callie placed her hands on her hips to keep them off of Pooky. "Let me try to put this in perspective for you."

Pooky pursed his lips to hold in his tongue. He hated when she talked to him like a two-year-old, but he also knew it was just a reflection of her anger. And he noted for the first time that Callie was truly fearful of what this Julian Cruise could do to them and their small business. "I'm listening," he stated while folding his arms across his ample bosom.

"This man is one of the top financial advisors in the country. He deals with people from all over the world, powerful people, important people. People who could wipe our little operation off the face of the earth." She nodded toward the magazine still in Pooky's hand. "You see how *Craine's* described him as a 'bulldog in a business suit'? That means he's a ruthless bastard. Capable of doing anything and everything to get what he wants." Callie turned and began pacing the concrete floor. "And trust me, people like that don't file lawsuits on a fluke. No. They plot and plan their revenge." She stopped on the far side of the garage and turned to face Pooky. "And for what we did to his classic car, no matter how innocently it occurred, he's going to want retribution." With that statement, she turned and stormed through the door leading to the small apartment they shared over the garage.

Pooky watched her go, twisting his mouth in an exaggerated pout. "And people call *me* a drama queen," he muttered. He stood thinking for several seconds. Finally tossing the magazine and summons on a counter, he grabbed his purse off the coatrack near the door and headed out.

Pooky didn't completely agree with Callie regarding Julian Cruise's supposedly unquenchable thirst for vengeance, but he was smart enough not to underestimate the possibility that they might need more help.

He climbed into his sport-utility vehicle and started the engine. Taking a deep breath, he turned the steering wheel in the direction of the street and pulled out of the garage parking lot.

Julian could still feel her every curve, every dip of her soft, little body welcoming the slow stroking of his fingers along her bare skin. He shifted, needing to feel her beneath him, needing to open her up and finally know what it was to love this woman. His heart was pounding with his greedy hunger. From the moment he'd first touched her, she'd haunted his dreams, teasing and taunting and always remaining just out of reach. A beguiling little elf, making him feel things he'd never felt, want things he'd never imagined. Now it was her turn to want and need. Before the night was through, she'd call his name and beg him to take her again and again. He pushed against the mattress, feeling the soft petals of her womanhood open to him—

Urrrgghhh!!

The startling screech of his bedside telephone sounded loudly. Julian shot straight up in the bed. The thin, damp sheet fell around his waist. His heart was still pounding in alarm.

Urrrgghhh!! The phone screeched again, and Julian disregarded it, looking around the empty bed to realize in painful disappointment that he was alone.

Urrrgghhh!! He reached over and grabbed the cordless phone. "Hello," he answered gruffly, knowing the listener would assume the grainy sound of his voice was due to his interrupted sleep, not his unfulfilled lust.

"Hey, man, what's up?" Sam Fremont, Julian's mechanic, called cheerfully from the other end. He loved Sam like one of his own brothers, but his nocturnal habits sometimes put a strain on their lifelong friendship. Julian, being a man of order and routine, insisted on getting eight solid hours of sleep every night. Sam, a true night owl, had no respect whatsoever for that schedule and tended to call whenever the mood struck him; like now.

Julian glanced at the clock on the nightstand. "Why are you calling my house at four-thirty in the morning, Sam? And keep in mind that anything short of a death is an unacceptable answer."

"I'm dying all right." Sam chuckled. "Dying to get out of Detroit."

Julian scooted back against the headboard. "Okay, I'll bite. What are you talking about?"

"Tami started hinting at marriage last night. I've decided to hide out in Traverse City for a few days, hoping she'll get off this particularly pointless kick."

"I thought you really liked Tami."

"I do, and I'd like to keep seeing her, but you know how I feel about husband-hunting women."

"Sam, you are thirty-two. Don't you think it's time you started thinking about settling down with one woman?"

"What are you talking about? We're the same age, and I don't see you running to the altar."

"The difference is, I'm not running from it either. I just haven't found the right woman." He ran a tired hand through his short-cropped hair, briefly remembering the lustful dream Sam had interrupted moments ago. "At least not a real-life one," he muttered as an afterthought.

"What's that supposed to mean?"

"Never mind. Look, you can't play your whole life. As much as I hate to say this to you, it's time to grow up, Peter Pan."

"You're more than mature enough for both of us."

Julian chose to ignore the remark. He'd heard statements similar to that one enough to last a lifetime, and from several different sources. Sometimes his family and friends treated him as if he were some kind of soulless android. "You never did say why you were calling."

"I got your message off the answering machine earlier. I was just returning your call. What's up?"

"I was in an accident a few days ago."

"Are you all right?"

"I'm fine, but Baby's not."

"How bad?"

"I don't think there's any engine damage; mainly bodywork."

"Humph," Sam said while thinking. "Tell you what, there's a mechanic on the East Side—"

"Sam! Don't do this to me. You know I don't take Baby to just anyone. Only you."

"I know, I know, but this is one of my apprentices, and believe me, she knows as much about classic cars as I do—maybe more."

"*She*? You're sending my Baby to some *wannabe* female mechanic?"

"Better not say that to her."

"I can't believe you're doing this to me."

Sam's ever-present playful tone changed to that of a concerned friend. "Julian, I would never send you to anyone I did not trust completely. She knows her stuff, and she'll treat Baby like the treasure she is."

Julian sat silently on the other end, pressing his temples between his thumb and index finger, wondering if the situation could get any worse.

"I'm telling you, man, you won't be sorry," Sam continued. "It's a small garage, but don't let that fool you. Just swing by, check her out, and then decide. Got a pen?"

Reluctantly, Julian wrote down the address of the garage. "Okay, but that's all I'm promising, so if you are expecting some kind of kickback for recommending me, don't count on it."

"You've more than done your part to fatten my pockets over the years," Sam boasted, referring to the many profitable financial tips Julian had given him over time. "I'll let the finder's fee slide. I'll give you a call when I get back in town."

"All right, just make sure you don't put me in the middle of this thing with Tami, the way you did with Char."

"Don't worry, I've learned my lesson. I can't believe I actually thought the Boy Scout would cover for me. Later, man."

Julian placed his receiver back on the base and sat up in the bed, thinking about his commitment-phobic friend and all the opportunities he'd had to marry. Sam had a way of attracting passion-filled and sometimes emotionally unstable women who had always baffled Julian. They flocked to him like magnet to metal and fawned over him as if he were the best thing to ever happen to them. And even when he rejected them, they still wanted him. But not one had ever gotten him within twenty feet of a church or a justice of the peace.

Julian frowned thoughtfully, considering the difference between Sam's relationships and his own. The women who Julian always attracted were the complete opposite. Always career-minded and ambitious, marriage was the furthest thing from their minds. Many of them attempted to use Julian's social and political connections to advance their own interests. He always recognized the ladder climbers and never really minded their blatant exploitation since his own reasons for dating them weren't much different.

Early in his career, Julian had discovered the precarious position he put himself in every time he showed up at a party stag. Middle-aged, married businessmen were never fond of a handsome, single young man hanging around their wives no matter how much of a financial wizard he might be. And Julian knew their fears were not without reason, considering the slips of paper he sometimes found in his coat pocket and the occasional wink of an eye he caught across a crowded table. He found deflecting flirtations from dangerous women and feigning ignorance for jealous husbands consumed his time when all he wanted to do was talk business.

When he'd met and first started dating Celeste, he knew from the start that she just wanted to use him as a stepping stone to advance her future. But she spoke three languages, was a connoisseur of fine art, and was an expert in fine wines, and his influential clients loved her. Of course, once she'd achieved her goal, she'd dumped him. Celeste was *very* goal-oriented.

Then there was Helen. Helen spoke only two languages, but she was brilliant when it came to international business. She dumped him after only four months.

Then there was Irene and Saundra and so on and so on. And he soon realized he was continuing to date the same woman; she just had a different name. The same look, the same personality, the same cold, robotic lover each and every time.

In fact, Julian realized the only woman he'd met who'd come even close to being the type of passionate, exciting woman who plagued Sam constantly was the one who now haunted his dreams. And frankly, Julian often wondered if the response he'd felt in her body when he touched her wasn't mostly in his head. After all, he'd had one brief, albeit memorable, moment with a total stranger. Not exactly the kind of foundation anyone could build a future on. Truthfully, given her shabby appearance and strange companion, he had no delusions that she was probably not anyone he would have wanted to get to know better.

He turned over and began to pound his pillow into a comfortable position while considering his options. He could wait until his fugitive friend returned to town—and who knew when that would be—or he could try to find another repairman on his own, which was always a gamble. Or trust Sam's judgment about this woman mechanic.

As much as he hated to admit, the decision was already made. The only person he could ever trust with his precious Baby was be Sam or someone trained by Sam.

Burrowing into the covers, he closed his eyes, and instantly the dream woman appeared. Straddling his chest, staring down at him. Strong muscular legs gripping his hips. Her clear brown eyes watching him, steadily and seductively, begging him to take her. He rubbed his hand over his face, wishing she would return to the deep recesses of his mind and stay there.

Chapter 5

It was chaos, utter and complete chaos. Every corner of the small workshop was strewn with the strangest menagerie of items he'd ever seen collected in one place. In one corner were mountains of metal and piles of plastic. In another was a motley pile of damaged bicycles, everything from the three-wheel preschooler style to the more expensive mountain bikes used by serious bikers, each with a twisted wheel or bent bars, all seeming far beyond the help of anyone. The pile of bike parts was outlined by a white sheet that hid God only knew what. In the middle of the floor was a large, metal vehicle lift holding up a small brown sedan, which was obviously in the process of being repaired. But there was a sense of order. Julian could see it. Despite the clutter, the shop was rather neat. There were no oil stains on the light concrete, and he silently wondered how that was possible. The walls were lined with tools, each seeming to have its own place.

One-fourth of the larger room composed a smaller one. A paint shed, built from concrete with runner doors, and bright, halogen lights set deep inside the walls. From the well-used look of the paint shed, Julian concluded this was a working body shop. A good sign.

Two framed pictures hanging on the wall just above the sales counter caught his attention. The first one appeared to be two women, one rather short and one rather tall, both smiling happily while posing with Snoopy. The words Cedar Point Amusement Park and a date from the previous year were scrawled across the bottom in marker.

The other picture showed the shorter woman posing with the pit crew of a red racing Mustang in the background. The words Indy Five Hundred at Belle Isle Park were scribbled across the bottom of it.

Something about the women in the picture seemed familiar. Julian approached the picture slowly. Once he was close enough to fully recognize the images, he froze and sucked in his breath, not believing his eyes.

That's when he heard the slight jingling noise of metal on metal and realized he was not alone in the garage. Quietly, he circled the sedan on an overhead lift and saw someone standing beneath with arms lifted above their head. Taking in the shapely body beneath the fitted coveralls severed any doubts he may have had. It was her—it had to be her. Julian was certain he would recognize that body anywhere since it had haunted his dreams for the past three weeks.

The elf.

She was completely oblivious to his arrival. Whatever she was doing under the car had her full attention. She was shaking her hips to the sounds of a popular R&B song coming from the radio on the counter, and every once in a while she sang a few words to the chorus.

It was the hip shaking that convinced Julian to stand as still and quietly as possible. Every male instinct in him pleaded not to interrupt the seductive show. He found himself mesmerized by the gentle movement.

Suddenly, she stopped pulling at the defective part. Instinctively, Callie knew she was no longer alone. She lowered her arms and backed from beneath the raised vehicle. When she turned to face her visitor, she would've sworn her heart stopped beating for a moment.

All Callie had were vague memories of a peacefully sleeping angel, but now a very conscious man was standing in the middle of her shop floor. This was the man she'd feared would be trouble the first time she'd laid eyes on him. He wore neatly pressed tan Dockers, a sage-green pullover, and leather loafers, but even his casual attire could not create an image of warmth and approachability.

There was something very menacing about him, and she knew without a doubt a very real threat had just strolled into her garage. What was he doing here? Had he come to check out the garage? To look over his future property or to attempt more intimidation like the night of the accident? He'd become enraged once he realized Pooky was a man. He'd vowed that they would pay, and then two weeks later the summons had appeared.

Now here he stood.

Out of curiosity, Callie glanced around him and spotted the shiny, black Avalanche sitting in the garage entrance. *Nice backup car*, she thought, feeling bitter envy for a brief moment. She and Pooky had struggled just to make ends meet for so long it seemed like forever. And now here was this man, threatening to take what little they did have when he obviously had so much more.

Callie's eyes narrowed in anger as she considered his possible motives. If he wanted the only remaining legacy she had from her father, then he had better be ready to fight for it. "What do you want?" she asked with her hands fisted on her hips.

Julian's dark eyes skimmed over her small form, thinking what a loaded question that was. In his obsession with her body, he'd forgotten how lovely her face was. Small, delicate features set in golden brown skin, but her most stunning feature was the clear brown eyes, almost the color of topaz, which were now bright with silent warning.

She was dressed as she had been the night they met—in ugly green coveralls. She still wore the same oil-stained baseball cap with the bib turned back. In truth, Julian thought there was nothing appealing or alluring about her appearance at all. She was in no way sending out the typical female invitation. And yet, everything male in him was screaming yes in answer.

"Are you a master mechanic or still in apprenticeship status?"

Callie's heart skipped a beat. She'd often wondered what his voice would sound like. The deep baritone sound was very close to what she'd imagined. His lips were pressed in a thin line, but Callie knew that when they were relaxed, they were soft and full. The memory of touching them would be forever ingrained on her brain.

"I said, are you a master mechanic or an apprentice?" he asked again. His large, imposing frame filled every inch of the small space as he surveyed his environment in such a way that let Callie know important decisions were being made beneath that cool exterior.

When his eyes fell on her again, Callie could almost feel

gentle fingers tickling her skin. Why would he care if she was a master mechanic or still in training?

Unless…

Callie wasn't the slightest bit modest about her abilities. She knew that she had a reputation in the tristate area for being somewhat of an expert in antique cars. And he did have an antique car that needed repairing, right? Could it be that he was here for a totally different reason than she'd first suspected?

"That depends." She folded her arms across her chest.

Piercing dark eyes scorched her skin. He folded his muscular arms across his chest to match her pose. And Callie silently wondered how crazy it was to bait a bulldog.

"On what?"

"On why you want to know."

Julian found himself gritting his teeth. "I was told you specialized in classic car repair. But I won't deal with an apprentice. If you are fully certified, I might have a deal to offer you."

She slowly moved toward her workbench to collect an oilcloth. "I'm fully certified." Callie's mind was running a thousand miles an hour. "But I'm not sure I would be interested in any deal you would be offering," she answered with her back to him, slowly wiping her hands on the cloth.

Julian took several aggressive steps forward and stopped. A game of cat and mouse was being played, and he had a sneaking suspicion he was the mouse. "Why not?"

She swung around to face him. "Did you honestly think I would repair your car when you are *suing* me?"

"I would think that you would be more than willing, considering you're the reason it needs to be repaired in the first place."

"I told you then and I'm telling you now," Callie said between her teeth, "we were not responsible for that accident!"

A long silence fell over the pair as they came to a stalemate. At some point since he'd walked through the door, Julian thought she'd discovered she had the upper hand and was playing it like a pro. Of course, he could simply take the car to another garage. But despite everything, something about the fierce, little beauty standing in front of him in stained coveralls spoke of competence and expertise.

"Will you repair my car or not?" Although he looked completely calm while examining the few tools on the counter, Callie could hear the underlining menace.

"First let's hear this offer." Callie leaned back against the counter.

He crossed the room to stand directly in front of her, only a few inches of precious air between them. And Callie found herself fighting a trembling that seemed to increase with his proximity.

As if reading her thoughts, Julian's mouth spread in a slow, heart-stopping smile. "You fix my Corvette, and I'll drop my lawsuit against you and your friend." He made a hand gesture. "That seems like a fair trade."

Callie lowered her eyes, trying to understand the intense physical response this stranger was creating in her. "When?"

"What?"

"When will you drop the lawsuit? Today or when I'm finished with your car? What if you decide you don't like the work and sue anyway?"

She knew she should feel guilty about what she was doing, but desperate times called for desperate measures. By some twist of fate, this man who she at first believed was holding all the cards was apparently missing the ace of spades.

Julian's eyes pinned her to the ground. "Are you calling me a liar?"

Callie fought the temptation to retreat, knowing if she did

she would lose any advantage she may have had. "I don't know you well enough to call you anything."

"I said," he started slowly, "I would drop the suit, and I will."

"Immediately."

"No!"

"I guess I can't help you then." Callie shrugged her shoulders. "With all these legal fees, I have no money left for parts or a garage to work in." She took a deep breath and braced herself for whatever offensive statement would fly loose from his lips. It was blackmail, pure and simple. But as far as she could see, she had no other choice.

Julian paused for several moments deciding, and Callie waited patiently. A person wasn't blackmailed every day. She could afford to give him some time to come to terms with the situation. Besides, she needed some time herself to try and understand the magnetic pull he seemed to have on her.

Finally, he nodded. "Okay then, you've got a deal." Before he could reconsider, Julian bent his head forward. "And to seal it…"

When Julian felt soft lips meet his, he had to fight the urge to force his way into her mouth. Something shifted in the universe, and he felt the kiss all the way to the tips of his toes. Using control he'd never needed, he let her lips skim over his, letting her guide it. She would decide when he could come inside. Julian was so focused on the tender kiss, it took a minute to realize his arm had snaked around her waist. For the life of him, he could not remember ever reaching out to her.

His tongue pressed against the smooth surface of her teeth for less than a second, and she opened her mouth and let him inside. She parted her lips as her small hands circled his neck. Lust flooded his body, and all his intentions of moving slowly and allowing her to set the pace disappeared. All that was left was the rising bulge in his slacks, his pounding heartbeat, and three weeks of dreams filled with erotic images of this woman. Callie's soft body responded eagerly as if she had read his thoughts and agreed completely.

Julian held on to her small frame, pressing her body up against his own. What was it about this elf that felt so good, so *right*. Pressed against him, Callie could do nothing to hide her body's response. She knew she should've pushed away; she shouldn't have let him kiss her, but she just couldn't find the will to do it.

Wrapping his hands around her bottom, and without allowing their lips to part, he lifted his small burden up against him. Callie's legs parted to straddle his muscular thigh, feeling as if she would never get close enough to him. Feeding on his mouth in wanton abandon, she reveled in the most glorious feeling she'd ever known. The feel of Julian's hands on her body made her question every relationship she'd ever experienced. Nothing—*no one*—had ever made her feel this way with just a kiss.

Julian felt himself stiffening at the image of the beauty in his arms; her body was responding magnificently. He knew if they stayed on their present course, they would make love right then and there. Neither one was giving a care about anything outside their perfect little bubble. And Julian suddenly realized this was the most freeing experience of his life. *This* was the passion other men spoke of, which up until now he had only imagined. His large hand curved around her thigh, almost intuitively being drawn to the warmth emanating from the center of her being.

Feeling his questing hand in places no man had gone in quite some time, Callie was rocketed back to earth. *What am I doing?* She began pushing against his hands.

"Wait, stop!"

Julian's trembling hands froze in place, one beneath her bottom, the other holding her firmly around the waist. "What's wrong?"

Julian felt something in his heart snap as he looked into her eyes. He knew in that moment that she would not go through with it. The bubble was busted. He let his arms drop to his side as she slid down his leg and took several steps back.

Callie quickly folded her arms across her chest to hide the most obvious sign of her arousal. "Umm, look." Callie cleared her throat loudly. "I don't usually do things like this."

"Don't," Julian snapped. His body was still in overdrive, and despite whatever she may be thinking at the moment, he had not a single regret. He held up his hand to still the apology. "Don't say it!"

Callie jumped at the harsh tone. Just a reminder, she thought, of how little she knew about this man. "I just meant I don't jump on every man who comes through my front door, that's all."

Julian took several steps from the temptation she represented. "I never thought you did."

Callie's eyes narrowed in anger. "Well, I don't!"

"I never thought you did!"

"Maybe you should go."

Julian ran his hand over his short-cropped hair, silently warring with his instincts. He knew she was right—the only way to end such an awkward moment was to walk away from it and never look back. So why was he having such a hard time convincing his body to leave?

Julian was mystified by what was transpiring between them. She was so wrong in every way, but his crazy male hormones just didn't seem to care. He cleared his throat. "I was serious about the deal. You fix my car, and I'll drop the suit. We'll just call it even."

Maybe things were going to work out after all. Callie nodded in agreement.

His eyes slowly slid over her again. He held out his hand. "Deal?"

Callie stared at the large hand for several moments. It was just an ordinary hand, with strong, well-defined fingers, but Callie felt that if she accepted this handshake, she would be agreeing to a lot more than a few car repairs. She stepped forward, looking up into his dark eyes with determination. She took the hand and shook it. "Deal."

Chapter 6

"**Y**ou do understand, Mr. Harding, that you have only three CDs left in your portfolio." Harold Presner, the bank's in-house investment advisor sat across the table from his strangest client.

Pooky nodded solemnly. "Yes, I understand."

"Let me strongly caution you—"

Pooky smiled beautifully and reached across to table to touch the other man's hand. "Harold, can I call you Harold?" Pooky asked sweetly. "Harold, I understand your concern, and I truly appreciate it, but I really need to cash one of my CDs. And quite frankly, I'm in somewhat of a hurry. Besides, I still have my Chrysler stock, and last I checked, it was doing quite well. Not to mention that sweet little mutual fund you set up for me a few months ago. Right?"

Harold nodded dumbly, flabbergasted by the way a smile transformed the face of this person. "Well, yes, but—"

"Harold—" Pooky's voice dropped an octave, reminding

Harold Presner that he was indeed dealing with a man "—I need to cash that CD. Please don't give me a hard time."

Harold Presner hated to see his clients—any of his clients—make a bad decision. But his job was only to offer recommendations, and he'd done that. "All right, I'll be right back."

Pooky sat back in his chair. He watched Harold Presner let himself into the money cage, and only then let his guard down enough to bite his lip, which was a nervous habit he'd had since childhood. He had no idea what the future would bring, but the ten thousand dollars from this CD would help for a while. But he could not ignore the fact that Harold Presner was right. Over the past five years, he'd cashed in over 60 percent of his significant investment portfolio, both in an attempt to help Callie and to get his own enterprise off the ground. When Callie had come to him all those years ago, he'd been more than willing and able to help her. But for reasons beyond their control, the garage had not been able to turn a profit. Not a lot of people trusted a female mechanic.

Pooky knew that Callie did some of the finest work in the city, and he was certain that once word got around, their business would boom. He just had to keep them afloat until then.

Julian stood towering over his fourteen-year-old daughter. She looked so timid in the large wingback leather chair. Her small hands were cradled in her lap, her head downcast in shame. She looked like the epitome of remorse, and Julian wasn't buying it for one second.

"Olivia, look at me," he said in his most stern fatherly voice.

Olivia lifted her head and looked at her father with large brown eyes. The long ponytails falling over her shoulders were the perfect touch to her act of innocence.

"Did you do it?"

Her long dark lashes fluttered innocently. "No, Daddy."

She looked so repentant; a lesser man would've been easily suckered. It had been a painful education, but Julian was slowly learning the ways of his daughter. He crossed his arms behind his back and studied her.

"Olivia, this is the third suspension in four months!"

Olivia's brown eyes flashed with hidden fury, but she quickly suppressed it. "I *said* I didn't do it. The head mistress is a liar—an ugly, toad-face liar!"

"There's a liar here," Julian's deep voice growled, "but it's not the head mistress!"

Olivia was on her feet in an instant. Having inherited her father's height at fourteen years old, she stood just beneath his chin. "You'd believe a stranger's word over your own daughter's?"

Julian had had enough of her dramatic performance. She was guilty as sin, and they both knew it. "Go to your room! And don't come out until I tell you to!"

"Fine!" Olivia spat, turning and storming away.

"Fine!" Julian called after her. He listened as the door slammed shut. He turned and went back to his desk and tried to immerse himself back into his work, but he was still too angry. Angry at his inability to control his own child, angry with Rachel for giving him such a monumental task with absolutely no guidance. In one afternoon, she'd changed his life and placed him in a role he doubted he would ever be suited for.

He was angry with Sam for sending him to his apprentice. Angry that ever since his first encounter with the elf, he'd not been able to shake her image from his mind. That perfect little body that called to him, along with those seductive bedroom eyes that revealed such a passionate nature. Angry that he'd come so close to having her, but instead was left feeling as frustrated as ever. He was angry at the whole world!

In a rare fit of rage, he used his long arms to rake his desk clear. Roaring in anger, he pushed his desk blotter, penholder, brass paperweight, empty cola can, and piles of papers onto the floor.

A soft tap on the door interrupted his tirade. "Um, did I come at a bad time?"

Julian looked up into the face of his eldest brother, James, who was also one of his business partners. Together, the three brothers formed Cruise Corporation, which was quickly becoming one of the most influential financial consulting firms in the world. This was due mainly in part to Julian's computer-like brain, a fact neither brother would dispute.

Julian was never surprised to look up and see the members of his family roaming freely through his house. Unfortunately for him, his mother had insisted on a key to his eighteenth-century brick home when he moved into the exclusive Sherwood Forest area years ago. *In case of emergencies*, she'd said. What she did not say was that she intended to make a copy of the key for his father and each of his two brothers. Or that any time, day or night, qualified as an emergency.

Julian slumped back down in his chair. "Unless you are bringing me good news, you can go back where you came from."

James smiled. "Well, then I guess I'm bringing you good news."

Julian suddenly sat up. "Please say we won the bid for CompuTech?"

The brothers had bid against three other top financial firms for the right to consult with one of the fasting-growing computer software companies in the country. The account not only held a significant financial gain, but it was a matter of prestige as well. CompuTech's reorganization was in the news every day, and so would the name of the financial firm that managed that reorganization.

They knew the competition would be stiff, so Julian had bid lower than market expectation. It was a ploy that had worked for him more than once.

James rubbed the back of his knuckles against his chest, smiling in pure satisfaction. "Okay, we won the bid for CompuTech."

Julian jumped to his feet. "Don't play with me, man."

"Really, we did."

"Yes!" Julian felt the sweet victorious feeling he always got whenever he managed to underbid the competition. With such a large part of the auto industry collected in one place, Detroit could be a very competitive city at times.

James cast his eyes in the direction of the family room that attached to Julian's home office. The couch was empty, which it rarely was on a weekend. "Where's Olivia?"

"Don't ask."

James heard the subtle warning and left the matter alone. He'd witnessed more than one battle of the wills between father and daughter. He held his tongue this time, but on more than one occasion, James had dared to point out the obvious to Julian. As far as he could tell, the main point of contention between parent and child was the similarities in their personalities.

In truth, Olivia looked more like her mother, but in spirit and mind she was most definitely her father's child. Strong-willed to the point of being insufferable, highly intelligent and fiercely independent, they shared a very aggressive personality. The two souls were mirror images of each other, and their inability to deal with each other was proof of just how difficult that personality really was.

Julian bent and began picking up his items. "How long do we have to prepare our presentation?"

James came around the desk to help him, noting that the laptop computer was still sitting perfectly safe and sound on the desk. "They want to meet at the end of the month."

"That's less than two weeks."

"I know." James frowned.

Julian slumped back down into his leather desk chair; he was already creating the plan in his mind. "That's okay. We can do it."

James took up a position on the edge of the desk. "I've already got Jonathan working on the format."

Julian nodded his head. Jonathan, the youngest of the Cruise brothers, had only recently graduated from Northwestern and had been brought into the fold. But like any new recruit, he had to pay his dues, which meant running miscellaneous errands for the business and doing the tedious stuff neither Julian nor James wanted to do.

"Great, I'll get started on the financial plan tonight."

"All right, I'll devise a timeline. I think that's what swung the bid in our direction—we were the only ones who could meet their time constraints."

"Make sure we do," Julian said gruffly, already scribbling ideas across his legal pad.

James shook his head, knowing that casual conversation with his brother had just come to an end. His mind was turning inward to that wonderful place that was making them all very rich young men. Julian had a gift for determining the direction of the economy and the best investment strategies. His abilities greatly resembled fortune-telling.

He could examine the financial data of any struggling company and determine what they were doing wrong in a matter of minutes. But the true skill—the one that had made him one of Detroit's rising stars—was that he could give them a way to fix it. A way that, according to his record, worked 95 percent of the time. And when it didn't work, it was usually because of circumstances beyond anyone's control. Realizing he'd been dismissed, James let himself out of the house. Julian, who was pecking at the keyboard, barely noticed.

Julian was working at his desk several hours later when the melodic voice of a woman interrupted him. "Hello," the voice of Pam Cruise drifted into his home office as a blurred image of his mother, and a ceramic pot of what smelled like her irresistible clam chowder, breezed by his doorway, moving quickly toward his kitchen.

Julian shook his head, wondering if there would ever come a day when his relations would knock upon entering his house. He glanced at the clock and realized he'd been working for close to two hours straight. At the insistence of his growling belly, he decided to take a break.

By the time he reached the kitchen, his mother and Olivia were hunched over the pot, inhaling the wonderful smell emanating from it.

"Umm, Grandma, that smells wonderful!" Olivia practically cooed.

As Julian entered the kitchen, he felt his jaw flex. Olivia was supposed to be in her bedroom. He circled the counter, placing a quick kiss on his mother's cheek. "And to what do we owe the pleasure of this visit?"

Pam tilted her head and glared at her middle son. "Do I need a reason to visit my child?"

Apparently this visit was not what it appeared. His brain quickly calculated the possibilities. Either James had called their parents and cried foul about his treatment of Olivia or…Julian cast a suspicious look in his daughter's direction. *I knew giving her a telephone in her bedroom was a bad idea.*

Pam Cruise was a devout parent to her three offspring. Having been a housewife since the age of twenty-two, she'd had years to perfect the art of motherhood. For the past thirty-five years, her children had been the center of her universe, and although Julian and his two siblings had all flown the coop, her nesting instincts were as strong as ever. Especially when it came to her only grandchild.

"Where's my boy?"

Pam smiled at the familiar gruff voice of her husband calling from the hallway.

Julian shook his head. "I really wish he wouldn't do that."

Suddenly, the older and much more relaxed of the Cruise males appeared in the kitchen doorway. He was dressed in a royal blue velvet leisure suit and expensive running shoes. His perfect smile was proof that good teeth were hereditary.

"There he is." James Cruise Sr. appeared in the doorway. "My boy, my boy." James Sr. stood grinning at his son from the door. "Damn, I've got some good genes."

Julian and his mother's eyes met across the room, and they both simply shook their heads. Julian, along with his two brothers, were quite used to their father claiming complete credit for their creation. According to James Sr. he alone was responsible for not only their lives, but also their individual success.

James Sr. was an affectionate man and always greeted his sons with a hug. "How are you, son?"

"Never better, Pop," Julian answered, his attention returning to the item that brought him to the kitchen in the first place: the ceramic pot. "I really wish you wouldn't call out down the hall to me like that. What if I had a client here?"

James Sr. shrugged his shoulders. "What if? They would've heard me looking for my son."

Julian shook his head. He'd asked his father a countless number of times not to call to him from the other end of the long corridor leading from the front entrance to his home office. Being self-employed, he often used his home office for the occasional necessary meeting.

James Sr. ignored his son's disapproving look and moved around the kitchen island to his granddaughter. "How's my baby?"

Olivia wrapped her arms around her grandfather and squeezed tightly. "Okay, I guess. Although, Daddy's put me on punishment again." She cast a smug look of triumph in the direction of her father, and Julian knew instantly that his parents' visit was no coincidence.

His father's casual smile disappeared. "Again? What did she do this time, sneeze too loud for you?" He swung around to Julian. "She probably committed the carnal sin of coughing in public."

Julian stood with his legs braced apart, determined to stand his ground with his father. And disgusted to realize he'd been set up by a fourteen-year-old girl.

When it came to Olivia, his father could be quite obstinate. As far as James Sr. was concerned, his one and only grandchild could do no wrong. And Olivia was very good at using her resources, a skill Julian had been repeatedly told she'd inherited from him.

"She was suspended from school—again."

James Sr.'s dark eyes flashed. "If you'd stop sending her to those stuck-up private schools and try sending her to a regular school with regular kids, maybe she'd stop getting suspended!"

"The problem is not the school, Pop. It's Olivia. She's defiant!"

"So were you, but your mother and I never shipped you off anywhere!"

"Grandpa?" Olivia's timid voice interrupted the battle.

Julian glared at his daughter. Her lips were trembling, and she'd even managed to summon water to her eyes. *She is good*, Julian thought, *very, very good*.

"Oh, Grandpa, I'm so sorry. That mean old woman picks on me. I don't know why."

"Shh, it's okay. Grandpa's here now." He stroked her long ponytails and cooed gently.

Julian felt a fury building in his chest. He'd specifically told Olivia not to come out of her room until he told her to. Now, to send her back, he would have to go to war with his father, and Olivia knew it. He was seriously considering turning his *little girl* over his knee and showing her a side of her father she'd yet to see.

Julian looked to his mother for support, but as always, Pam was just taking in the scene. He knew she would make her judgments later, but they were usually in favor of her husband. Sometimes Julian felt as if he had to fight his whole family for the right to raise his daughter the way he saw fit. And it was times like this when the weight of the challenge seemed too much to bear.

Frustrated beyond belief, he grabbed his keys off the counter and headed for the door. "When I come back, I expect you—" he pointed to Olivia "—to be in your room." He was almost to the door when he paused. He grabbed a bowl from the cabinet and filled it with his mother's homemade clam chowder, then headed out the back door.

"Where do you think you're going?" James Sr. called to his son, still cradling his granddaughter in his arms.

"Out," Julian called over his shoulder, never breaking his stride.

Chapter 7

"He's just soo sexy."

To his credit, Pooky paused only momentarily, although the heartfelt statement was shocking. Up until then, the only bodies he'd seen his little cousin get lustful over were usually metal. He continued to unpack the grocery bags while listening quietly.

"But he's the enemy, right?" Callie stood leaning against the wall on the opposite side of the small kitchenette.

"If you say so." Pooky shrugged and reached up to place a few cans of vegetables in the top shelf of the cupboard.

"He tried to sue us, and may still if he's not satisfied with the work I do."

"He'll be satisfied."

"I mean, who cares if he has the most perfect lips you'd ever want to see and perfectly flawless chocolate-brown skin. Who cares if he kisses like an angel—right?"

"Right."

"Or that incredible body. Like a…a…"

"Bodybuilder?" Pooky offered helpfully.

"No." Callie shook her head thoughtfully. "He's leaner. He's muscular, but not too much. Know what I mean?"

"I'm sorry I missed him. I've never seen him in a vertical position."

"He is definitely something worth seeing." She laid her head back on the wall. "His smile is like sunshine."

"Watch yourself, girl. This brother's bringing out the poet in you."

Callie's head came up, and her eyes narrowed in suspicion. "What's that supposed to mean?"

"Just that I know you, my darling. I know you very, very well. So when are you planning to see him again?"

"When he brings the car, I guess."

"No, I mean socially?"

"Have you heard a single word I've said?"

Pooky's professionally arched eyebrow went up in response to the fierce glare Callie was giving him. "I've heard every word you said." He bent to place the dishwashing detergent in the cabinet under the sink. "I even heard the words you *didn't* say."

Callie threw up her hands, realizing there would be no sympathy forthcoming. "I hate it when you get philosophical!" She stormed out of the kitchen.

Callie was not looking to be analyzed. She'd waited most of the afternoon for Pooky to return for one simple reason: she needed the kind of unconditional support she could only receive from her best friend.

Callie flopped down on the couch. She needed to get her mind off of *him*. Something she'd been unable to do all day. Callie had hoped that once Pooky returned, he would tell her in no uncertain terms that the man was a monster and that she'd done the right thing in rejecting him. She should've known all Pooky would want to do is delve into her psyche. He considered himself something of an amateur therapist.

Pooky came and braced his tall form in the doorway. His buttercup jumper was the perfect accent to his caramel coloring. His make-up, which he wore almost twenty-four hours a day, was applied with perfection as usual. His exceptional instinct for color and style along with his naturally refined features made the double take a standard reaction. More than one brother had his head turned by the tall, superfine *sista*. But under close scrutiny, the truth was revealed. And there was absolutely no cosmetic help for his deep, husky voice.

"Did I say something wrong?" he asked innocently.

"Yes."

"What'd I say?" He crossed the room and sat down next to Callie, lifting her short legs onto his lap. He began to untie her workboots.

"You broke the best friend oath. When I say a guy—any guy—is a lousy, arrogant SOB, you are supposed to agree without hesitation. When I say he's a class-A jerk, you are suppose to say *absolutely*."

He pulled off Callie's slipper footies and began massaging her feet as a peace offering. "Oh. I forgot about the best friend oath."

Callie lay back on the sofa as she felt her whole body relaxing in response to the foot rub. "Yes, you did." She nodded in agreement.

Pooky's magical fingers were working their wonder, and soon she felt the tension flowing from her body. She would never admit it, but Pooky was right. She would most definitely have to watch herself with Mr. Julian Cruise.

With one touch, he managed to inflame her senses to the point of lost reason. When he held her against his hard body, nothing else had mattered. Not the lawsuit, the garage, even the harsh words spoken between them. All that had mattered was the burning passion she felt emanating from her core and the hungry desire she saw reflected in his black pearls.

Overcome with fatigue, Callie spoke her thoughts. "I want him, Pooky." The words were more of a whispered sigh than a statement.

Pooky recognized the sound. Many days Callie worked herself into a complete state of exhaustion. In her efforts to keep the garage open, she often worked ridiculously long hours and took on repairs for a fraction of what the competition would charge.

"Shh, hush now," Pooky cooed lovingly. He thought about the check he had tucked neatly in his purse. At least it would hold the wolves at bay another couple of months.

Despite what he'd told Callie, Pooky was concerned about Julian Cruise's mysterious arrival at the garage. If it was coincidence, then it had to be one heck of a coincidence that would bring him to them. And if it was not, then the man was definitely up to something.

Standing, Pooky stretched Callie's feet out on the couch and went in search of a blanket. He knew she was out for the night. Some days, like today, Callie worked so hard that wherever she finally stopped was where she slept.

Covering her with a blue blanket he found in the linen closet, he stood looking down at a young woman who'd seen more grief in her twenty-eight years than some women had in a lifetime. He only hoped this enigmatic stranger wouldn't be more of the same.

* * *

Callie was awakened to a beeping sound she recognized as a truck-backing signal. She sat up and took in her environment, realizing she'd fallen asleep on the couch again. Pushing back her blanket, she stood and stretched. That's when her mind finally registered just how close the beep-beeping sound was. It sounded like the truck was backing inside her garage!

Callie raced down the stairs and came to an abrupt halt at the bottom. A tow truck driver was just stepping out of the truck and coming around to the back to lower his platform.

He took one look at Callie in her disheveled state and coveralls and nodded. "Are you the mechanic?"

"I guess so." She yawned, trying to get a look at the vehicle up on the flatbed. She never scheduled appointments this early in the morning, so whoever it was had to be a walk-in. She came along the side of the truck, stretching up on her tiptoes, and instantly recognized the little red Corvette sitting in shambles.

Realizing Julian Cruise had wasted no time in getting his vehicle into her shop, Callie wondered if the car's owner was soon to follow. Just then, Pooky came sashaying down the stairs with all the urgency of molasses.

"Morning, sunshine!" He pecked Callie on the cheek as he came to a halt in front of her. "Well, well, what have we here? Callie, you didn't tell me we were having company."

Callie twisted her lips in derision, knowing Pooky recognized the car as easily as she had. Why did he insist on making everything into a production?

A shadow fell over her at the same time that she realized Pooky was standing with his back to the vehicle. He couldn't even *see* the car on the flatbed. So that could only mean…

"Good morning."

The deep baritone voice that had been resounding in her

head over the past twenty-four hours resonated from only inches behind her.

Pooky's eyes twinkled with mischief as he took in the man who was only slightly taller. "So, sleeping beauty…we meet again."

Julian glared hard at the other man, hoping to intimidate him into fleeing the building in terror. But from the playful wink he received, there was not an ounce of fear in his polyester-clad heart.

Julian took in his stylish ensemble of light blue bodysuit and cream-colored Capri pants. The man was completely accessorized, from the perfectly matching blue stiletto sandals and cream-colored scarf tied around his neck to the light blue eyeshadow that outlined his eyes. Julian begrudgingly admitted that on a woman the clothing combination would've been quite appealing.

He glanced down at the tiny woman standing directly in front of him. He couldn't see her face, but then again, he didn't need to. It was embedded in his memory. Just when he was about to speak to her, they all heard the driver calling from the back of the truck.

"Whose gonna sign this requisition?"

"I will." Julian moved around Callie and Pooky to take the clipboard from the man, and Callie got her first glimpse of him.

He was dressed casually in a dusk-colored light knit sweater, khaki jeans, and loafers. His neat, graying hair was freshly cut, and his full mustache was neatly trimmed.

Callie's eyes fell on Pooky, who was watching her and grinning with such joy he bordered on giddy.

"What?"

"You look like hell."

Callie's eyes widened in stunned disbelief. She suddenly

realized she must've looked like she'd just rolled out of bed, considering *she had just rolled out of bed*!

"Oh no, Pooky. You've got to cover for me," Callie whispered.

Pooky cast a glance over his shoulder at the man speaking with the tow truck driver. "I'll give you enough time to get back upstairs; then I'm out of here. That man has *homophobe* written all over that gorgeous body of his, and if I stay here, I'll be too tempted to try to kiss him again—and I don't even want to think where that would lead."

"Pooky! Keep your talons off of him."

"Feeling possessive?"

"Feeling desperate!" she hissed in a whisper. "He's agreed to drop his lawsuit, but if you go pawing all over him, he just might change his mind."

"All right, all right, but you better go while that driver's got his attention."

Callie tried to circle around the other side of the tow truck, but when she reached the staircase, she realized the unloaded car was cutting off her path. *Damn!*

Callie heard the truck's engine turn over and stepped back as the driver pulled out of the small garage.

"So? What do you think?" Julian spoke to her from the other side of the small sports car now sitting on the floor.

Callie heard Pooky's faint snickering as he hurried out of the garage. *You better run,* she thought. So much for any possible escape.

Callie realized there was no hope but to hold up her head and try not to get too close to him with her morning breath. She walked back a few steps and began to seriously consider the damaged vehicle. "Wow, it was mint, wasn't it?"

"Yes."

"I'm going to have to replace the door. Too many pieces

missing and a lot of cracks. There's no way around it. I'm certain I can find a replacement on eBay, but it will no longer have all its original parts."

"What exactly is involved here?"

"Well—" Callie walked along the vehicle, taking in the damage "—the good news is that the door is fiberglass, not metal. And these steel rods here and here." She pointed to a place down between the door, as Julian bent over her shoulder to see. "Those are there to protect the glass window, and it worked. Your window can be reused."

"How long is this going to take?"

Callie rubbed her chin thoughtfully. "Let me see…with ordering parts, glue, sanding, and painting…a couple of weeks."

Julian ran his hand over the cloth top, sadness etching his face.

Callie mimicked his caress on the opposite side, running her hand along the smooth material. "Not to brag, but when I get finished, you won't be able to tell the difference. Unfortunately, you can no longer sell it as mint."

"I know. Just fix it. I'm more attached to it sentimentally than I am financially."

"I understand why. He's a beauty."

"He? Aren't cars and ships referred to in the feminine?"

"That may be okay for some. But for me, something this fine and well put together could *only* be a man."

Julian chuckled. "How did you get into this line of work anyway?"

She shrugged in false modesty. "I cut my teeth working with my dad on antique Fords and Chevys." Her eyes clouded, remembering the 1957 Chevy Belaire, the pride of their collection. Paul had sold it in the estate auction along with all her other childhood memories.

"My dad and his friends were part of the Woodward Dream

Cruise Society, so I grew up around every kind of antique known to man." Callie's mind was in a distant past. "I learned everything I could about them."

Julian felt his heart skip a beat as her eyes lit up with pride when she spoke of her work. Her small smile was playing with his hormones. And he wondered for the hundredth time what was wrong with him. Looking at her in her present condition, there was nothing enticing about her appearance at all.

She was crumpled and wrinkled beyond help, and he was certain those coveralls were the ones she was wearing the day before. He recognized the small oil stain near the collar, and that didn't say much for her hygiene.

The only thing neat about her was her freshly braided cornrows. So why was it, every time he looked at her, his body screamed *gimme*!

Callie was busy pulling at the damaged door, trying to pry it free. "Can you pass me that crowbar over there?" She jerked her head to the right.

Julian stood his ground.

After a few moments, she realized he hadn't moved. "It's right over there." She motioned again.

"You are not taking a crowbar to my Baby."

"I have to get this door off somehow, and it's ruined anyway."

"You are not taking a crowbar to my Baby," Julian repeated.

Callie realized nothing was going to get done with Baby's overprotective father standing guard. "Okay. By the way, I want to apologize for my appearance. I never expected you this early. If you don't mind, I'd like to go freshened up. Can I give you a call later with an estimate of what needs to be done?"

Julian knew she was trying to get rid of him, but what was he supposed to do, tell her she couldn't shower?

"No problem." He smiled insincerely. As he crossed the

room, he pulled his wallet from his back pocket and took out a business card. "Call me on my cell," he said, placing the card on the counter. He then picked up the crowbar and headed toward the garage entrance without ever looking back. "I'll be waiting to hear from you."

Callie shook her head. Well, at least he has peace of mind, she thought, climbing the stairs to her bedroom. And, of course, there were two more crowbars under the counter, one of which she had every intention of using once she showered and changed. As far as she could tell, it was a win-win situation.

Paul DeLeroy stood on the empty People Mover platform outside of the casino, staring down at the raised tracks wondering how he'd managed to get into this mess.

Ten years ago, he'd had more money than he knew what to do with. He'd liquidated his stepfather's assets, sold off almost all his property, and by rights he should never have had to work again.

He'd quit his job, and he and his wife, Mona, had been living large. The problem was spending more time together—they were getting on each other's nerves. So he started hanging out, and more and more often found himself sitting at a crap tables in one of the local casinos. He found he had a knack for the game, but unfortunately his winning streaks never lasted long enough. And the last few months his losing streak had been so bad he'd been forced to start borrowing against the house.

But tonight when he tried to secure the loan with his credit card, he discovered there was nothing left on the card. He pulled another from his wallet, and it was also rejected, as was another. When he pulled his checkbook from his pocket, he tried to remember when the last time was he'd balanced his account and realized it had been weeks. He did a quick mental calculation and came up with a number very close to zero. Somehow, almost overnight, he'd gone from millionaire to flat broke.

How was that possible? *Maybe I could get a job.* Then he remembered he hadn't worked in years. And if he recalled correctly, he'd told his last boss to go to hell when he quit, so he really couldn't expect a recommendation from that quarter. Maybe he could mortgage the house? But how could he face Mona? Beautiful Mona. He'd always known she married him for his money. So what would she say when she found out? Would she leave? So many questions and none with answers. This left him here, thinking how easy it would be to step off the stone platform and end it all. He could wait until the train was right upon him, and just one step forward...

"Are you the one looking for Silver?"

A deep voice spoke from a few feet behind him. Paul started to turn around.

"Stay where you are. Just answer the question."

Paul swallowed hard and wondered briefly if his decision to do business with a loan shark was any better than falling on the train tracks. "Yes, I'm the guy. Are you Silver?"

"No."

Paul waited for some further explanation, but none came. "Does he know why I'm looking for him?"

"Yes. He sent me to check you out, make sure you're legit." The man paused for several long seconds. "He also wants to know how you heard about him."

"I used to work with a guy named Felix Harris, said Silver helped him out this way a few years back."

The other man said nothing. He recognized the name Felix Harris. As Silver's enforcer he was intimately acquainted with all of his late payers. Felix was a chronic late payer and had more than one permanent physical injury to show for it. He wondered if the man standing in front of him was aware of Silver's "late fees." Not his problem; he was just supposed to check the guy out, and he could tell to Silver with a clear conscience that the terrified, trembling, desperate man standing in front of him was no cop.

"Be in front of the park by the old main library tomorrow at ten P.M. I recommend you be there a few minutes early. Silver has this thing about punctuality."

Paul, who'd been holding his breath for fear of being rejected, sighed in audible relief. "Thanks, man. Thank you so much. Tell Silver thanks."

As the man faded back into the shadow he could become at anytime, he was wondering how that gratitude would hold up under the first beating.

Chapter 8

"Pooky, you are magnificent!" Thomas Johnson, better known to the world as Cassandra, held the bright red formal gown in front of his body, watching how the light shimmered off the sequined fabric. "This is exactly the effect I wanted and more."

Pooky bit his lip, fighting his instinct to agree with the man that he was indeed brilliant and magnificent and so much more. Callie had scolded him recently on his lack of modesty, so he'd resolved to try to be more humble. But it was hard being humble when he knew for a fact that he was fabulous.

"Thank you so much!" Cassandra reached across the couch and hugged his friend. "This would've cost a fortune from a real designer. I mean—" Cassandra instantly began backpedaling "—you know, someone famous." The image of his beautiful dress disappearing in front of his very eyes was enough motivation to shut him up.

Pooky sat glaring at his friend, knowing if anyone other

than this man had made a comment like that he would've already been out the door. But he and Cassandra had too much history. Twenty years ago, the high school friends had come out together. Although the relationship had not worked out, they continued to be there for each other over the years, providing moral support through the many turbulent years that followed while they struggled to find their places in an intolerant world.

"Just try it on so I'll know if it needs any adjustments." Pooky responded dryly.

"I'm sure it doesn't. Everything you do is always so perfect." Cassandra was still trying to dig out of the very deep hole he'd fallen into.

Pooky twisted his mouth in derision as he watched his friend shovel bull as if his life depended on it. "Just go try on the dress. I've got to get going."

Cassandra hurried behind the screen that served as a room divider. "How's Callie?" he called over the wall.

"Okay. She's still stressing over the money man and his lawsuit threat."

"I thought you said they'd come to an agreement about the car?"

"They did—about the car. It's the hopping-in-the-sack part they can't seem to find peace with."

Cassandra's black wig bounced as his head came around the side of the screen. "What? When did that happen?"

"It hasn't." Pooky leaned back into the sofa. "That's the problem. He's been there six times in six days *supposedly* checking on his car repairs, but the only rear end I see him eyeballing is Callie's. And she's just as bad. I swear her coveralls have gotten tighter and tighter with each passing day. I'm amazed she can still breathe. And, girl, you won't believe this!"

Cassandra had completely stopped dressing to listen to the latest gossip about their baby girl. When Callie had shown up on Pooky's doorstep ten years ago with nothing, she had not only been taken in by Pooky, but by a small and loving band of cross-dressers as well. "What?" Cassandra asked anxiously.

"Yesterday she had the nerve to pull her braids back into a ponytail with this big floppy green bow to match her coveralls! The thing was hideous!"

Cassandra burst into laughter. He could clearly see the big green bow sitting atop the mass of jet-black braids. And he knew as well what an affront that would be to Pooky, whose sense of style was unquestionable. "What did you do?"

"Naturally I snatched it off her head as soon as I saw it. And not a second too soon—Mr. Fine came stepping through the door shortly thereafter. That thing would've turned him off like cold water on a hot fire."

"She's so lucky to have you for guidance."

"I know, which is why I have to hurry back. I still have a few errands to run when I leave here, but I really can't leave her to her own devices too long."

"Ta-da!" Cassandra appeared from behind the screen in the gown. The red sequins sparkled in the afternoon light, from the strapless top to the fishtail bottom. "How do I look?"

"Wonderful," Pooky stated, examining his creation with a perfecting eye. The dress needed no adjustments whatsoever. "What's it for anyway?"

"We are doing a stage version of *Sparkle* at the senior center. I'm Sister."

Pooky bit his lip again. Callie had also scolded him about his rude comments. So telling his friend that even on an excellent day he was no Lonette McKee was definitely out of the question. "Gotta go." He gave the other man a peck on the cheek as he breezed by on his way out the door.

"Give Callie my love!" Cassandra called.

"Will do."

"Pooky!"

Pooky paused in the door.

"I know you said she had the thing with the lawsuit worked out, but tell her if she needs some cash, I've got a little bit in savings. She's welcome to it."

Pooky smiled. He knew in the ordinary world, he and his friends were seen as freaks and outcasts. But he also knew it was this very status that caused them to have more compassionate hearts and generous natures. It was days like today when he considered it a privilege to be counted amongst the outcasts. "Thanks, I will."

Julian stood leaning against the counter, his eyes frozen on the sight of the woman squirming beneath his car. He'd never imagined he could be jealous of an inanimate object. His dark eyes widened as she shifted into a position that was so blatantly erotic, he had to wonder if it was done intentionally.

The cell phone attached to his belt gave off a musical note. "I've got to take a call; I'll be right back," he called to Callie, who was under the car carriage.

"Um-hum," she mumbled, too caught up in what she was doing to care.

He cleared the garage's entrance. "Hello?"

"Julian? Hi, it's Denise."

"Hey, Denise, am I still picking you up at seven-thirty?"

"That's why I'm calling. My boss just called me. He needs me to fly down to our corporate headquarters in Arizona to-night. I have to sit in his place at a board meeting first thing tomorrow morning. I'm so sorry for the short notice, but I have to cancel our dinner date."

"Denise, you can't do this to me. This was more than just a dinner date. I'm meeting with some very important potential clients."

"I'm sorry, Julian. This is my job we're talking about. I have to go."

Julian felt his forefinger and thumb automatically go to his temples. He could already feel a migraine coming on. This was the most important dinner engagement of his career to date and now he was dateless. "All right, I understand."

"Again, I'm sorry."

"It's okay. Good luck with your meeting tomorrow."

"Thanks for being so understanding."

"No problem."

Julian clicked the END button on the phone and stood looking up at the afternoon sky. In less than six hours, he and his brothers were going to have the most important meeting of their career with the CEO and CFO of CompuTech, one of the largest growing software companies in the world. They catered to the auto industry but had found that their growth exceeded their financial structure. They needed financial guidance and Cruise Corporation had won the distinct honor of providing it. But Julian understood that at this early stage in the relationship, that agreement was like the wings on a butterfly—incredibly fragile. And even something so slight as an off-numbered dinner party could kill the relationship.

Denise had been the perfect dinner partner. She and Julian had tried the relationship thing years ago and had found that they made much better friends. She was beautiful, suave, and intelligent. She was all the things needed in a dinner partner for a meeting of this magnitude without any of the relationship pressures. Where was he supposed to find a replacement for someone like her on such short notice?

He thought about perusing his little black book for a willing ex but then decided that was asking for trouble. *Maybe James can hook me up. He has pretty good taste in women*, Julian thought, considering his sister-in-law, Maya. Then he shook his head in doubt. No, James had been out of the game for almost five years now; he wouldn't know anybody. *What about Jonathan?* No. He shook his head much more emphatically. Knowing Jonathan, he'd hook him up with a call girl. *Sam?* God only knew where he was hiding. But then again... Julian turned in a slow circle. Maybe Sam had already given him a woman.

As Julian reentered the garage, he was forced to question his sanity along with every survival instinct he had. He was actually considering inviting a sexy little grease monkey to the most important dinner of his career. Obviously, his hormones had finally won the battle for dominance over his mind.

Of course, even if he did invite her, she probably wouldn't accept. He had no idea if she was as attracted to him as he was to her. Quite frankly, he wasn't even sure she liked him. All he had to go on was one kiss. Okay, one unforgettably delicious and breathtaking kiss. But still, just one.

Since Callie had begun working on his car, they'd fallen into a kind of unspoken partnership. She'd been very patient with his overprotective attitude toward his Baby and took the time to explain in detail everything she was doing. They'd shared ideas, and she'd even asked his opinion on occasion.

Sam was right, the lady definitely knew her cars. He was more impressed by her knowledge and expertise with each passing hour spent in her company.

"Okay—" she came toward him, beaming her incredible

smile "—I just need to put on the finishing touches and he'll be ready to go."

In a distant portion of his mind, Julian heard and understood the words, but the majority of his consciousness was centered on her smile. "Will you go out with me?"

"What?" Callie's eyes widened. She took a step back, wondering why she was so surprised. This is what she'd been hoping—actually angling for—over the past few days. Callie had used every feminine wile in her collection to turn the man's head, but every day he'd just come in, prop himself up on the bench, and watch her work. Never saying anything that remotely resembled flirting. In the process, Callie had discovered just how uncomfortable it was to try to work in tight clothes and that there was something about green bows that seemed to set Pooky off. Now he'd finally said something interesting and she was too shocked to respond properly.

Seeing the expression on her face, Julian was already regretting his words. "Never—"

"Yes."

"No, it's okay."

"Really, I want to go out with you. You just surprised me, that's all."

Julian studied her eyes and felt everything inside him begin to relax. "Are you sure?"

"Yes. I'd love to go out with you. When?"

"Tonight."

"Tonight!"

"I know it's short notice; it's okay if you can't."

"No, no, tonight's fine."

"Great, I'll pick you up at seven-thirty."

"Okay. I should have your car ready by then as well."

"That's perfect."

"Okay, I'll see you at seven-thirty."

Julian turned and hurried out of the garage. Everything in him wanted to jump up and shout. He finally did, cruising down the I-94 interstate when his excitement found release in the form of a "Yeah, Baby!!" that reverberated off the walls of his SUV.

Pooky leaned back and studied Callie with intense concentration.

"What are you doing?" she called over her shoulder, still searching through her closet.

"Trying to decide what color would look more spectacular on that wonderful skin of yours…turquoise or red?"

Callie came to a red linen pantsuit Pooky had designed for her a few years back and pulled it out. "This is all I have in red," she said, holding it up. "And I have nothing in turquoise."

Pooky just frowned and shook his head. "Oh no, that will never do." He turned and walked out of the room without another word.

"Where are you going?" Callie called after him.

"Shopping. I need fabric."

Callie ran out into the hall, but Pooky was already halfway down the stairs. "You don't have time to make a dress! This dinner is tonight!" she called over the stairwell railing.

Pooky stopped and stared up at his cousin in disgust. "Who do you think you're dealing with? I'm *Pooky*, baby! All I ever really need is two hours alone with my machine and a fine piece of fabric to make *any* woman fabulous, but you—" he popped his fingers "—I can do in one and a half." He turned on his heels and bounded down the stairs, his shoes clicking loudly against the wood. "Be back soon—you just make sure his ride is ready to roll when you are."

Callie's mouth flew open, and her eyes widened. In her panic to find something appropriate to wear, she'd completely forgotten about the partially dismantled Corvette in her garage.

When Pooky returned one hour and forty-five minutes later, Callie was bent over the car, wiping down the hood with a soft cloth.

"Whoa," Pooky said in genuine awe, "this doesn't even look like the same car that was towed in here two weeks ago."

Callie, wiping her hands on the cloth, was examining her completed project with pride. "Well, it's as close to its original condition as it will ever be."

The little red car glistened like a showroom model under the bright shop lights, and Pooky would've sworn that if the thing had a personality, it would've been smiling in smug arrogance.

Shoving the rag into her back pocket, Callie approached her cousin warily, eyeing the plastic bags he carried like one may have contained a rattlesnake. "Well, what do you have for me?"

Remembering his purpose, Pooky smiled widely. "Darling, I've had an epiphany." He turned and hurried toward their upstairs apartment. "It came to me in a vision while I was driving."

"That's scary."

"No—inspired."

"By?" Callie asked, following close behind. She was secretly excited and was fighting to contain her curiosity.

"By the challenge of your height." He entered his workroom and carelessly dropped the bags beside his sewing machine.

Callie stopped in the door with her hand on her hip. "What's that supposed to mean?"

"Let's face it, sweets, you're not exactly a mountain."

From anyone else, those would've been war words, but this was Pooky. They had discovered early on in their codependent relationship that there was very little they would not put up with from each other. Besides, she was still too curious about what was in the bags.

With the flick of his hand, Pooky pulled off his short black wig and skullcap and tossed it on the coatrack. He ran his hands over his smooth scalp. "That thing was starting to drive me crazy. Now, come here. Let's get your measurements."

Callie came forward hesitantly. "As many times as you've done this, I would think you'd have them memorized."

"I have a fair idea, but you've been making a lot of lunch-time runs to Burger King lately. I'm not taking any chances."

"Hey!"

"Turn," he commanded, completely ignoring her outrage. He stretched the measuring tape along her body in several vertical angles, then around her breasts and hips. Callie, quite used to the routine, stood perfectly still until he was finished.

"Okay, now go." He shooed her with the wave of a hand. "I've got work to do." Bending to collect the bags he'd brought in, he shot back up when he felt Callie slap his bottom on her way out the door.

"Brat!" he called after her, rubbing his stinging bottom.

"Queen!" she called back from down the hall.

"Damn right, and don't you forget it!" He laughed playfully and continued organizing his materials to begin working on the dress. Pooky noticed the clock—he had less than five hours to create the image in his head. Always a perfectionist when it came to his work, he was more so with anything he designed for Callie. Her outfits were always labors of love, his silent thanks for her presence in his life.

Callie stepped out of the shower and wrapped the towel around her wet body. She glanced at the clock on the wall and bit her lip. In thirty minutes, Julian would be arriving to pick her up. Most of the afternoon, she'd heard the buzzing of the sewing machine in every part of the garage. But now there was complete silence.

When she entered her room, the bright turquoise dress draped across her bed was the first thing she saw. The iridescent fabric made the vividly colored gown impossible to ignore. Lying beneath it on the floor were a pair of high-heeled slippers that matched the color exactly.

Across the room stood Pooky hunched over her small jewelry box. "No…no…no," he mumbled to himself, picking through the small selection. "There's no hope for it. I'll have to let you borrow some of mine," he said to Callie without looking at her. He'd sensed her presence the moment she entered the room. "I'll be right back." He turned and hurried past her. "That wet kitten look doesn't really work for you, darling. Hurry and dry off. Mr. *So Sexy* will be here soon," he called back.

Callie was still staring at the beautiful gown with moon-struck eyes. How could anyone create something so beautiful in such a short time?

She crossed the room. Holding the towel against her wet body with one hand, she ran the other over the soft, paper-thin silk fabric.

Pooky came blazing by, headed in the direction of the jewelry box. "I saw a silver ring that will go perfectly with this."

"Oh, Pooky." Callie's full attention was still focused on the dress. "It's so…so…oh, Pooky."

Pooky stopped picking through the costume jewelry and turned to face Callie. The sound of pure joy and adoration in her voice was breaking his heart. She always worked so hard and had so little to show for it. Almost every penny she made went right back into the garage, and it was still not enough to pull the small shop out of the red. She didn't have anything left over for beautiful baubles and gorgeous gowns. But of course, like any woman, she loved to look beautiful.

For the look of happiness on her face right now, Pooky thought, he would make her a thousand gorgeous gowns. "Okay, enough of the ooohing and aaahhhing. Time to get dressed."

He came up behind her and began toweling her dry.

"Stop." Callie's vocal cords gave up a shaky sound as Pooky shook her left and right. "Stop! I can do it."

"Then do it. Prince Charming is on his way."

Callie dropped the towel and lifted the dress. Holding it against her naked body, she stood in front of her full-sized mirror, simply admiring the image—something she didn't do often. "I must admit, I do feel a little like Cinderella."

In the mirror's reflection, Callie could see Pooky place both his large hands on his hips and twist his mouth into a full pout. "I know you are not comparing my genius with something a bunch of mice and birds threw together!"

Unable to stop herself, she swung around and hugged her cousin fiercely. "What would I do without you?"

Pooky returned the hug and fought to hold back the tears forming in his eyes. "You'll never have to know, because I'm not going anywhere." He sniffed loudly. "Now let's get you dressed."

"Really, Pooky, I've got it."

"Okay." He turned and headed toward the door. "Be down in fifteen minutes or I'll come drag you out."

"Yes, ma'am," Callie said formally, but the twinkle in her light brown eyes contradicted the serious tone.

Pooky huffed loudly, "You go ahead and think I'm joking. If you're not down in fifteen, you'll find out just how serious I am."

"Pooky," Callie called just as he disappeared from the doorway.

He stuck his head back in. "Yeah, sweets?"

"Thank you."

"You can thank me by having a fabulous time with Mr. *So Sexy*." His ruby red lips spread into a wide mischievous smile. "Don't forget to give him a kiss for me."

"Get out!" Callie reached behind her, grabbed a pillow off the bed, and tossed it toward the now-empty doorway. Pooky's cheerful laughter carried all the way down the hall.

Chapter 9

Julian sat in his Avalanche outside the garage for almost twenty minutes. Earlier that day he'd floated along on the anticipation of spending the evening in the company of the most interesting woman he'd met in a long time. But, as he began to dress for the evening, the reality of the situation began to sink in.

He was about to take a woman he barely knew into a situation where her behavior and conversation could determine the outcome of his future. *What was I thinking?*

What if she and her drag-queen cousin had the same taste in clothes? What if she ate with her fingers? *My God! What if she votes liberal?* He banged his head against the back of the seat. There was no help for it now; the wheels of fate had been set in motion. He took a deep breath and opened the door of his truck.

The first sight that greeted him upon entering the garage was not comforting. Pooky appeared to be packing up his sewing materials as if just completing a project. Julian said a silent prayer that the sewing project had nothing to do with his dinner companion.

Seeing Julian, Pooky called up the stairs, "Callie, your date is here!" Pooky turned, smiling at a delicious-looking Hershey bar dressed elegantly in a navy blue suit. His neat, short fade was accented perfectly with the white wingtips at each temple. His Billy Dee Williams mustache was perfectly trimmed. *Why are all the cute ones straight?*

"Evening, Jules!" Pooky chirped happily.

"Don't call me that," Julian corrected.

Pooky's pleasant expression faded. "Then what should I call you?"

"My name is Julian."

"Isn't that what I said?"

"No, it's not."

Pooky hunched his shoulders and returned to his packing. This conversation was getting too complicated.

Julian's eyes landed on his car sitting on the other side of the garage. He walked across the room and ran his hand along the shiny red fiberglass. He leaned to the side and considered the body of the vehicle intently. There was no way to tell with the naked eye that the door was not part of the original body. He was examining the uniformity of door to fender when he heard Pooky approaching. He pretended not to notice, hoping he would go away. It didn't work.

"Callie is awesome when it comes to cars."

Julian squatted down in. "Yes, she is," he whispered, studying the shiny, chrome-side pipe.

"She's like the Michelangelo of metal." Pooky laughed at his own joke.

Julian glanced up at the man standing with his hands on his hips. His short leather skirt and matching silk blouse looked like party clothes. He had on his blond wig again, and as always, his make-up was applied with an almost professional flare. Julian wondered briefly how long it took him to get dressed up like that. He had a fair idea for women, having watched previous girlfriends go through the rituals. But a man? And if you accounted for pantyhose and false bras, that had to be extra. "Do you always dress like that?"

Pooky's eyes widened in surprised. "Do you always dress like that?"

Julian simply shook his head, realizing he would probably never get an answer to his question. He ran his finger along the grating in the pipe, tugging a little to check stability. All the while hoping the conversation was over. It was not.

"Ever hear of the White Elephant Club?"

"No."

"You should check it out sometime. Their décor is done in stark white; it's like a lab or something. But beyond that the food is great, and it has a really large dance floor."

"Um-hum."

"Of course, the crowd that hangs out there is probably a lot different from any you are used to." Pooky let his eyes roam over Julian's long form in a suggestive way. "They would eat you alive."

Julian's head snapped around as he recognized instantly that the man was intentionally trying to make him uncomfortable, but Julian Cruise wasn't about to be intimidated by anyone. He stood and was just about to fire off when he heard a light rustling on the stairs.

After a couple of seconds, Callie came into view, and Julian felt his heart in his throat. She smiled in that way that boiled his blood and Julian knew that he'd made the right decision tonight. This was definitely the woman he should be spending the evening with.

"You look lovely."

Callie's smile widened. "Thank you. Let me grab my shawl and I'll be ready to go."

Julian watched her cross the room to the drafting table and collect what looked like a scrap of cloth until she picked it up, and he could clearly see it was a silk shawl made from the exact same material as the dress.

"The car looks great," Julian said, coming around the side to open the door for her.

"It came out better than I thought it would. I don't think anyone other than an expert could tell the difference," Callie answered as she climbed into the bucket seat.

"Have fun," Pooky called as he pressed the button to raise the garage door.

He watched in fearful anticipation as the little sports car pulled out of the driveway. Anybody with two eyes could see the electricity flying back and forth between the pair. They wanted each other so badly they were practically salivating. But they were as different as night and day.

Pooky picked up a small clutch purse, checked his wig and make-up in the reflection of the glass door, and headed out to his favorite nightspot. As he started the engine of his car, he wondered if two people so poorly matched stood a chance. He hoped so, for he feared his little cousin had already lost her heart to "a bulldog in a business suit."

The ride to the restaurant was filled with sexual tension. Every time Callie moved even the slightest bit, Julian heard a rustling of fabric that sounded like silk sheets. She smelled like honey and spice and everything nice, and the scent was creeping into his nose and wrecking havoc on his senses. Then there was that one bare shoulder that kept peeking at him every once in a while when her shawl would slip down her arm. That shoulder was begging for a kiss and a caress. How could someone who worked in dirt and grease every day have such incredibly beautiful skin? It was like…liquid gold.

What was the acceptable sex date, again? It had been so long since he'd dated anyone he'd forgotten. Was it the fourth or the fifth? Could he wait that long? Or was it the sixth? Six dates before he could make love to her. It could take weeks to squeeze in six dates! How was he supposed to wait that long?

"So…you wanna do it?"

Hell, yeah! Wait. What is she talking about? "I'm sorry, what was that?" Julian asked innocently while pulling into the parking lot of the restaurant.

"I was saying that if you wanted me to, I could take care of this." Her finger slipped through a tiny hole in the red fabric of the dashboard.

Julian pulled to a halt in front of the valet check-in point. "Where did that come from?"

Callie put up both hands defensively. "Hey, I was only responsible for the damage outside the car. But that could easily be fixed with a little fabric repair."

He took a minute to look at the tiny damaged spot. "Thanks, I'll just leave the car with you when I return you home tonight." He stepped out and waited for Callie to come around.

As soon as the valet opened her door, Callie bolted out of the car. The cool night air felt like glory on her hot skin. The thirty-minute ride from the garage had felt more like three hours in a furnace. What was it about this man that set her on fire?

When Julian stepped out of the car, his back was to her,

and Callie took a stolen moment to just look at him, at his unusual height and those broad shoulders that needed no assistance with padding. *There should be a law against looking that good.*

Turning her attention to the familiar old home that had been renovated into a five-star restaurant, Callie felt a tinge of something like sorrow touch her heart. This was her father's favorite restaurant, and she'd shared many meals with him here. But that was a lifetime ago, and now she was questioning her reasons for being here tonight.

When Julian turned and gave her that half smile that spoke of secrets and promises, Callie remembered exactly why she was here. She wanted this man, like she'd never wanted anyone in her life. She needed to touch him, to lie with him, certain it was the only way to get him out of her system, out of her mind. And tonight she'd resolved to do just that. She wasn't exactly sure why he'd suddenly asked her out tonight, but she knew opportunity when it knocked.

She came around the small car and placed her hand in his and immediately felt the spark of electricity that seemed to be ever present with him. It was a sexual thing. That was all. Once she got that out of her system, she could get him out of her mind; she kept repeating the same refrain, *Out of my system and out of my mind.*

"Ready?" He smiled, and Callie felt her knees go weak.

"Yes."

He led her up the stairs into the restaurant.

Twenty-five years of experience and training had taught Henry, the maître d', how to seem oblivious to couples arguing right in front of him—like the couple arguing in the corner of the small lobby right now.

When they'd entered moments ago, he would've sworn they were newlyweds. They had that look of new love about them. Then Henry made the apparently critical mistake of recognizing the man and speaking to him in a familiar way. All he'd said was that the party of eight they were dining with had already arrived.

This was news to the young lady in his company, and from the look that came across her face, it was not good news.

"How many did you say?" she'd asked Henry.

"Four couples." Henry had looked to Mr. Cruise in confusion. Mr. Cruise's reservation had been for five couples, and their arrival completed the party.

The lovely young woman then turned to her dinner companion and glared. "When were you planning to tell me we were dining with four other couples?"

"Does it matter?" Mr. Cruise had asked.

Henry could've told the man it apparently did but knew better than to speak when not spoken to.

"Of course it matters! What is this all about, Julian?" she'd asked.

"It's about dinner. We just happen to be having it with my brothers and a couple of business associates."

Henry was no expert on women, but when this woman's small fisted hand rose to rest on her hip bone, he knew it was not a good sign.

"Our first date is a business meeting?"

Henry could tell by the startled expression on Mr. Cruise's face that the man was finally beginning to understand this was not going to just be smoothed over.

"Okay, I apologize. I guess I should've said something earlier."

"Damn right you should've said something earlier—like

when you invited me out." She tilted her head to the side in thought. "Wait a minute. Wait just one minute. Am I a last-minute fill-in date?"

Henry shook his head subtly at the dumbfounded expression on the face of a man caught in his own trap. Poor Mr. Cruise.

"Callie, it's not like that. I wanted to go out with you, really. It just happened to be convenient—"

"Convenient?"

"Okay, not the right word." He held up his hands. "I just meant that this worked out perfectly."

She shook her head sadly. "Take me home, Julian."

"Callie, please. You've got it all twisted around. It's not like that."

"Either you take me home or I'll call a cab. Either way, I'm leaving now."

Julian took her by the arm and led her farther from the restaurant entrance and Henry's big ears. "Callie, please, don't leave. I need you."

She folded her arms across her chest and glared at him. "Apparently not. You have eight other dinner companions to keep you company."

"Okay, okay. I admit, I handled this poorly. But believe me when I say no one in that room can take your place tonight. This is the most important meeting of my career, and yes, my dinner date cancelled at the late minute. And yes, I asked you on the spur of the moment. But not because you were handy—because you are beautiful and charming, and I wanted to spend some time with you."

He ran the back of his hand down her cheek, and Callie felt the tingling all the way to the tips of her toes. How could she criticize him when her reasons for wanting to be with him weren't much better?

"Please, don't leave," he whispered, bringing his head down to hers.

Instinctively, Callie raised her head to his and parted her lips. She felt his large hand come around and brace her back. And in that moment, she wanted nothing more than for the kiss to go on forever. But after a few seconds he pulled back, his dark eyes pleading desperately.

"All right, I'll stay." She started to turn and paused. "But not because of that kiss."

"Of course not." Julian smiled triumphantly. "Thank you." He pecked her cheek and led her back into the restaurant.

Chapter 10

James Cruise felt his wife, Maya, thump his thigh and fought to the urge to grunt in pain. *What was that for?* He looked to her for an explanation, and she quickly jerked her head in the direction of the door.

James turned his attention in that direction and saw his brother entering the dining room, following a woman who barely reached his chest. He in turn thumped his brother Jonathan, sitting to his right.

Jonathan, unable to stifle his grunt, gained the attention of everyone at the table.

He wiped his mouth with his linen napkin. "Sorry, something caught in my throat," he quickly covered, and that's when he noticed his brother moving in their direction with a woman he'd never seen.

"Sorry I'm late, everyone." Julian smoothly guided

Callie around the table to the two empty chairs. He took a moment to shake the hands of the only two nonrelated men at the table.

Dan Hart, the CEO of CompuTech, looked at his watch. "Only you would consider three minutes late, Julian."

Julian pulled out the chair and waited for Callie to be seated. "You would be amazed what you could do with three minutes, Dan. Everyone, I would like to introduce Callie Tyler."

Callie smiled and gave the appropriate responses as Julian introduced everyone at the table. She couldn't help feeling the overattentiveness of the two men, whom Julian introduced as his brothers. Although the introduction would never have been necessary.

Callie felt as if she were sitting with the same man at three different stages in his life. Twenty-two and fresh out of college, Jonathan gave Callie a flashback to what Julian must've looked like ten years ago with the world just beginning to open to him like an oyster ready to give up its pearl. And to her left sat James, Julian a few years into the future when the graying at his temples will have covered his head, giving him a very dignified and regal appearance.

Each was coupled with a woman who seemed to suit their phase of life. Jonathan's date, introduced as Keisha, was no more than twenty-two herself, and her flamboyant lime-green leather suit could've rivaled anything in Pooky's closet. James's wife, Maya, on the other hand, was pure elegance in a crème-colored wool pantsuit. Her green leather days were behind her. Now she was a woman comfortable with her station in life and confident in herself. And that confidence was reflected in everything from the way she sat in her chair to the twinkle in her eyes when she smiled.

The other four people, two older white couples, introduced

as Dan Hart, the chief executive officer of CompuTech; John Jamerson, the chief financial officer; and their wives, Carol and Moira, respectively.

Although it was obviously a business meal, everyone radiated with a warmth that Callie could not associate with the cold, calculating image of business dealings she had in her head. The men were friendly and jocular, and the women were funny and open.

A pretty young server came to take their order, and before long, the table was strewn with a wide assortment of excellent foods. No one at the table questioned the restaurant's five-star rating.

As Callie cut into the succulent beef roast she'd allowed Julian to order for her, she decided that all in all their party of ten was a nice collection of unique and pleasant personalities, and she was glad she'd decided to stay.

The hours passed quickly, and soon the bus boy was clearing the dishes and everyone was sipping on the last drink of the evening. Julian sat back in his chair feeling like a man truly blessed.

Not only was Callie holding her own, but she also had Dan and John eating out of the palm of her hand. Julian had been nursing the same glass of wine all evening, and now he took the final sip wondering why he hadn't thought of this earlier. He'd hunted from one end of Detroit to the other to find an appropriate dinner date, sure that his sophisticated and refined clients would want to spend their time in the company of like-minded women. But all they really wanted was one of the fellas. Someone they could talk sports and cars with. Someone like Callie.

"I'm sure you know your stuff, little girl," Dan Hart said,

"but you'll never convince me that a HEMI could rival a 396 like what Julian has in that hot little red pepper."

Callie took a sip of her wine and smiled sweetly. "I don't have to convince you, Dan. Just give me a time and a place; you bring the Corvette, and I'll bring *anything* with a HEMI and let you convince yourself."

The table burst into laughter.

"This one's got some lead in her pants, Julian," John Jamerson said, completely ignoring the elbow jab he received from his wife for the inappropriate remark.

"How long have you been fixing cars, Callie?" Maya asked.

"Since I could reach the fender, I guess. My father started me almost from the crib, and from what I told it was to my mother's dismay."

"What does your father think of you doing it professionally?" Moira Jamerson asked.

Callie paused. She was having such a good time, she'd almost forgotten that these people didn't really know anything about her. "Both my parents died several years ago."

The startling announcement was followed by a brief hush that fell over the table.

Julian broke the silence with a loud clap of his hands. "Well, ladies and gentlemen, this was a both productive and pleasant evening. And, Dan, we'll have the formal proposal on your desk by the end of the week." He glanced at both his brothers for confirmation and received nods in both directions.

"Julian, before this evening, I knew Cruise Corporation by reputation only." Dan wiped his mouth one final time and tossed his linen napkin on the table. "But after spending some time discussing your ideas and plans with you and your brothers, I believe that reputation is well deserved." He stood and offered his hand to Julian, then to

James and Jonathan. "I look forward to doing business with you."

Jonathan volunteered to collect the coats and wraps while everyone was saying their good-byes.

Ten minutes later, Julian and Callie were back in his car and headed to Callie's home. Julian chuckled to himself, remembering how hesitant he'd been about bringing Callie. He had no way of knowing for certain, but he was pretty sure without her the meeting may have gone a lot differently.

"What's so funny?" Callie asked. She lay with her head back on the seat; her window was cracked, and she was enjoying the night air as it breezed over her skin.

"Just that people are rarely what they seem."

"I take it you are referring to me?"

"You, Dan Hart, Superman, you know, people."

Callie sat up. "Superman?"

"You know what always bothered me about Superman?"

Callie's head fell back again as she studied the handsome man sitting beside her. She was certain Julian had had only one glass of wine, but now she was beginning to wonder. "No. What has always bothered you about Superman?"

"How can one pair of glasses make that much of a difference? Glasses on, he's Clark Kent, but remove the glasses and suddenly he's Superman."

"Superman was made for kids, Julian. Kids don't question that kind of stuff."

"Smart kids do."

"Were you a smart kid?"

Julian gave her a look as if to say, "What a ridiculous question."

Callie smiled and shook her head.

"Thank you for staying."

"I'm glad I did. I had a really good time."

"Me, too," Julian said. "In fact, I hate to see the evening come to an end."

Callie felt her heart skip a beat, realizing this was the opening she'd been waiting for. It was now or never. "Who says it has to?"

Julian's eye widened to the size of half-dollars, but that was the only indication that he was surprised. "Umm, certainly not me. Would you like to come back to my place for a nightcap?"

Callie braced herself, knowing they were now speaking in code. Accepting his invitation would be accepting more than just an after-dinner drink, and they both knew it.

"I would like nothing more. I'll follow you back to your place in my own car so you won't have to drive me home later."

The pair drove on in silence for the next ten minutes until Julian pulled into the garage parking lot. He pulled up to the garage entrance and waited for Callie to get out and press the button for the door lift.

"How long do you think it will take to repair that hole?" Julian asked, stepping out of the Stingray.

"A couple of days if I have everything I need in the patch kit." Callie considered telling Pooky where she was going but decided she could do without the twenty questions that would bring on.

As she came along the side of the car, Julian's arm swept out and pulled her to him. Suddenly his mouth was on hers, and she felt his warm tongue prying her lips apart.

Soon he was inside her mouth, and Callie could barely breathe around the erratic thumping of her heart. Her arms rested on his broad shoulders, and she rose to the tips of her toes.

It was not close enough for Julian. Callie felt his large hands cupping her bottom and lifting her even higher, pressing her hard against his chest.

Finally, he pulled back and rested his chin on the top of her head while trying to regain some control over his breathing. Julian had never wanted a woman the way he wanted this elf. *What is she doing to me?*

He sat her back on her own feet, and using his thumb and forefinger he lifted her chin. "Callie, are you sure you want to do this?"

Callie smiled in reassurance, seeing the expression in his eyes. She wasn't the only one who was nervous. "Yes, Julian, I'm sure."

Julian kissed her gently once more and held her close to his body. Okay, he'd done the gentlemanly thing and given her one last chance to escape. But she'd willingly declined the offer, which meant he got to keep her fair and square. That's the way the rule worked. As he held her in his arms, feeling her warmth and steady heartbeat against his, he wondered if the keeper rule could last for a lifetime.

Chapter 11

Julian tossed his jacket and tie across the back of the sofa as he watched Callie cross his living room. His complete attention was riveted to the way the shimmering turquoise dress moved with her body. The light glistening off her shiny, thick cornrows gave evidence of her healthy hair. Julian briefly considered the lengthy task of unbraiding her hair just to put his fingers in it.

She bent at the waist to peer into his large exotic fish tank, and Julian was forced to grab the back of a nearby lounge chair to brace himself. *This is getting ridiculous.* He shook his head in silent scowling.

"Care for something to drink?" he asked. Turning from the temptation of her upturned bottom, he moved toward the wet bar in the corner.

"Sure," she called over her shoulder, returning her attention to the single large fish that occupied the tank. "Wow. What is this thing?"

"A lionfish."

Callie's eyes widened in surprise as she took in all fifteen inches of the exotic fish. Brown stripes punctuated his pale skin and fanned fins. "It's huge, and I love those fins. Did you name him?"

"Simba."

She bit her lip to keep from smiling. "Very original."

"Thanks. I thought so."

"Hello, Simba." She gently placed her hand against the tank. "Aren't you adorable."

"He's also poisonous and aggressive."

"Oh." Callie quickly took several steps back from the tank as if the fish could jump out and grab her. She turned toward Julian with pure seduction in her eyes, crossing the room to accept the drink being offered. "I should've known not to trust anything that cute."

He watched her approach, still amazed that the beauty sauntering in his direction was who she was. "I still have a hard time accepting that you're a mechanic." He put up his hand in defense of the fire that blazed through her amber eyes. "Not that I'm questioning your ability. I've seen your work firsthand, remember? It's just…"

Callie accepted the drink and smiled. "You can say it. I've heard it a thousand times."

"I've tinkered with cars all my life. I know the type of heavy, hard work involved sometimes."

She shrugged and took a sip of her champagne. "You get used to it. I've been doing this all my life." She sat the drink on the counter and lifted her bare right arm into an L shape. "Feel that."

Julian shook his head at her brazenness. "That's okay, I believe you. You are a regular Xena."

She frowned at his subtly patronizing tone. "No, I mean it.

Feel." She leaned across the bar to give him easy access, but instead he circled the bar and came up beside her.

His large arm circled her waist, and he gently pulled her against his body. "You don't have to prove anything to me." He bent his head and touched his lips to hers. As always when he kissed her, it was as if her body understood exactly what he wanted and immediately responded.

Callie's arm instinctively went around his neck; her eyes closed, and her mouth opened to his gentle prodding.

Julian squeezed her tightly against his body, which was becoming quickly aroused. He feared this was just another of his frustrating dreams, that if he did not hold tight, she would vanish as she had on so many nights. She felt so right, each and every time he touched her. His lips found their way along her neckline, and he breathed her scent into his lungs.

"Can I make love to you, Callie?" he whispered against her skin.

She leaned against his arm for support, certain she could not stand on her own if her life depended on it. She smiled with satisfaction, her amber eyes opening just enough to see the anxious expression on his face. "Do you have to ask?"

Julian knew a yes when he heard one. He braced her back and knees, swooping her up into his arms and heading in the direction of the hall. Her slight weight was nothing against the driving desire to have her in his bed.

He took the stairs by twos and reached the upper landing in record time. He moved swiftly down the hall, pausing only long enough to find her lips again. "I'm going to make love to you all night long."

Callie laughed at the intensity in his words. She understood completely, considering she was as aroused as he was. "That's what they all say," she teased.

Julian froze four steps from his bedroom door. His dark eyes fastened on the woman lying helplessly in his arms. Callie's heart skipped a beat at the way his intensity had transferred from pure lust to pure anger so quickly.

"What do you mean *all*?" His eyes raked her luscious form, his body warring with his mind. He knew this was no virgin he was about to bed, but the thought of her having been with several men tore like claws.

"It was just a joke," she said quietly, realizing she'd inadvertently hurt something deep inside him. "Just a joke," she whispered, lifting her head to his.

Once her lips touched his, all other thoughts vanished. Who gave a damn how many men she'd been with? Julian thought. Tonight she was his. And he would do his very best to wipe away the memory of anyone who'd come before him.

As they entered the bedroom, Callie turned her head left and right trying to look around from her unique vantage point. She had a feeling the real Julian resided in this room, and after his little display of jealousy in the hall, she was suddenly feeling desperate to know this man she was about to make love with.

Done in hues of plum and bronze, the room was classic masculine elegance, just like everything else about the man. It had lush plum carpeting so deep that she felt Julian sink down into it with the additional weight of her body. The wood furniture was light oak, which surprised Callie a little. She would've pegged him as a mahogany man. Dominating the center of the room was a massive four-poster bed. The plum-and-bronze coverings and many pillows only added to its imposing appearance.

"Does Paul Bunyon know you stole his bed?" Callie tried to hide the new nervousness creeping up her spine. *What am I doing? I barely know this man!*

Julian laid her across the bed as if she were made of glass. "Well, he won't be getting it back tonight." He ran his hand along the outline of her frame with a sculptor's touch. Gently gliding over her arms, the edges of her breasts, her rounded hips, finally wrapping his large hand around her firm thighs. "You're so beautiful."

Callie couldn't help being flattered by the reverence she heard in his voice. She was certain it was more lust than eyesight speaking, but she wasn't about to dispute him.

Julian stretched out beside her. In just the short time since he'd lain her down, his body was already missing the close contact. His hungry eyes eagerly roamed over the feast, unsure where to start. He'd dreamed of this moment for weeks, and now she was finally here. This was his chance to show her all the wonderful things a man could do to a woman he desired. The problem was, he felt as nervous as a schoolboy and just about as clueless.

Giving in to instinct, he bent his head and placed a gentle kiss against the nipple protruding against the thin silk material of her dress. Realizing there was no barrier between the dress and the woman, he placed another, and another, finally sucking the breast into his mouth, dress and all. Wrapping his arms around her, he lifted her body up to him as his suckling became ferocious.

Her startled gasp caused him to pause, and when he did, he was shocked to realize what a painfully tight grip he had on her. His eyes came up to meet hers, and they shared a look of genuine surprise. Both realized for the first time that whatever the attraction was between them was not purely physical.

"What is this?" Callie whispered their shared thought out loud. "We've just met."

"I don't know," Julian answered, his words mumbled against the skin of her neck.

"Maybe this is not such a—"

"Shh." He silenced her with a kiss. With the slightest pressure, her lips parted under his. His tongue found hers and began a silent duel as he drank her in. She tasted just as he'd known she would, all sweet honey and nectar. Her clear eyes were clouded with lust, and Julian fought the urge to shout in male triumph, "I've wanted you from the moment I was aware of your presence in the world." He lifted her small hand and pressed it against his heart. "Feel my need for you."

Callie's eyes widened. His heart was pounding like a drum against the wall of his chest. She smiled into his dark eyes. This man was so different from the one she'd imagined him to be. "You are not at all what I thought you would be like."

His lips twisted in a smirk. "Considering how we met, I'm not sure I want to know what you thought I would be like."

She shrugged, and when she did, the thin spaghetti strap slid down her arm. She subconsciously reached out and lifted it back into place.

Julian waited patiently for her to position the strap before reaching up, looping his index finger around it, and sliding it back down. He slid the strap even lower until her upturned breast was revealed. His attention was immediately focused on the perfect golden breast, and all other thoughts were set aside in favor of exploration.

Callie closed her eyes, reveling in the feel of his soft mouth skimming over her chilled skin. Slowly, he pulled the silk fabric from her body as if peeling the skin from a luscious piece of fruit. Every inch of brown skin that was revealed was kissed, caressed, and fondled until Callie thought she was going insane.

Once the dress lay in a heap at the foot of the bed, Julian sat back on his haunches to study his handiwork. "Do you have any idea how many times I've imagined you like this? How many times I've made love to you in my mind?"

Callie smiled seductively, feeling the power of a desired woman. "Maybe half as many times as I have."

He shook his head slowly while unbuttoning his snow-white shirt. "No, try twice as many times. And still I never imagined you would look like this." He paused in his undressing long enough to cup one breast, and without meaning to, his mouth followed his hands.

When she felt his mouth close around her hard nipple, Callie began pulling at the shirt. She wanted to feel his skin against hers, press her face against his warm flesh. Julian understood her need, and working together, soon he was as naked as she was.

Without ceremony, Julian parted her thighs and placed his hand against her warm center to confirm what he already knew. She was as desperate for him as he was for her.

Callie parted her thighs wider in silent invitation. The amber of her eyes had darkened to a deep bronze in her lust, and they begged him without words to complete the ritual.

Reaching into his bedside table, Julian donned a latex shield, lifting each of her legs around his waist. "This is more than sex, Callie. You do realize that, don't you?" His breathing was labored, but he wanted assurance that she was feeling the same magnetic pull, the same strange energy that he was. Something was happening between them, and Julian knew this was more than just a romantic interlude.

Instinctively, he knew that once he entered her body, they would both be changed in some irreversible way. He needed to know she understood this as well as he did.

"Please, Julian," she whispered, holding on to his shoulders. She pushed her open body against his throbbing penis. "I need you so much," she cried.

Her want was too strong for him to fight. Holding her small bottom in his large hands, Julian slowly entered her body. Immediately he recognized the tightness of her. It was both wonderful and alarming at the same time.

The rightness of her, the perfect molded shape of her. The amazing discovery that her body seemed to be designed just for him. And that was as far as his analytical mind could get before his carnally driven body took over. Holding her tight against him, Julian plowed into her willing body, again and again, trying to consciously force himself to remember her unusual size, trying not to crush her petite body with his driving need to consume all of her.

Her response was his reassurance. For every forward thrust, he was met with an equally forceful pull. She clung to him like a dying woman, touching and kissing every ounce of skin her mouth could reach. Pressing herself against him until she could get no closer. The frantic need of their coupling brought them to the pinnacle much sooner than either wanted to.

As Julian felt her body tremble in his arms, he was certain that the moment when God fashioned his soul and sent him into the world, this small part had somehow gotten separated from him. Julian knew he'd never felt more complete and total.

Callie opened her eyes sometime later, surprised to realize she'd fallen asleep. She twisted her head to look into the face of the man who still held her tightly, even in sleep. Her mind flashed back to the incredible lovemaking they'd experienced earlier that evening. It was supposed to be a "wham-bam, thank you, sir," but the intensity of it was mind-altering, and Callie knew she'd made a drastic error in judgment. *Making love was supposed to scratch the itch, not give me full-blown poison ivy.*

That was not at all the way she'd seen it happening. He fit, like no one ever had. From the first moment their bodies connected to the last, it was pure bliss. *But you don't have time for bliss*, her skeptical mind intervened. She was trying to build a business. Where did someone like Julian Cruise fit into that plan? That was the problem—he didn't.

She felt the slight shift of his body as Julian repositioned himself. He turned over, still holding her tight, and she rolled with him. Everything in her screamed, "Run for your life," but she just didn't have the will to pull herself from his hold, or his bed. So, she closed her eyes and snuggled into his warmth. She would deal with her conflicting emotions in the morning. Things were always much clearer in the light of day.

Chapter 12

Callie was not given the reprieve she sought. Less than an hour later, her eyes snapped open and her body came alive to the feel of something wonderful being done to her. She became fully conscious, moaning in pleasure at the feel of Julian's mouth in places she'd only dreamed of.

She reached down between her legs and felt his curly head slowly moving back and forth. "Oh, Julian."

His head came up, realizing he'd achieved his goal. "You like that?" He smiled sinfully, running his large thumb over the protruding tip.

Unable to stop herself, Callie twisted and writhed on the bed, trying to complete what he'd started.

Sensing what she was doing, Julian removed his hand and held her legs. "No, baby." He touched his lips to the inside of her thigh. "You go there with me or not at all."

"Please, Julian," Callie cried, needing the release his warm mouth promised and not caring at all how desperate and needy she sounded.

"Shh," he cooed, returning his fingers into her soft warmth. "It's okay. I'm here now." Soon his mouth followed his fingers, and moments later Callie felt herself falling and falling into the sweet abyss.

As she drifted into sleep for the second time, Callie considered the words she'd heard whispered in the dark: *You go there with me or not at all*. No. Callie yawned tiredly. There was no place for Julian Cruise in her life.

Callie opened her eyes again to find two obsidian jewels focused on her face. How long had he been watching her sleep?

Julian reached up to touch her cheek. "Do you realize how lovely you are?"

She smiled to hide her embarrassment and looked around the room seeking a clock. "What time is it?"

"Does it matter?"

"It's probably getting late. I'd better be going."

"Callie, it's almost two in the morning. Just stay the night."

"Easy for you to say. You don't have a garage full of cars with impatient owners waiting for you."

Julian propped himself up on one elbow. "What, are you trying to tell me that people pick up their cars at two in the morning?"

Callie rolled over with her back to him. "Of course not."

"Okay then, stay the night." He scooted in close behind her and nibbled her collarbone. "I don't spend the night with beautiful women on a regular basis." *Especially not tiny, heart-stealing elves*. "Why do you think my brothers were giving you the third degree? Even they understood they were witnessing a historic moment."

Callie laughed. "Okay, I'll stay the night, but first thing in the morning I have to get going."

"First thing in the morning."

Callie studied his serious expression, wondering if he knew that his mischievous dark eyes gave him away.

Instead of sleeping, they spent the early morning hours talking and sharing the secrets of their lives, past and present, their fears and triumphs, and those things of which they were uncertain.

Julian was telling Callie about the day he opened his front door and found Rachel and Olivia standing there. Callie twisted in his arms until they were face-to-face.

"Julian, it's not your fault."

His dark eyes twinkled in the reflection of the moonlight. "Yes, it was. If I had searched harder, I could've found where her father moved them. I should've kept looking for her."

"You were a seventeen-year-old boy!" She took a moment to regain her composure. "You offered to marry her. You tried to do the right thing."

"It wasn't enough. Every time I look at Olivia, I think of how hard it must've been on them, struggling over the years while I was living the good life."

Callie reached up and took his face between her hands. "Julian...when Rachel needed your help the most, she found you, right?"

He nodded once.

"Obviously she knew where you were all along. Baby, don't do this to yourself. Guilt and regret can eat you up inside if you let it. Believe me, I know."

Julian tightened his arms around her waist and pulled her closer. "Some days I'm certain Olivia hates me. I think she blames me."

"Does she know about the addiction?"

"I don't think so. Rachel brought her here before things got too bad. I'm hoping she never saw her mother…"

"High?"

He nodded.

Callie snuggled against his warm flesh. "Julian, I'm no expert, but it sounds to me as if both you and Rachel have been given something few ever receive. Thanks to you, she has a second chance at a clean life. And thanks to her, you now have a second chance to know your daughter. I just hope you both understand what a rare privilege you have been given and make the most of it."

Julian rested his head on her shoulder. Looking out the window at the velvety night sky, he considered her words. They lay quietly in the dark until Julian heard the sounds of soft snoring. Knowing it was selfish, he nibbled at her shoulder. He knew he ought to let her sleep, but he feared his time with her was limited, and he didn't want to waste one moment.

She smiled drowsily. "Don't you ever sleep?"

"Yes—" he placed gentle kisses along her neck "—just not tonight."

An hour later, the couple was snuggled in a blanket on one of the loungers on Julian's bedroom balcony, watching the stars twinkle across a clear night sky.

"Why did you become an accountant?" Callie yawned, trying desperately to stay awake when her body was blissfully exhausted.

"What else would I have done?" He looked down into her face with a confused expression.

"I don't know. Maybe marketing and sales, or medicine. Dr. Cruise has a nice sound. I'm sure you could've been the next Evel Knievel if you tried. Anything. So why sit behind a boring desk and punch numbers all day?"

"Ah, you see, that's the difference between me and Evel Knievel. I don't think numbers are boring. Numbers are consistent; numbers are reliable."

She huffed. "If you say so."

"Seriously. Think about it. How many things in your life can you say will always be the same no matter what else changes? Numbers never change. One plus one will always and eternally remain two.

"And that's important to you?"

"Obviously you're not a control freak."

"You call yourself a control freak?"

"No. The world calls me a control freak. I just answer to it."

Against the still of the night, Callie's soft laughter sounded much louder than it was and Julian thought it was as sweet as any melody he'd ever heard.

After a second short nap, they'd given up on sleep, both truly amazed at how easy it was to confide in the other. Callie was sharing things with this man she'd never shared with anyone, not even Pooky. And she was finding there was a great relief in speaking her pain aloud.

She'd explained to Julian how she came to own the garage. Giving him an overview of the pampered life she'd lived under the warmth of her father and stepmother's love. How it had all come to an end when the court made her stepbrother her guardian. She spoke with malice of how easily Paul had ruined her father's company and stripped her of almost everything. She felt Julian's grip tighten on her through the blanket as if he could literally share the hurt and devastation she'd experienced at the tender age of fifteen.

"Where is he now?" Julian was asking in casual tones, but

there was nothing casual about his words. Callie knew that if she did not want to become a party to murder, she'd better not give up the requested information.

"Not certain," she answered, which was in part the truth. She had some idea, but she wasn't certain if he had moved from his last known address in the ten years since she'd seen him. "No one in my family would help me—except Pooky."

Julian twisted his mouth in consternation. As much as he hated to admit it, he owed her strange and constant companion a debt of gratitude for protecting Callie. Her fate could've taken her to the worst parts of life if she'd not had Pooky on her side. His mind briefly flashed on Rachel in the rehabilitation institute, and how easily a person's path could be altered.

Julian nodded in the direction of the orange globe that was just appearing beyond the horizon. "Here comes the sun."

Callie smiled, amazed at the clear view they had from their vantage point. It had been years since she'd taken the time to just enjoy the rising of the sun and the beginning of a new day. "It's beautiful. How can something so ordinary still be so extraordinary after thousands and thousands of years?"

Julian smiled, wondering if she had any idea just how *extraordinary* she was. After everything she'd been through, she could still find joy in life. Even though her stepbrother had tried to cut her off from the world, she'd still managed to carve out her own little niche.

They stayed on the balcony until the sun was fully above the horizon. Afterward they returned inside to Julian's bed, which had become their own private haven of warmth and loving. By late morning, without realizing it, they had both fully entrusted the other with the secrets of their souls.

Chapter 13

"Hello," Jonathan Cruise answered sleepily.

"Hey, it's me." Julian spoke barely above a whisper. "I need you to do me a couple of favors."

Jonathan rubbed his sleepy eyes and scooted from the bed, trying not to awaken his girlfriend, Keisha. He grabbed the notepad he kept by his bedside for mornings like this when his big brother awakened him with an inspired thought for their business. An occurrence that happened quite frequently.

Once he was through the bedroom door, he yawned loudly and flopped down into a hallway chair. "Okay, shoot."

"First, I need you to take my ten-thirty meeting with HP Products. Something's come up, and I can't make it."

"I don't have my Palm Pilot, but I'm pretty sure my morning is free. What's the other thing?"

"I need you to find out what you can about a man named Paul DeLeroy. He's somewhere between thirty-five and forty and used to live on the East Side. I think he went to school up north somewhere."

"And…"

"There's no *and*; that's all I know."

"That's not enough information. There could be ten guys that fit that description. Why are you whispering?"

"Look, if you find ten guys, fine. Give me the information and I'll sort it out. I just need you to get cracking on this today. And I'm not whispering."

"Wow, this is news. They usually don't last the whole night. And you two just met."

"Just get that information together."

"Fine, keep her a secret as long as you can. We both know in this family that's never very long."

"Will you do it or not?"

"I'm already on it."

"Thanks, man. I owe you one." Julian hung up the phone and surveyed the tray of delectables. He had a full pot of coffee, a colorful plate of breakfast pastries, and a small bowl of healthy-looking fruit. Yes, he thought, this should be enough to fortify the elf for now. Maybe for lunch they would have something delivered.

He'd already called James and asked him to handle his only appointment later that afternoon, so now he was free to spend the whole day with the tiny treasure that had somehow fallen into his lap.

He climbed the stairs to his bedroom and gently pushed the door ajar. She was still fast asleep, curled on her side like a contented kitten. Julian stood staring down at her in wonder. Who would've thought this perfect woman was hiding in an auto shop on the East Side? He huffed. No wonder it took so long to find her.

He placed the tray on the nearby dresser. Tossing his robe across the end of the bed, he reached into the bedside table and took out a condom. He quickly slipped it on with no problem; just the sight of her was enough to prepare him. He quietly climbed into the bed behind her.

Julian scooted his long body as close to her curled form as he could get and buried his head against the skin of her shoulder. She smelled wonderful, he thought, breathing in her skin. All feminine musk and faint perfume, and…his lips twisted into a satisfied smirk. *Me. She smells like me.*

He kissed her shoulder gently, pulling back the covers to further explore her naked body. He'd spent almost a full night getting to know that body, but it wasn't nearly enough time. "Wake up, sleepy head," he whispered against her neck.

She mumbled sleepily and turned over, curling against his bare chest. It wasn't exactly what he was going for, but the feel of her soft breasts against his bare chest was not something he could argue with. He kissed her neck and her shoulder; wrapping his large hand around her bottom, he pushed her up against his stiff manhood. The effect worked better than any alarm clock known to man.

Callie's eyes opened, and a soft smile came to her mouth. "I see someone is already wide awake."

Julian chuckled against her breast. "Umm," was his only answer. Turning her flat on her back, he used his knee to part her legs. "If you weren't so enticing, maybe I could leave you alone for more than a few minutes."

Callie eagerly opened her body to this man she'd never imagined existed, more than happy to accommodate his ferocious appetite. "Do you hear me complaining?"

He touched her core, assuring himself of her readiness before entering her body. Once he'd reached her center, he stopped moving, content to stay there, enjoying what he felt had to be a brief glimpse of paradise. He braced himself on his elbows and looked down at her rapturous face, needing to know she felt the same way he did at that moment.

Slowly he pulled back and sunk himself to the hilt again. Her soft cry of satisfaction was all the assurance he needed. "Can I live here?" he teased, while struggling to control his breathing.

Callie's mischievous streak surfaced. Holding tight to his shoulders, she pushed herself up against him while at the same time contracting her vagina around his throbbing penis.

"Oh my God." Julian's breathing became more and more labored.

Callie repeated the action, and Julian lost all self-control. Roughly lifting her small body against his, he plowed into her again and again, losing himself in her soft, wet essence until finally, bucking hard, he exploded.

In the midst of his release, he felt her body give up its sweet nectar, and soon she joined him. As the pair went over the edge together, both knew they had never felt anything so utterly, perfectly sublime.

Almost an hour later, Julian sat propped against the headboard, supported by a pile of pillows with Callie straddled on his lap. He was still buried inside her body, for they'd discovered it was the only compromise—neither wanted to part long enough to eat. So, Callie fed him grapes from their fruit bowl while nibbling on the last bite of a chocolate donut.

Julian was thinking of the bright future ahead. Sharing his thoughts and body with someone who understood and accepted him. The trick was how to convince her that she was everything he wanted in a woman. Although they had only known each other a short time, he planned to spend his life getting to know her better.

Callie, on the other hand, was thinking along a totally different line. She knew what had happened between them over the past twenty-four hours was rare and special. It had never happened to her, and she was almost certain it had never happened to Julian either. But what did it mean? How could two people who'd spent only one night together fall in...

"Do you believe in love at first sight?" Julian asked after swallowing the latest grape.

She shrugged her shoulders carelessly. Statements like that gave her the feeling that the man was gifted with some kind of psychic ability. "I don't know. Maybe."

"Hmm," he muttered thoughtfully.

Callie wondered if the next statement from his lips would be a declaration of love, and the thought terrified her. Her heart was pounding as she watched his beautiful lips twist with the chewing of the grape.

"Callie, I—"

"I've got to go," she blurted out.

Julian lifted her body from his. "What?"

"Cars don't repair themselves, Julian." She gave her weak excuse, already climbing down off the large bed.

"Now? You're leaving so soon?" Julian scooted to the foot of the bed and paused to watch her cross the room to retrieve her silk dress and panties, which were neatly folded on the back of a side chair. She completely disregarded her nakedness.

Callie grabbed up her few clothes and headed to the bathroom. "It's almost noon, so it's more like a 'finally' than a 'so soon.'"

Julian watched in stunned silence as she gently closed the door. He ran both hands over his short-cropped hair and sat trying to understand what just happened. He heard the shower water start. One minute they were making love and feeding each other, the next she was running like a frightened rabbit.

Julian knew that he was in love. It was a simple fact. Nothing he could explain, of course, but he understood it nonetheless. Despite the many hours of lovemaking they'd shared, they'd spent a great deal of their time together just talking and getting to know each other. He felt they'd known each other for a lifetime; something in him recognized her spirit and just knew she was the one.

Could it be, he thought, rubbing the back of his hand against his bristly chin, that she just didn't feel the same way? The water stopped, and he heard the shower door sliding open. The mental image of her standing in the middle of his bathroom floor dripping wet was too much temptation. He stood and headed in the direction of the bathroom.

"Julian? Where do you keep the towels?"

When he opened the door, she was bent over, looking into the cabinet under the sink. In a flash, he was behind her.

The feel of his quickly rising bulge pressed against her wet skin was like jolts of lightning down her spine. "Julian," Callie whispered, "I have to go."

"No, you don't," he answered, already nibbling at her wet earlobe. Her cornrows were damp with steam and her skin was hot to the touch. "You can stay right here with me all day if you want." He reached past her to open a drawer. His fingers quickly touched on what he sought. Despite his trembling hands, he quickly donned the plastic sheath.

Even as she whispered, "No, I can't," her unruly body pushed back against his.

"Yes, you can," he answered. Holding her in place against the sink, he parted her and entered from behind. Within moments, all Callie's resistance was gone as she pushed back against him, trying to pull him deeper inside her.

Caught up in the splendor of her welcoming body, Julian almost missed it—almost. His eyes opened for only a second, just long enough to catch the combined look of joy and pain reflected in the mirror. Callie's light brown eyes were watching him the whole time they made love, watching him with a look of both hope and despair.

Julian felt the intensity of her feelings radiating off her in waves. His body reacted without warning, and as always, Callie's responded in kind. Her soft mouth parted on a moan as she found her release. Gently cupping her neck in his large palm, he kissed her with all the passion and love he felt in his heart, and she drank him in like a dying woman.

In that moment he understood that she was terrified of what she felt for him. More than likely because of the swiftness in which it occurred. Which was probably more natural than his eager willingness to accept and embrace the idea that they had fallen in love overnight.

His baser instinctive reaction was to tie her to his bed and never let her leave his house, reclaiming her again and again until she confessed what she felt for him. But the civilized part of him insisted he set her free and allow her to come to the realization that she loved him on her own. *But what if she doesn't?*

Rubbing against his skin, she practically purred with satisfaction. "Now see what you've done? I'll have to shower again when I get home."

"Why not shower here?" Julian asked, desperately seeking to hold her there. Some part of him secretly believed that if she left the house, he would lose her forever.

"I tried that and look what happened." She gently pushed

against him to get free. "No, it's best I go home." Turning, she collected her panties and started to dress.

Julian slumped against the sink and watched her in brooding silence. "How about dinner tonight?"

Handling it like crepe paper, she lifted the turquoise gown over her head and tried to shimmy into it without damaging the fabric. "Um, I don't know if that's such a good idea."

He moved forward to help her pull the dress down over her damp body. "Why?"

Once her face was free, she took a deep breath. "Look, this was great—really. But it was just one of those things, you know. Where did I leave my shoes?"

Julian followed her out of the bathroom, his mouth partially opened in stunned disbelief. "I'll be damned. You are going to pretend like this was some kind of fluke thing. Treat it like a one-night stand."

Callie had decided that because of his ability to read her mind, her best defense was to avoid any and all eye contact. She got down on her knees, looking for the shoes beneath the bed. "It *was* a one-night stand, Julian. We both knew that last night."

"Yes, but it became something more."

"Like I said, it was great, but anything more would never work." Her voice was muffled against the bedspread as her hand dug around beneath the bed.

Spotting something turquoise, Julian crossed the room and found the high-heeled slippers beside one of the side chairs they'd made love in last night. Julian briefly looked around the room, realizing they had utilized almost every piece of furniture in their sexual marathon.

"Here." Julian held the slippers up.

"Thank you." Callie accepted the slippers, still working to avoid those dark, all-seeing eyes. "I'm just saying that I think we were both a bit *deprived* last night, and that's why the sex was so good. But if we tried it again, it wouldn't be nearly so perfect."

Watching her lose the battle to keep her balance, Julian moved forward to help.

She leaned against him without thought, allowing him to slip one shoe and then the other onto her small feet.

When he finished, he wrapped his arm around her waist. With lightning speed, his mouth covered hers and she instantly responded. Julian pushed his way between her lips, savoring her unique flavor, trying to memorize the taste of her forever. Then slowly he pulled back, waiting and watching as she regained her sense of place and time. Her eyelids finally parted, and her puckered mouth relaxed.

He leaned close to her ear and whispered, "What's your excuse now?"

Her eyes widened, realizing how easily she'd been manipulated. She pushed away from his warm and all-too desirable body. "I'd rather leave with the memory of one wonderful night than mess it up by trying to repeat it. Good-bye, Julian."

He watched her collect her small purse and walk toward the door. She paused, and he could almost see her physically bolstering herself. Tossing out what they'd shared wasn't nearly as easy as she pretended.

"I'll see myself out, and I meant what I said." She stopped in the doorway and turned back to glance over her shoulder at him. "I had a great time."

Julian couldn't help thinking she looked like a diva from one of those old gangster movies.

"You are a special man, Julian Cruise." Her hungry eyes took in all of him, trying to burn the image on her brain. "Good-bye."

He smiled, slow and seductive. "Later."

Chapter 14

Callie kicked off her slippers at the bottom of the stairs. Pooky usually slept until close to noon, and when he was awake, he was working and rarely heard anything over the sound of his sewing machine. If she was very careful, Callie thought, she could creep into her room unnoticed. But, of course, stealth was no defense against a nosy queen.

Callie rounded the top of the stairs and found Pooky leaning against the wall with his arms crossed over his chest. "Well, well, well, look what the dog dragged in."

Unable to stifle a yawn, Callie covered her mouth. "I thought it was 'look what the cat dragged in.'"

"The cat came home five hours ago! I thought maybe you forgot where you lived!"

Callie pushed past her cousin. "Stop exaggerating."

"I hope he was worth keeping me up all night with worry."

Pooky followed her into the bedroom. He had a full night of venting to do. She wasn't about to get off so easily.

"You stay out all night on a regular basis."

"I *know* you're not trying to be like me. You can't be like me, little Ms. Amateur!"

Pooky paused, placing his large hands on his slender hip bone. "And at least I call to let you know I'm safe and sound."

Callie paused in her doorway, realizing that beneath the layers and layers of dramatics, Pooky was truly concerned. She felt a tinge of guilt slip into her shield of pleasant memories. "I'm sorry, Pook. I really didn't expect to stay all night. Before I knew it, we were watching the sun rise."

"That good, huh?"

"Better."

Pooky's mouth twisted in frustration, realizing he would have to give up his venting if he wanted to get the details. "You're lucky I enjoy a good story. Okay, what happened? He seemed so mild-mannered, I never would've imagined him taking you home on the first date. And I most definitely would never have imagined you accepting."

Callie stretched across her bed. "That's because he didn't take me home. I invited myself."

Pooky covered his mouth with both hands. "You tramp!"

Callie smiled, not the least bit offended.

Pooky flopped down beside her. "Okay. Details! Details!"

Callie curled on her side while her mind fought a silent battle. Some part of her wanted to hoard the memories in her mind and not share them with anyone. But this was Pooky, and she shared everything with Pooky. Well, almost everything.

"Pooky, I think I'm in love."

"*Damn!* That good?"

"He's sweet, and funny, and sometimes it feels like he's reading my mind. We are so connected."

Pooky sat silently listening. Some part of him was ecstatic with joy that his little cousin was finally feeling the finest emotion. But another part of him feared that no good could come of it in this particular instance. "Callie, be careful. This *is* the man you referred to as a 'bulldog in a business suit.'"

The dreamy expression disappeared from Callie's face, and Pooky felt like the greatest heel in the world.

"I know. That's why I had to get out of there this morning."

"Afternoon."

"What?"

"It's afternoon, not morning," Pooky corrected playfully.

Callie reached behind her head and pulled out a pillow. "Whatever!" She laughed, tossing the pillow at his head.

Pooky ducked the blow and stretched out on his belly beside his best friend and the only person he could say he truly loved. "Do you regret it?"

"No. It was a one-time thing. I understood it could never be more than that. But still…it was great while it lasted."

"Hello, Mr. Cruise. It's so nice to see you again." Delores Hillsdale smiled and extended her hand. "Please, have a seat."

Julian moved into the room cautiously and accepted the hand. Despite the woman's jovial manner, he knew this was not a social visit, nor was he here to receive good news. A principal rarely summoned any parent to the school for good news. And knowing his own child as he did, Julian was sure those odds were even more against him.

Taking the seat across from the desk, Julian unbuttoned his suit jacket. "Your message seemed urgent, Mrs. Hillsdale. Is there a problem?"

"Yes, I wanted you to come up here to see for yourself." She stood and approached the window that looked out over the north side of the building, motioning for Julian to follow. "In approximately five minutes, Olivia will be climbing back into the building through that window." She pointed to a window on the lowest level, near the back of the building.

"What?"

Delores turned and rested her hip against the windowsill. "Olivia has been skipping school on a regular basis. She usually leaves after second period, but she is always back by seventh so that she can exit the building with the other children and be outside when you arrive."

"Mrs. Hillsdale, I'm sure you are mistaken. Olivia is a straight-A student. Yes, she has some behavioral problems, but if she was missing that much school, it would show in her grades."

"You would think so, wouldn't you?" Mrs. Hillsdale said thoughtfully.

Julian was beginning to wonder if maybe Olivia had been correct in her assessment of Mrs. Hillsdale. "Are you accusing her of cheating as well?"

"Oh, no." Mrs. Hillsdale shook her head emphatically. "No. We've watched her work very carefully. Much of it she does during second period."

"I don't understand what you are saying."

"Aaah." Mrs. Hillsdale smiled with satisfaction. "Right on time."

Julian turned to see a pretty girl dressed in faded jeans and an oversized T-shirt lifting one leg over the windowsill. She looked in both directions and ducked her head through the small opening, disappearing inside.

Julian stood with his mouth gaping open. There was no

doubt as to the identity of the girl, but that was the only thing he recognized about the scene. Where was the school uniform she'd left the house in that morning? Julian felt a cold chill run down his spine. Where would a fourteen-year-old girl spend her days, if not in school?

Julian turned quickly and headed in the direction of the door, multiple punishments running through his head as he tried to find the one most painful.

"Mr. Cruise, please wait!" Delores grabbed his thick upper arm in both her hands. She slid a little on the plush carpeting as she tried to hold a raging bull.

"I'm going to kill her," Julian mumbled his thought aloud.

"Mr. Cruise! Please! We need to talk." Delores knew she had no hope of holding the man if he was determined to leave, so she gave up the only bit of information she thought might pause his stride. "She goes to see her mother!"

It worked. Julian froze in his tracks. He turned in a slow circle. "What did you say?"

"I've had her followed for the past two days. I wanted to have all the facts when we spoke. She leaves here and catches the city bus across town to see her mother."

Julian felt his knees go weak. *She knows?* Olivia not only knew her mother was in rehab, but she also obviously knew where. What else did she know?

Delores, seeing the stunned expression on the man's face, guided him back to the side chair. "One of our security personnel has been shadowing her ever since we discovered she was leaving the school grounds. He said she goes to the rehabilitation center, but she does not go inside. She just sits on a bench in the park across the street, staring at the building.

"One day, she apparently even took some seeds for the birds in the park, but she has never tried to enter the building.

We are almost certain her mother doesn't know she's there. Which is why I called you today. This is about a lot more than missing a few days of school, Mr. Cruise."

Julian buried his head in his hands. "She knows," he whispered.

Delores rested her hip on the edge of the desk in front of him and waited patiently while he tried to collect his thoughts. When Julian had enrolled his daughter in the exclusive prep school, he'd told the principal the whole story, knowing Olivia would need an adjustment period. He wanted the staff to be prepared for anything that might come up.

He'd tried so hard to hide the truth from his daughter; he had even gone as far as to enlist the help of his family members. *Did my parents tell her? James? Jonathan?* No, he decided, his family would never betray him.

"I assume you have never spoken with Olivia about her mother's recovery program?" Delores asked.

Julian shook his head numbly, still shell-shocked. "No. I thought it best that she know as little as possible. I thought that maybe if Rachel was able to get well, she would never have to know."

Delores returned to the seat behind the desk. "Mr. Cruise, remember what you asked me a moment ago? You said if Olivia was missing that much school, it would show in her grades."

"Right." Julian was struggling to find the thread of the conversation. "What does that have to do with anything?"

"The reason Olivia has been able to maintain her grades and miss five out of eight subjects over the last several days is because she studies ahead. She does the work *before* it is required, which means she's actually learning it on her own— teaching herself. She's a gifted child, Mr. Cruise. Too intelligent to be kept in the dark about anything for long."

Julian had always known Olivia was a clever girl, but up

until now, he'd only seen that clever brain at work scheming against him. It had been very hard to see it as a positive thing.

"May I recommend something?" Delores wrote a name and number on a sheet of paper. "Take Olivia to see this therapist. He has a lot of experience dealing with children of addicted parents. He may be able to help Olivia confront whatever it is that takes her to the door of the rehabilitation center, and then no farther."

Julian reached forward and accepted the paper. He glanced at the name of Eric Powers and the string of credentials that followed it. Up until the moment he watched Olivia crawl through that downstairs window, Julian had felt he was in complete control of the situation with his daughter. But now he wasn't so sure. Maybe this man could help. At the very least, it couldn't hurt.

"Mr. Cruise, may I make another recommendation?"

Julian looked up from the paper in his hand, trying to keep his mind on the conversation and not on the many questions running through his brain.

"I wouldn't tell Olivia about what you discovered here today. At least until you have a chance to speak to a professional therapist. Right now she's simply spending her afternoons sitting on a park bench, and I will make sure someone is watching over her the whole time she is off school grounds. But your relationship with your daughter is still new and somewhat fragile. If you try to confront her now, who knows how she may act out in retaliation."

Julian nodded, deciding to accept the advice. One day prior and he might have argued, believing he knew what was best. But that opinion had been drastically altered in just a matter of minutes.

Chapter 15

Callie ran her finger over the sills and along the edges with a smile. The repair on the dashboard hole was finished, and no one could tell with the naked eye that the paneling had been replaced. The true sign of a professional job.

She backed out of the car and stood to stretch her back where she had been humped over for the past ten minutes. She lifted her arms over her head and paused, sensing a presence behind her. Arms came around her waist, and she felt warm lips on her neck.

"I've missed you," Julian spoke into her ear.

"Just in time." She turned in his arms.

"Just in time for what?" Julian asked the question, but his attention was focused on the best angle from which to kiss her.

Callie wiggled out of his arms. "I just finished repairing that hole in the dashboard. Check it out."

Julian completely ignored the car and watched the tiny

woman who'd captured his heart saunter across the room. He knew she was putting distance between them in more than just a physical way, but at the moment he had no idea how to undo it.

He glanced at the new dashboard paneling once. "When can I see you again?"

Callie put on a false smile. "You're seeing me right now."

Julian realized she was not going to make this easy. "Callie, don't do this. What we shared was special. Don't throw it away."

"I really don't have room in my life for a relationship right now, Julian. Please respect my wish in this, and let it be."

"I can't do that. What we shared is once in a lifetime. If we let it go, we may never get another chance like this." He walked toward her until he came to the large air compressor, which was bolted to the floor, separating them. "Are you trying to tell me I'm the only one who thinks something special happened between us?"

Callie turned her back to him, knowing that was not a lie she could tell with any believability. "I'm just saying that special or not, it won't work. We're both entrepreneurs, which basically means we're married to our businesses. And you have the extra burden of trying to get to know your daughter for the first time. When would there be time for anything else?"

"We'll make time."

"It's not that sim—" When she turned to face him again, her heart constricted at the pain on his handsome face and she knew instantly something terrible had happened since they'd last seen each other. "Julian? What is it?"

"Olivia's been skipping school and going to the rehab center to see Rachel."

Callie covered her mouth with both hands. "How did you find out?" She came around the compressor to stand beside him.

"Her school discovered she was skipping and had her followed."

"Oh, Julian, I'm so sorry." Callie instinctively wrapped her body around his large form, not caring that her actions completely contradicted her words.

Julian was smart enough not to comment. He needed her warmth, her gentle understanding, and he wasn't about to do anything to ruin it. Instead, he returned the embrace.

"Have you said anything to her about it?"

"No, the school recommended I speak to a therapist first."

"I know how important it was for you that she not know her mother's situation."

Julian took Callie's face between his hands, bringing her eyes to his. "Callie, you were right. Few are given second chances. I'm trying hard not to blow my second chance with my daughter, but I don't know how to talk to her. Everything I say is wrong. This afternoon when I saw her climbing through the window, my instinct was to string her up by her toes until she's twenty-one. It never even occurred to me she was going to visit Rachel."

"I'm no parent, but I think the 'stringing her up by her toes' thing is a perfectly normal reaction to discovering your child is skipping school. Just be glad her principal had the wisdom to handle the situation the way she did."

The ringing of a cell phone interrupted her. Julian pushed the small button at his waist. "Hello?"

Callie backed up to give him some physical room and to give her mind some as well. What was she doing? Saying no with one breath and crawling all over him in the next. But when she sensed his hurt, his pain, she *needed* to comfort him. There was no doubt about it; she was in love with Julian Cruise. A situation that could only lead to heartbreak.

Julian quickly completed the call and returned to her. "I've got to go. James is having some trouble with the CompuTech proposal. But can I see you later? Dinner at my place?"

Dinner will lead to lovemaking, which will lead to my downfall. "Yes."

Julian smiled. "I'll pick you up about six."

Callie could no more resist Julian's charm than she could not breathe. "Don't bother. I'll meet you at your house."

Julian paused in doubt.

She smiled, sensing his hesitation to believe her. "Don't worry, I'll show."

With one quick peck on her lips, he was out the door, his mind already onto his proposal and what needed to be done.

Callie stood in the garage doorway and watched his SUV disappear into traffic. Try as she may, she could not see any good end to a relationship between two people so different. But, good or bad, her path had been chosen. She had given her heart to a bulldog in a business suit; now all that was left was to wait and see what he did with it.

"Hello?" Paul crept across the creaky floorboards of the abandoned house with hesitation. "Hello? Is anyone there?" He paused and looked back at the open doorway, wondering if he had completely lost his mind.

When the man he only knew as Silver's advocate called his home, his first reaction had been fear, and with good reason. He'd only spoken to the man one time on the People Mover platform downtown, and during that brief conversation he had not shared his home address or phone number.

When the man told him he was calling to tell Paul when and where to pick up his loan money that fear turned to instant relief and gratitude. But now that he was standing inside a run-down home in the worst part of town, he had to question what had brought him to this place in his life.

How desperate did he have to be to meet a dangerous stranger in a place like this to collect an illegal loan? The events of the last few weeks played back through his mind. The constant rushing to get to the phone before Mona when he suspected the caller to be a bill collector. Stealing her jewelry out of her box in the dead of night so he could run off to the pawnshop the next day and cash it in, hoping and praying the whole while that she would have no cause to check her box anytime soon. The humiliation of being thrown out of his favorite casino after he'd made the mistake of having his name added to the compulsive gambler list and then getting caught trying to get back in.

The heel of his shoe moved and the floor creaked loudly. Paul spun around at the sound of scurrying and shuddered when he noticed the small, dark shadow shuffling quickly across the room. His eyes lifted to the figure that had materialized in the doorway.

The man stepped forward into the light, and Paul found himself staring into the lightest eyes he'd ever seen on another black man. Eyes so light they almost glowed in the bright sun were set in deep mahogany skin. The effect was at once both eerie and surprisingly beautiful. It all made sense now. *This* was the reason the ruthless young gang lord was known on the street by one word…Silver. With a heart as cold as ice and eyes like molten steel, what else would he be called?

"Hello, Paul." The coarse, tenor voice revealed his true age.

Paul felt his gut clinch. This was no hardened old man he was dealing with. The boy was barely out of his teens, maybe not even that.

"Are you Silver?" Paul decided that despite those eyes,

given what he had heard about Silver, there was no way this child could've done those things.

The young man reached into his jacket pocket and pulled out a large brown envelope. He looked at the packet for a moment. "Does it matter?" He smiled, but there was nothing friendly about it.

Paul stood frozen in place. Accepting this money was the most dangerous gamble he'd ever taken. But he was certain that if he could get a winning streak going again, he could pull himself out of this debt. Give this gangster his loan money back, return Mona's jewelry; all he needed was a few lucky hands. He stepped forward to take the envelope when the other man grabbed his arm, spun him around, and placed a gun firmly against his temple.

"The interest on this loan is one hundred and fifty percent, and I expect your payment on the first of every month promptly for the next twelve months. If you are late…" His silver eyes cut to Paul, and Paul was certain he saw hell swirling in their glassy depths. "Believe me, Paul, you don't want to be late."

Just as quickly as he was grabbed, he was released and pushed across the room with the envelope balled in his tight fist. Just as quickly as it appeared, the gun disappeared as if it had never existed.

Paul watched him turn to leave. "Wait! Where do I bring the payments?" He looked around in disgust. "Do I come back here?"

The gangster stopped in the doorway with his back to Paul. "Don't worry. When the payment is due, I'll contact you. You just make sure you have it when I call." With those gravelly words, he rounded the corner and disappeared.

Paul leaned against the wall, not caring about the dirt and

grime that covered it. The feel of the cold steel both against the side of his head and staring into Silver's eyes was not a sensation he would soon forget. Despite Silver's youthful appearance and voice, Paul knew for certain that he had just encountered Detroit's most vicious warlord face-to-face. He swallowed hard when the full impact of what he had done finally sunk into his numb brain.

Callie was stretched out on the rack beneath a '98 Pontiac Grand Am when she heard the familiar, loud clippity-clap of Pooky's trademark stiletto heels coming across the concrete floor. Unfortunately, her cousin had the double-whammy curse of having both very large and very flat feet. He tried so hard to be the dainty, feminine creature he envisioned in his mind, but the reality was so far from that dream it was a shame.

"Callie! You are not going to believe this, girl!"

Callie turned her head to see two lime-green, open-toed shoes complete with ten lime-green painted toenails directly in her face. "Let me guess, Marshall Field's is having a sale." She returned to the task of air-drilling the muffler into place beneath the car.

"This is serious." Pooky bent as far as his straight skirt would allow. "Somebody has been calling our friends asking about Paul."

"What?!" With one push of her heels, Callie cleared the vehicle and bounded to her feet. "What are you talking about?"

He placed his large hand against his hip bone. "Just what I said. Someone's been calling our friends asking about Paul."

"Who has been called?"

"Well—" Pooky leaned against the car, settling in for the long version of the story "—I stopped by Cassandra's, and he told me first. In fact, he said because of the kinds of questions this person asked, he thought maybe the guy was working for you."

"What kind of questions did he ask?"

"Things like—" Pooky began counting off on his fingers "—how Paul treated you, what they knew about your father's will, how Paul took all your money, did any of them ever remember you saying anything about where Paul lived, that kind of stuff."

Callie pulled her rag from her back pocket and wiped her hands. That was all ancient history. Who would care about how her stepbrother treated her ten years ago?

"So," Pooky continued, "after I left Cassandra, I went by the old apartment building on a hunch, and sure enough almost all of our friends had been contacted. Diva Dale, Go-Go, Tanya, Ms. Dory, and even our old landlord, Mr. Agnes. And they had all been asked the same questions—how Paul treated you and so on."

Callie rested her elbow on the roof of the car. "But why?" she said, more to herself than to Pooky.

"Wanna know what I think?"

Not really.

"I think it's Paul."

"And why would Paul call to ask questions he already has the answers to?"

"I think he found out that you opened the garage again, and he's just trying to deflect suspicion. You know, see if he can dig up something he could use to rob us blind."

Callie crossed the room to place the air drill back into its holder. "There's just two things wrong with your explanation, Pooky." Callie stood with her back to Pooky, staring out the garage door. Her mind was running a thousand miles a minute trying to interpret the meaning of this bit of surprising news.

"You are always so critical of anything I say! Like you are the only one who can have a good idea." Pooky pouted. "Okay, Ms. Smarty Pants, what's wrong with my explanation?"

"First of all, you said yourself this person is not asking questions about me, just about Paul, right?"

"Well…yes." Pooky reluctantly agreed.

"Secondly, Paul already took everything from me ten years ago, except this garage, which hasn't turned a profit since we opened the doors. In short, it can't be Paul trying to take anything from me—because I don't have anything worth taking."

Pooky's finely arched eyebrows crumpled in defeat. "Oh. I see your point. Well then, who do you think it is?"

Callie was racking her brain trying to find just that answer. A light went on in her head as she suddenly recalled the most recent conversation she'd had regarding Paul. It was curled in the warmth and shelter of Julian's arms as he drilled her on the whereabouts of her stepbrother.

She turned to face Pooky. "I don't know who has been making these calls, but I may know on whose behalf they are calling."

Chapter 16

"This is it?" Julian sat behind his desk reviewing the scant report on notebook paper given to him by Jonathan. All it contained were the names of a bunch of drag queens and their answers to Jonathan's ridiculous questions. "What am I supposed to do with this?"

"How would I know? You are the one who wanted this information. You said bring you what I could find out and you would do the rest." Jonathan sat slumped in the wood chair on the other side of the desk. He gestured to the fives pages of notes he'd collected. "There it is. The rest is up to you."

Julian flipped back through the pages in disgust, looking for anything that might be helpful.

"Look—" Jonathan sat forward in his chair "—maybe it would help if you told me why you were looking for the guy. I mean, all you gave me was a name, where he once lived, and his connection to Callie. Pretty skimpy information, really."

Julian shook his head. "You are right. I should've just hired a professional to begin with. Your time would be better served helping James with the CompuTech proposal. He's having trouble researching the history of some of the accounts."

"Sorry, man. I did the best I could given what I had." Jonathan stood from his chair. "If we are done here, I'm going to head over to James's place."

"All right. Thanks anyway." Julian was still skimming the pages when he heard his brother's surprised gasp. His head came up to find Callie standing in the doorway to his office.

Instantly Julian was on his feet. "Callie, what are you doing here so early?"

Her surprised eyes went back and forth between the two men. "Sorry to just barge in, but the front door was open."

The two brothers exchanged a concerned look, both wondering how much she had heard.

"It's okay, come on in." Julian came around the desk to greet her.

"Later, man," Jonathan tossed back over his shoulder. "It was nice seeing you again, Callie," he said as he passed her in the doorway.

"You, too," she answered, but her eyes and attention were focused on Julian coming toward her.

Julian took her in his arms and held her. She didn't *feel* angry, he thought. Her soft, warm body was as relaxed and welcoming as always. Maybe she'd just arrived and hadn't really heard any of the conversation.

"Well, you're early for dinner, but I can think of some interesting ways to pass the time until then." He nibbled gently at her neck.

"Why are you looking for Paul?"

Julian considered telling her the truth for all of a second. "What are you talking ab—"

Callie quickly placed a hand over his lips to still them. "Don't insult my intelligence by denying what we both know."

He put his arm around her and led her to the leather couch. "I did it for you. From what you told me, this man is still a threat to you and your business. I thought it best if you found him before he found you."

Callie settled back on the couch. "I appreciate the thought, Julian. But Paul is my problem, not yours."

"Don't you understand? Your problems are my problems."

Callie turned in his arms. "Julian, we spent one night together. One night. That's all. You don't owe me anything."

Julian felt his temper flare briefly. When would she accept what had happened between them was love and stop belittling it and making it sound like some cheap booty call?

"We shared something wonderful, Callie. I know what it is, but you are not ready to hear it yet. Still, I can't let you sit here and act like it's nothing." He took her slender shoulders in his hands. "Tell me you don't feel something more than lust for me, something much more real and important. Say it, right now."

One look in his dark eyes and Callie knew that was impossible.

His soft mouth twisted in triumph. "That's what I thought."

"Honestly, Julian, I don't know what I feel." She broke his hold and stood. "But regardless, Paul is my problem, and I have to deal with him the way I see fit."

Julian stood as well. "Don't you see? You don't have to do it all alone anymore. You've got me now."

"Julian, you can't just come in and take my life over."

"I'm not trying to take over; I'm just trying to be a part of it. I want to help you any way I can."

"Then help me by letting me handle this my own way. If this relationship stands any chance of working, you've got to understand at least this about me—I fight my own battles."

Not anymore. "All right." He took her into his arms.

Callie pulled free and stood back from him. "Julian, I need your assurance."

"Okay," he said with a shrug of his shoulders.

"No." She shook her head emphatically. "When I was a little girl, my parents would make me heart promises when something was really important, because a heart promise can never be broken."

Julian's eyebrows crunched in confusion. "Oookay," he said slowly.

"A promise of the heart is an unbreakable promise, Julian. You must keep it because the heart will accept nothing less than the absolute truth." She looked into his dark eyes, searching. Did he truly understand the importance of a heart promise? "I need your *heart promise* that you will not try to find Paul on your own."

Julian braced himself with as serious an expression as he could muster. He had no idea what this heart promise non-sense was about, but her level of intensity had tripled in the past few seconds. He was certain of only one thing—whatever this was, it meant a great deal to her. The last thing he wanted to do was insult her.

"Promise me, Julian. Promise me that you will not look for Paul on your own."

Julian, ever the strategist, honed in on the loophole to the promise. He could make this promise in good conscience, because the truth was he had no intention of trying to find Paul DeLeroy on his own. He was going to hire a professional.

He held up his right hand. "I promise."

"A heart promise?"

He cleared his throat. "I make a *heart* promise that I will not try to find Paul DeLeroy on my own."

Callie threw herself against him, holding him tight, and Julian returned the embrace, certain that their future was sealed. She loved him as much as he loved her; eventually she would accept this, and once the monster of her past had been dealt with, their lives could move forward without concern.

Callie was chopping tomatoes for the tacos they were preparing for dinner when she heard the back door creak open. She knew who it was without turning to see. Julian had already prepared her for the arrival of his daughter. She took a deep breath and painted on her most flattering smile.

"Hello, you must be Olivia."

The teenager stopped in the doorway, surprised to find a stranger in their kitchen. "Hello," she answered tenuously.

Callie wiped her hand on the apron Julian had lent her. "I'm Callie. Nice to meet you."

The girl stared at the hand for several seconds. "Nice to meet you," she muttered.

"We're making tacos. I understand they are your favorite." Callie was fighting hard to keep the nervousness out of her voice.

The beautiful child standing in front of her was not what she expected. At fourteen, Olivia was already half a foot taller than Callie and looked nothing like her father. And thankfully so, Callie thought. Julian's ruggedly handsome features were wonderful on a man but were not made for a woman.

The girl's sculpted features were refined and delicate and set in olive skin. But one look in her eyes, and Callie felt as if she were looking into Julian's. The shade of brown was lighter, but there was that same keen intelligence, that sense of too much awareness. Their eyes, both Julian and his daughter's, gave a person the impression that every word they said was being dissected and examined, making one very conscious of what was said in their presence.

Just then, Julian reentered the kitchen trying not to make eye contact with his daughter. He'd just gotten off the telephone with her principal and knew that she'd gone to the rehab center again today. Apparently, this time she got as far as the front door. She was hurting inside, and Julian felt helpless.

"Hello, sweetheart," he called over his shoulder as he went to the stove to stir the meat sauce. "I see you've met Callie."

"Want to help us make the tacos?" Callie offered cheerfully. "The lettuce still needs to be sliced, and the cheese needs to be shredded."

Olivia looked from one to the other. "I've got a lot of homework." She turned and headed toward the front part of the house.

"Olivia," Julian called to her as she passed him.

She stopped and turned to her father.

Julian froze. There was so much he wanted to say, so much he could've said, and yet none of it seemed right at that very moment.

Olivia tilted her head to the side, sensing the hesitation in her father. "Yes, Daddy?"

Julian forced a small smile. "Never mind, sweetheart. Go get started on your homework. I'll call you when dinner is ready."

Olivia paused for a moment longer before going to her bedroom and closing the door.

Julian felt Callie's arms close around his waist. He quickly turned in her arms and pulled her against him. How had he managed to come this far without her? He lifted her against him and kissed her passionately, squeezing her tightly again.

"I don't know how to help her. I don't know what to say," he whispered against her ear.

"You are giving her your patience and understanding, Julian. That's what she needs right now," she answered softly. Both were wholly aware of the other person in the house.

"I've scheduled an appointment tomorrow with the therapist the school recommended."

"Have you talked to Olivia at all about it?"

"No. I was just going to pick her up from school tomorrow and take her there."

Callie pulled back from him a moment. "No, Julian." Callie shook her head. "Don't do that to her. Give her the ability to prepare herself; tell her."

"I don't know how she will react."

"Imagine her reaction to arriving at the therapist's office when she had no idea you were even aware of the situation."

"Stay the night with me, Callie. I need to hold you tonight." His large hand curved around her bottom, lifting her against his hard body.

It took every ounce of her will power, but Callie pushed back from him. "You need the time with your daughter more."

Julian had not said more than ten words to his daughter since he'd seen her returning to the school two days ago. He did indeed need the time alone with Olivia, and even though his selfish heart wanted to wallow in Callie's warmth and gentle loving, he knew he had a more important commitment to his daughter.

After Callie left, he would talk to Olivia and clear the air. He was not able to be there for the first thirteen years of her life, but she needed him now, and he would do everything in his power to help her.

Despite the colorful display of Mexican food on the table, the overall mood of the dinner was bleak. The only thing resembling entertainment for Callie was watching Julian try to eat his taco remnants with a fork.

Callie's three attempts to engage Olivia in conversation had all failed miserably as Olivia continued to halt the exchange with clipped, single-word answers.

With each rebuttal, Julian's thick eyebrows seemed to come closer and closer together, and Callie was fearful that he would eventually explode at his daughter for her rude behavior. That would, of course, end any chance she had of befriending the girl.

"So, Olivia," Callie began again, wondering if she was just a glutton for punishment. "How do you like school?"

"I don't." Olivia glared at her father. "I wish I was back in my old school with my friends. I hate it here."

In a strange way, the angry response was an improvement, Callie thought. It was the most words she'd said all night.

"I told you, Olivia," Julian interrupted, "your school is on the other side of town. There's no way you can get back and forth on your own, and I can't take you and pick you up every day. I have to work."

Olivia was instantly on her feet. "Is that supposed to be a crack against my mother?"

Julian jumped to his feet as well. "Of course not! When have you ever heard me say anything negative about your mother?"

"You may not say it, but I know you think it. You think you're better than her!"

Callie sat stupefied. The girl had gone from corpse to raving lunatic in under sixty seconds.

"I never said that either. Don't put words in my mouth, Olivia."

"You think I don't know what this is all about? Bringing *her* here?" She pointed an accusing finger at Callie.

"What are you talking about?" Julian's arms flailed wildly. "This was supposed to be a nice family dinner."

"Family? With her playing mommy?" She turned to give Callie a scathing look. "I'd rather be an orphan." With that, she stormed out of the room. Seconds later, they heard her bedroom door slam shut.

Julian stood in front of his chair, his eyes wide in shock, his head throbbing in pain. "What just happened here?"

"I'm not really sure."

"One minute we were eating, and the next—"

Callie stood. "Maybe I should go."

"Please don't leave me alone here with that." He nodded in the direction of his daughter's room. "I don't care what I say, it's never the right thing."

"There is no *right* thing, Julian."

"I'm not ready to let you go home."

"You need to talk to your daughter. Talk, not yell—talk."

"What if she's not willing to listen?"

"I think once I leave, she will be. That little girl has got a whole lot going on in that head of hers. She needs to get it out. Talk to her, Julian."

Callie crossed the room to him with outstretched arms. Julian eagerly accepted her offering, squeezing her small waist between his large hands, knowing she was right and hating that she was right so much of the time, especially in an arena where she had less experience than he did. Maybe it was instinct; he wasn't sure, but he knew this was what had been missing from his life. Someone to bounce ideas off of and share problems with.

His family tried to be there for him and help with Olivia, but inevitably, the tough decisions always came back to Julian alone. But not anymore, he thought; whether Callie knew it or not, they were a team for life.

He nibbled at her neck, loving the way she felt in his hands. "Sure you don't have time for a quickie?"

"I don't think you know the meaning of the word."

Chapter 17

"Olivia? Do you know why your dad brought you here today?" Eric Powers reclined in his leather lounger. Everything about his appearance and demeanor gave the impression of a relaxed and casual observer. But the oversized black cardigan and crossed ankles were a cover for the very intense study being conducted.

He was making mental notes about everything from the way the young girl held her hands in her lap to the way her eyes darted over his degrees and credentials that lined the walls. He knew he was being sized up. She was trying to calculate how much of a threat he was to what she felt was her superior intellect.

Olivia tried to ignore the older white man sitting a few feet from her. But with them being the only two people in the room, it was impossible. If she could just keep quiet for the next hour, he would have nothing to report back to her father. She knew that anything she said would be analyzed, so her best strategy was to say nothing.

"Olivia? Do you know why you are here?"

She huffed in her chest. He was obviously going to be persistent. "Yes."

"Would you like to talk about it?"

"No."

Eric gently placed his notepad and pen on the side table and leaned forward in his chair. "You know, if you don't talk to me today, your dad's just going to bring you back next week, and the week after, and the week after that. He's the kind of man who insists on results, and we'll keep doing the same thing over and over again until he finally gets results."

Olivia quirked an eyebrow. "Is he your patient as well?"

Eric fought to hide a small smile. "No. That was a freebie."

Olivia wanted to smile in return. She felt herself softening. She never imagined she might actually like the guy. But she quickly shook off the warm feeling and put her armor firmly back into position.

"You know, we don't necessarily have to discuss your reasons for being here today. We can talk about anything you like."

Olivia's mouth twisted in disbelief. That was a trap if ever she saw one.

"Okay, have it your way. But in a couple of weeks when you find yourself still sitting on that couch, you'll realize that my analysis of your father is right on the money and that the only way you are going to get rid of me is to cooperate."

"I don't see what the big deal is anyway. So I go visit my mother every now and then. So what?"

"Come on, Olivia, don't throw up that ole no-big-deal smoke screen. We both know it's not that easy. Your mom left you with a father you never knew so that she could check into a rehabilitation center for her cocaine addiction. And you say that's no big deal?"

Olivia's brown eyes shot daggers across the room. "You don't know anything about me or my mother."

"But I want to know."

"No, you don't! You're just like him, just like all of them! They pretend they care and say all the right things. But they don't care! None of you do!"

Eric felt a burst of relief. Finally, they were getting somewhere. "Your father cares."

"That hypocrite! He's worse than all of them! He thinks he's so smart with his big house and fancy cars. He thinks he's better than us!"

"Us? You think your father believes he's better than you, Olivia?"

"Of course! Why else wouldn't he have come looking for me? He knew he had a child! If Mama hadn't found him, he would've never come looking for us."

Eric ignored the water that was now streaming down her face; his mind was riveted on the river flowing much deeper. The one that troubled her young soul. "And you resent him for that?"

"Wouldn't you?"

Julian stood staring out his office window at the pouring rain, considering all he'd learned in the past week. His worst fears had been confirmed. His daughter hated him. Not true hate, but more a deep resentment for his lack of presence in her life for the first years.

According to Dr. Powers, Olivia was transferring the hurt and anger she felt toward her mother onto him. She needed to blame someone, and Julian, the estranged, unknown rich father, was the perfect target.

His desk phone rang, startling him out of his contemplation. He crossed the room and answered it quickly. "Julian Cruise."

"Hi."

Callie's soft voice was a balm to his troubled soul. He slumped down in his desk chair. "Hey, what's up?"

"I was just calling to ask you the same thing. Did you get Olivia moved out okay?"

"Yes," he said with regret. After her second session with Dr. Powers, Olivia had announced her decision to live with her grandparents. Julian's first reaction to this decision had been a swift and emphatic no. His second was to fire the therapist who seemed to be only making matters worse.

But after talking with the doctor, Julian had decided to go ahead and let her move into his parents' home for a while. It broke his heart, but he was willing to do whatever was necessary. And according to Dr. Powers, Olivia needed to put some physical distance between them so that she could give her mind some room as well.

"Yes, I took her this afternoon." His eyes were drawn back to the window. "The house feels emptier already."

"Do you want me to come over?"

Julian sealed the yes that came instantly to his lips. Much to his disappointment, Julian had recently discovered that his daughter wasn't the only one trying to distance herself from him. But Callie had chosen a different tactic.

Olivia had chosen to move out. Callie had chosen to move in. Lately she was spending a great deal of time at his house, and at first Julian had been pleased with the surprising turn of events. Until he began to notice the pattern. She only came late in the night, spent a couple of hours in his bed, and then waited until he fell asleep to disappear again.

Julian tried often to have serious conversations with her regarding their relationship and the future. Up until last night, Callie had avoided it with a kiss or a joke or a carefully timed seduction. But last night, Julian had insisted on an answer, something to suggest she planned to stick around. That confrontation had lead to a heated argument. But unfortunately, when she began rubbing against him, he realized he wanted her more than he wanted an answer. They'd made love. They'd fallen asleep. When he'd awoken, she was gone, and he still had no definitive commitment. Did she really think she could just crawl back into his bed tonight like nothing ever happened?

"Where are we in this relationship, Callie?" The phone line was silent for so long, Julian feared she'd hung up. "Callie?"

"I don't know, Julian. Why can't we just enjoy what we have right now and let the future take care of itself?"

"That's not how it works, baby. You have to choose to love; otherwise it can just slip through your fingers."

"I told you in the beginning that I was not interested in anything serious."

"Then what are we doing?"

"Having a good time."

"Please," he huffed in exasperation. "I'm too old for that mess. I need something more than that, Callie. I need to know you are going to be in my life…" Julian paused to choose his words carefully. The last thing he wanted to do was give her an ultimatum, since he most assuredly knew what her answer would be. "I need to know that somewhere down the line this thing will become permanent."

"I can't promise you that."

"Do you love me or am I crazy? Am I imagining this thing between us?"

"Love's not enough, Julian. Believe me. I have lost a lot of people I loved." She chuckled humorlessly. "Love doesn't guarantee anything."

"Yes, it does."

"People who believed themselves in love get divorced every day, Julian. What did love promise them?"

"Hope."

"Not enough."

"But it's a start."

"Do you want me to come over or not?"

"Are you coming as my *lover* or my *love?*"

"Why are you making this so hard? Why can't we just enjoy each other, and stop worrying about the future?"

"Because you can't go back in time. I love you, Callie. And I believe you love me, too. How can I hold you in my arms, come inside your body, and not want to know you feel the same as I do? I feel like we're stranded in the middle of the ocean together, and you're the only one with a life vest."

"Julian, please," Callie pleaded. "Don't complicate this. Let's just enjoy the moment."

Julian knew he was about to take the chance of a lifetime, but he had to. Her soulful plea was weakening his resolve. "When you are ready for something more than right now, let me know. I will be here. For you, I will always be here." With that, Julian gently replaced the receiver, fearing if he remained on the line, she would eventually break down his wall of resistance.

Julian tossed and turned for most of the night, finally falling asleep around midnight. Late that night, his drowsy eyes opened to a bumping sound coming from downstairs. The bumping got louder as he sat up in bed. Then he recognized the knocking. He glanced at his clock, which read 3:42. Who would be knocking on his door in the middle of the night?

Instantly he was on his feet and running across the room as the answer came to him in a flash. He had to get downstairs quickly or she might change her mind and leave. Bounding down the stairs two at a time, he was at the front door. Without even checking the peephole, he pulled the door open and felt as if the angels of heaven were singing just for him.

Without a single word, Callie circled around him and into the house. Julian watched her slow motions as he relocked the front door.

She stood with her back to him, studying the large foyer as if she'd never seen it. "If this doesn't work…"

He came up behind her and wrapped her in his arms. "But it will."

Callie accepted the warm embrace. This is what she'd come here for. This was what she'd been unable to sleep without, and it bothered her to realize how much she needed to be held by this man.

"I do love you, Julian. But I can't afford to lose another person I love. It costs too much in here." She touched a place near her heart.

"You won't lose me, baby. I will be here through the good, the bad—come what may." He smiled. "No matter how annoying you may find me, I will be here."

Callie turned in his arms. "You better be," she whispered, rising up on her tiptoes to press her lips to his.

Chapter 18

Callie watched Pooky as he slung his leather portfolio across the desk and kicked off his navy blue heels.

"Another no thank-you." He pouted and sank down on one of the stools sitting near the work counter.

Callie took in his neat navy pinstriped skirt set. Today's wig was pinned back in a neat bun. But unfortunately, it was late in the day, and his five o'clock shadow was showing. He looked like some kind of Miss Manners mutation. "Have you ever once considered going on a job interview dressed as a man?"

"Why would I?"

"Just a suggestion." Callie hunched her shoulders, having been down this road too many times to try again.

"This is who I am. If they can't accept that, then I don't need their stinking job anyway."

"But we agree that you do need a job, right? No more dipping into your trust fund."

Pooky twisted his mouth in sarcasm. "Of course."

A thought occurred to Callie, and Pooky watched her facial expression change.

"What's wrong?" he asked, pulling off his snap-on pearl earrings.

"It just occurred to me that I never received the electric bill for this month, but yet we still have lights on."

"Hmm," Pooky said, standing to collect his items. He tried to appear nonchalant as he made his great escape. "That's odd."

"Oh, Pooky, you can't keep doing this. Your parents left that money for your future. That's *your* nest egg."

"Exactly, *my* nest egg. To spend any way I want." Pooky picked up his portfolio. "Callie, you and I are mirror images of each other."

Callie almost laughed at the comical comparison, knowing there were no two people more different. But her cousin was serious.

"We both were blessed to be raised in loving homes by parents who allowed us to be ourselves, parents who planned for our futures, parents who died at young ages," he continued. "The only difference between you and me is that I did not have a conniving stepbrother waiting to take everything from me."

"I appreciate the thought, but I won't spend up all your money this way. No more trips to the bank."

"Okay." He hunched his padded shoulders. "Anyway, I've got two more interviews lined up tomorrow. Who knows, maybe one of them will be the one." He picked up his navy pumps and sauntered out with all the arrogance of true royalty.

Callie watched her cousin disappear up the stairs into their apartment and silently wondered what was wrong with her.

Every single day this man was rejected on so many levels, and yet every evening he returned with his spirit intact, ready to go out and party the night away. The world's cruelty never entered his own heart. Through it all, Pooky remained hopeful, trusting, and generous despite universal disdain.

Callie had been a constant part of his life for ten years. She knew how inhumane some humans could be, and yet every time a harsh word or cruel gesture broke his heart, Pooky simply swept up the pieces and glued them back together.

So, Callie thought, why was *she* so terrified of loving one man?

Julian pulled up in front of his parents' home and blew his horn. Within a few seconds, his daughter came out. He watched as she climbed inside the vehicle, wondering if it was his imagination or if she had grown in the last few days.

"Hi, sweetheart," he said, fighting the temptation to kiss her, unsure if it would be accepted. Although she had been a part of his life for only a little over a year, Julian felt as if she had always been there. He found that in the past few weeks since she'd moved out he'd missed her terribly.

"Hi, Daddy," Olivia answered, clicking her seat belt and settling in for the thirty-minute ride.

Julian pulled from the curb, deciding that today he would not try to force conversation with her, which was customary on these long trips to Dr. Powers's office. It was the only time he saw her, and he wanted to hear about everything that went on in her life while they were apart. But not today, he decided. Today he would allow her privacy and solitude and content himself with just her presence and knowing she was okay.

That lasted for all of two minutes. "How was school today?"

"Okay." She was looking out the window at a group of kids walking in the other direction.

"Anything new going on?"

"No."

"Were Mom and Dad home?"

"Yes."

"Are you getting along with them okay?"

"Yes."

Julian was frustrated but not surprised. This was pretty much the way the conversations had gone on these trips. She was never rude or disrespectful, but she was a far, far cry from congenial.

Out of desperation, Julian turned on the radio, hoping it would in some way affect her mood. He even turned it to the local rap station, which was not his kind of music. Still, she stared out the window at anything that happened to pass by.

He was changing lanes when he realized the radio was no longer on.

Olivia turned the knob slowly and shifted in her seat. "Daddy? Why didn't you ever come looking for me? I mean, you knew Mom was pregnant when she moved."

Although Dr. Powers had warned him to prepare for this conversation, he found he had no answer. According to the therapist, this conversation was a good sign, a turning point. But now that it was here, all the rehearsed responses would not come.

"Olivia, you are fourteen years old. Do you realize your mother and I were only three years older than that when you were conceived?"

Her thin brows crinkled in thought.

Julian checked traffic and pulled over to the closest parking space. He turned off the ignition and rotated to face her. "I'm not trying to make excuses, but I want you to understand. We were both very young and unfortunately still under our parents' rules." Julian paused, not wanting to place blame on

Rachel's father, although he secretly held the man responsible for hiding his daughter.

"Mom told me you tried to marry her. She said her father came home one day and announced they were moving. She said he hired a moving company and everything. They came in and packed the whole house. She said her mom and dad argued all that night, but they still ended up moving the next day. She said it was the saddest day of her life."

Julian listened attentively. This was the first time he had ever gotten an account of events from Rachel's point of view. And of course he should've assumed that Olivia would've adopted that same point of view. What other information about her father did she have for those first thirteen years except the information given to her by her mother? He also noted that she referred to Rachel's parents as her mom's parents and not as Grandma and Grandpa, which were the names she'd almost instantly began calling his parents. Which led him to believe Rachel had grown apart from her family.

"It was the saddest day of my life as well," Julian said quietly. "I never thought…I mean, I just never imagined he would go to such lengths to keep us apart."

"But why didn't you look for us?"

"Olivia, I have no excuse except immaturity and ignorance. Once you were gone, I felt as if I had no power over the situation. My parents tried to help me, but after six months or so we accepted that I would never find you. So, I went on with my life as best I could, but you've got to believe that I never forgot you. I often wondered if you were a girl or a boy, what you were like." He lifted her chin with his large hand. "When you two showed up on my doorstep, it was like a miracle."

Olivia turned her head to stare out the window again.

"Callie believes that Rachel and I have been given a rare

second chance—Rachel, a chance at a clean life, and myself, a chance to know you."

"She said that?"

Julian sat studying her profile, realizing how much he'd lost in not knowing this special child for all those precious years. "Yes."

Olivia was quiet for a long time, and Julian waited for her to say something more.

Finally she said, "I'm never having children until I'm at least twenty-five and married."

"Can I give you away when you get married?" he asked.

She was unable to suppress a small smile. "Sure."

Julian felt something like relief in the region of his heart. He started the car and pulled from the curb. He felt like he had learned as much about Olivia in their brief conversation as she had learned about him. Apparently the good doctor knew what he was talking about, Julian thought, feeling as if he and his daughter had finally made some kind of connection.

Julian bit his lip, remembering the rest of what Dr. Powers had said. He'd explained that this conversation would be the beginning of the healing process but in no way would it be the end. And Julian realized that although they might have just crossed an emotional river together, they still had an ocean ahead of them.

Chapter 19

"What are you doing?" Callie asked with concern, noticing that Julian was pulling out of traffic.

"I just have to make one quick pit stop."

She glanced at her watch, realizing that the truck had pulled to a standstill in front of a women's clothing store. "This is your pit stop?"

He smiled his devilish smile. "You could say that." He opened the door and bounded out of the vehicle.

"Julian, we're going to be late for the play," she called out the window. "We're already too late for any kind of decent parking."

"Just come on," he said, opening her door.

Callie sighed in resignation and climbed out of the vehicle, careful of where she stepped in her navy blue high-heeled sandals.

Julian guided her to the front of the store, and as the pair entered, they were greeted with enthusiasm. "Callie, this is Tia. Tia is an old friend of mine."

A middle-aged woman dressed in African apparel and sporting a short, neat Afro approached them like a long-lost friend. "Finally, I thought you'd never arrive! Girls! Our special guests are here," she called back over her shoulder.

Callie hesitated in the doorway, just now realizing that they were expected. "Julian, what's going on?"

He smiled, completely pleased with himself. "You'll see."

In seconds, Callie found herself encircled by four fluttering women. They were each measuring and comparing from different angles. As quickly as they appeared, the foursome disappeared behind a red curtain on the far side of the room.

"You were right, Julian, your estimations were almost perfect. We'll only have to make a few minor alterations," Tia said, studying Callie intently. "This is so exciting. We aren't often asked to do things like this—it really tests our skills."

Seeing she would get no cooperation from Julian, Callie decided to try her luck with this woman who appeared to be the proprietor, or at the very least, a manager. "Excuse me, but what was that all about?"

Tia was practically beaming with excitement as she shared a conspirator's look with Julian. "I was sworn to secrecy. But let me say this much at least—you are a very lucky lady to have a man like this."

Callie's patience had reached its limit. They were missing the show, and she didn't even know why. "What is going on here?"

Julian turned to her and took both her hands in his. "Callie, trust me on this. You're really going to like this surprise—and the play doesn't start until eight."

"You told me seven."

"I know," he said, looking over her head at the movement behind the red curtain. "I needed an extra hour for this."

"You lied to me?" She was shocked and appalled that he'd lied so easily and apparently was feeling no remorse.

"No, not a lie exactly, just a misplaced digit." He smiled and winked, turning his attention to the saleslady. "Are the accessories ready?"

"Everything has been put in place just as you specified," Tia said in her most professional voice.

"Thank you." Julian grinned his boyish smile, and the woman practically swooned. She glanced at Callie, wondering about the type of woman who would cause such a man to go to this great length to surprise her. She noted that the young woman did not look as excited as she should've given the circumstance. In fact, she looked rather ticked off.

Tia took in the rhinestone-studded blue jean pantsuit and matching soft hat. Even in her three-inch sandals, Callie's petite stature was obvious. The outfit was cute in a funky seventies way, Tia decided, but compared to her creation, it was a rag.

"Julian, I can't believe you're so nonchalant about a lie." Callie was looking up at the man she loved like he was a foreign being.

"Callie, you are making this a bigger deal than it is. Trust me, when you see your surprise, you'll forget all about that little white lie."

No lie is little, Callie thought, but decided to try to rein in her frustration. He obviously didn't understand how much she valued *complete* honesty, something they would have to talk about later. She folded her arms across her chest, deciding to be satisfied with the fact that they would not miss the show.

In a matter of minutes, the foursome reappeared carrying a short, black dress.

Callie's first instinct was to take in the lovely after-five dress with natural appreciation. It was lovely. The material had a velvety look to it, which reflected the light, showing the differing hues in the dark fabric. The shoulder straps were braided strands, which crisscrossed in the back and circled around the waist.

"So." Julian was watching her face. "What do you think?"

"It's beautiful," Callie said without hesitation.

"Yes." Julian came up behind her. "I picked it out a while ago but was uncertain of your measurements exactly. So you had to be fitted, but that would've ruined the surprise. This was the only way to do it and have it still be a surprise."

"What a wonderful gift. Thank you." She kissed him once with passion, expressing all the happiness she felt inside.

Tia was feeling triumphant. "Mission accomplished. Now let's get you changed so you won't be late for your engagement."

"What?" Callie asked in confusion, running her hand over the soft fabric.

"Baby, hurry, we still need to get across town in thirty minutes." Julian glanced at his watch.

"No problem, just let them pack my dress and we can get going."

"No, you need to change."

"Why?"

"I bought the dress for you to wear tonight."

"But I don't want to wear it tonight. I want to wear my blue jean pantsuit tonight. I bought it just for this occasion. You know that."

Julian and Tia shared a strange look, and Callie felt her blood boil. She remembered showing Julian the pantsuit over a week ago, when she'd first purchased it.

He'd nodded and pretended he liked it, but now she was wondering exactly when he commissioned Tia to design the dress.

As casually as she could, Callie smiled at Tia. "This is a such a wonderful surprise. How long have you two been plotting this?" she asked with playful mischief.

"Baby, we'd better get going," Julian tried to interrupt.

But Tia, being proud of her unique collection, wasn't about to be cheated out of the opportunity to boast. "Let's see," she said thoughtfully, "Julian came in for the first time about a week ago and picked out the dress, and then again three days ago with his estimated alterations. Of course, three days is not a lot of time, but we experts understand that sometimes you must do the impossible."

"Of course." Callie smiled at Tia and glared at Julian. "Well, I truly am both impressed by your work and flattered by the thought. But I think I will keep on my pantsuit for tonight and save this magnificent creation for a truly special occasion."

Tia smiled, sufficiently appeased. She, too, felt her beautiful dress deserved a more fitting occasion than an ordinary evening on the town. But she wasn't so wrapped up in praise that she'd forgotten who was paying the bill. She glanced at Julian. "We can wrap the dress to take with you?"

One look at Callie's stubborn expression and he knew there was no chance of getting her out of that pantsuit tonight. When she'd so subtly asked Tia about the date of the sale, he knew the jig was up. But what was he to do? There was no nice way to tell the woman he loved that she had horrible taste in clothes.

During her workday, she was forced to wear coveralls and work boots, but in her off time she tended to dress more like Lil' Kim than the future Mrs. Cruise should. The man in him had nothing but appreciation for the short skirts and halter tops she sported on a regular basis. Her small, athletic body was made to be shown off. He'd even come to accept the stares they tended to receive from other men when they went out in public. Okay, not really, he corrected himself. But he'd accepted that as long as they kept their distance, he'd keep his hands to himself.

He glanced down at the blue jean ensemble and decided that as far as Callie's taste went, this was actually pretty mild. At least most of her flesh was covered. But her taste in clothes did not go along with the plans he had for their lives—dinner parties with heads of corporation, political soirees with heads of state.

Callie was beautiful and charming and everything he could want in a lover and life partner. Despite her current circumstances, Julian knew by her speech and demeanor that Callie had been bred for better. Max Tyler had obviously had big plans and high hopes for his little girl. But life had thrown Callie Tyler a curve ball, and with strength and conviction she'd turned it into a fly ball. All Julian wanted to do was turn that fly ball into a home run.

But unfortunately, after living with drag queens for the past ten years, their poor taste had rubbed off on her. Callie had developed a bad case of hoochieitis. And it was his job as her man and future husband to cure her of it. But how?

"Yes, Tia." Callie smiled at the anxious saleswoman. "Wrap it, and please thank your staff for their hard work in getting this ready so quickly." With that statement, she turned and walked out.

Tia was still looking to Julian for direction.

"Go ahead and wrap it." He watched Callie leave the store. Through the glass windows, he watched her climb into his truck, shut the door, and sit staring ahead as if the past fifteen minutes had never happened.

Julian, having already paid for the dress a week ago, accepted the suit bag and accessories as he left the store. He hung the bags up in the backseat of the truck and climbed into the driver's seat. He knew just how bad he'd messed up when he realized she wouldn't even look at him.

"Sorry. I thought I was doing a nice thing," he offered.

"The next time you want to say something about my clothing selection, I would recommend you try *talking to me*. It will probably save you a lot of money."

Julian started the truck and pulled from the curb. Despite the dress fiasco, he was sure he could salvage the evening. She'd been looking forward to this show all week, and he knew once the curtains opened, all grudges would be forgotten. Blessedly, Callie wasn't very good at staying angry for any length of time.

One hour later, Julian glanced over at Callie as the curtains opened on act 1. She was smiling in anticipation. By the end of act 2 they were both laughing at the outrageous antics of the cast. After the show, they had a light dinner at a local bistro and returned to Julian's house. By midnight, much to his satisfaction, Julian had finally achieved his original goal of getting Callie out of her blue jean outfit.

Chapter 20

James and Jonathan Cruise each stood with an armful of manila files watching the laughing couple playing in the pool, not believing what they were seeing. Having known the man for thirty-two and twenty-two years, respectively, both knew Julian Cruise was not the frisky, frolicking type.

No, he was the serious-minded, pocket-protector wearing, calculator-toting type. Julian could give an accounting ledger hell, but playful and fun-loving? It had just never been done.

Yet, there he was right in front of their eyes, tossing Callie through the air to land in another part of the pool, struggling to catch his breath through his laughter.

When it seemed as if the pair was going to continue on in their fun forever, James stepped forward, and the movement caught Julian's eye. He looked up at his fully dressed brother standing at the edge of his pool. His black dress shoes were sprinkled with water droplets, and Julian wondered what they were doing there.

"Hey, man." He shielded his eyes from the sun and was only then able to see Jonathan standing in the background with a silly lopsided grin on his lips. "What are you guys doing here?"

"Hi, guys!" Callie called, swimming away.

Both men waved. James squatted down beside the pool and held up three fingers. "Three words for you: CompuTech future forecast."

"Damn," Julian hissed. "I forgot all about that." CompuTech was expecting a financial forecast of their future business based on Cruise Corporation's analysis so far. But right now, all Julian wanted to do was spend time with Callie. He was quietly considering a plan that would allow him to do both when his head disappeared beneath the water.

Sneak attack.

Seconds later, he resurfaced and looked in every direction for his attacker. He sighted a neon orange bikini bottom briefly surface and resubmerge. His target now spotted, he shot across the pool like a stealth bomber, completely forgetting the two men standing on his deck.

"Can you believe this?" James looked over his shoulder at his youngest brother.

Jonathan stepped up, still smiling. "Actually, no. I've never seen him like this. The man's a workaholic. Workaholics don't play."

James's head snapped around at the sound of a woman screaming, until he realized the scream was just high-pitched laughter. "Apparently, things have changed." He circled the edge of the pool. "Julian!"

Julian swiped the water from his face with his large hand,

still holding tight to Callie with the other. "Sorry, man, had to teach *someone* a lesson."

"Sorry to interrupt, Callie, but your man's got work to do," Jonathan called.

"It's okay," she said, still struggling to catch her breath. "That's where I should be as well."

"Don't go. We haven't made love today," Julian whispered, his hot breath against Callie's neck sending a chill down her spine.

She shivered. "You make me weak," she whispered in response.

"The feeling's mutual," he answered, using his tongue to lick up a water droplet behind her ear.

His brothers couldn't hear the words, but the way Callie moaned and leaned against Julian would've left a deaf-mute with little doubt as to the topic of discussion.

Julian looked up into the increasingly impatient face of his eldest brother. Then with one quick kiss on her neck, he set her free and swam over to the side of the pool. Using his strong arms, he pushed his body up out of the water.

"Can we postpone this until tomorrow?" he asked, grabbing a towel off the back of a nearby chair.

"No. We're pushing the envelope as it is," James said. "We are supposed to present our forecast to CompuTech tomorrow at two, remember? You put it off last week so you and your little mermaid could take a day trip to Frankenmuth. Then again this past weekend. I think you said something about staying in bed and watching some kind of movie marathon?"

Julian grinned. "I forgot about that." He wiped water from his ear while watching Callie climb out of the pool on the other side. The water beading in her glistening black braids and the sunlight reflecting off her golden skin completely erased his train of thought. He stood mesmerized by her curvaceous body until he realized she had the full attention of both his brothers as well.

"Let's take this inside," he said, and led the way into the house.

James and Jonathan exchanged a knowing glance; both men could appreciate how the beauty toweling off on the other side could wreak havoc on a man's mind. But neither was about to express that sentiment to Julian and run the risk of getting a busted lip.

The two men sat their heavy burdens down on the coffee table while Julian took the time to wrap up in his terry cloth robe. He sunk into his desk chair and pulled his own stack of files forward. He handed each of his brothers a small file from the top of the pile.

"I've already started working on the preliminaries, so this probably won't take as long as you think."

Jonathan sat down on the leather couch, and James took up a corner of the desk.

"And what do your preliminary numbers tell you?" James asked, skimming through the folder in his hand.

"It's not as bad as we thought. I think hiring us was more of a precautionary action than a true necessity. There are no immediate fires that need to be put out."

"Don't forget that copyright lawsuit from that techie in Illinois," Jonathan offered, referring to the only lawsuit that seemed to carry any possibility of financial repercussions for the megacorporation.

"What did Legal say?" Julian asked.

"Still waiting to hear back," Jonathan answered, jotting down notes to himself in his file.

"Still, even if the suit is lost, we're talking about what, two point three? Maybe three hundred thousand at the most. We'll calculate the forecast taking that possibility into account."

"Agreed," James answered, and Jonathan nodded solemnly from the couch.

"Now," Julian began, "if you look down toward the middle of page four, you'll see that sales—"

The soft tapping on the door interrupted him, and he looked up to see Callie fully dressed in her favorite attire: her Daisy Duke blue jean shorts and a snug-fitting halter top. Today the color was royal blue. "Just wanted to let you know that I was leaving."

Julian held his tongue, not willing to sacrifice his pride by begging in front of his brothers. But if they had not been there…

It had been almost forty-eight hours since she'd lain beneath him; by his calculation, that was forty-seven hours too long. "Dinner tonight?" He tried to sound casual, as if he didn't care but feared, to the men who knew him too well, the truth of his feelings was probably heard.

"Sorry, can't."

"Why not?" Julian asked the question before he could stop himself.

"Pooky found a new job yesterday. Some friends and I are taking him out to celebrate."

"Oh."

"You are welcome to come along," Callie offered tentatively. "I would've invited you, but I didn't really think it would be your thing. These are mostly our diva friends. Wasn't sure how you would feel about that."

Julian only heard the invitation to spend the evening in her company and completely missed the implication of the term *diva*. "Why not? I'm always up for new things."

James's eyes widened in amazement, and Jonathan had to stop himself from screaming, "Uh-uh."

Callie seemed equally surprised but quickly hid her stunned expression. "Okay. Can you pick me up at the garage around eight?"

"Sure. See you at eight."

Callie said her good-byes to the other men before disappearing around the corner and out the door.

Having the promise of seeing her again to look forward to, Julian was able to concentrate on his work. And within a matter of minutes of Callie's absence, the ole single-minded, control freak workaholic reappeared and then proceeded to send his brothers jumping through hoops all afternoon.

He threw out every possible scenario that could be presented by their client, leaving no stone unturned, no question unanswered. To Julian's thinking, nothing was worse than an ill-prepared presentation, mostly because a poor presentation could leave him and his brothers looking like incompetent fools. And no one knowingly trusted his or her money to incompetent fools.

By early evening, both James and Jonathan were seriously missing the fun-loving, frolicking guy they'd met at the pool earlier.

"I'm not going in there—that's a gay bar!" Julian turned and headed back in the direction of his car.

"First of all, it's a club, not a bar. And secondly, I told you we were meeting some friends of mine. Where did you think we were going?"

Julian stopped and turned to look at her like she was completely insane. "What are you saying? That all your friends are gay?"

Callie paused thoughtfully. "Pretty much."

His eyes narrowed as he studied the woman in front of him, once again wondering how his neat, orderly life had come to this. Here he was outside a gay bar, seriously considering going inside to send congratulations to some drag queen he'd almost run down and mistakenly kissed instead. *What the hell is going on with the universe?*

"I'm not going in there," he stated again, and continued on to his car.

Callie held her ground. "Suit yourself."

"You're staying?" He stopped dead in his tracks. "Without me?"

"This may come as a shock to your system, Julian. but I am perfectly capable of have a good time without you. Pooky's my best friend, my roommate, and my only family. He's busted his behind going on interview after interview over the past several months trying to get someone, *anyone* to look beyond his appearance and at the work in his portfolio. He deserves this celebration, and I have every intention of sharing it with him."

Julian hung his head in defeat. Was there anything he wasn't willing to do for this woman? "Let's go." He took her hand and led the way back to the front of the building.

As they approached the entrance, Julian began to take in the crowd with a different eye. From a distance, the club looked like any other club on a Saturday night. Throngs of people standing in groups, pushing forward in an effort to catch the eye of the burly man standing down front with his large arms folded over his chest, all hoping for some sort of special favor to be tossed their way.

But up close, you could see that this group was indeed different. Androgynous-styling made gender determination impossible. Men dressed to kill in women's clothing, and some of them were quite convincing. Women with short, cropped haircuts and tattoos that ran the length of their slender arms. Costumes that looked like they had come straight out of a *Star Wars* movie, and the occasional gothic rebel completed the strange collage.

Glancing at the flashing neon sign that read, WHITE ELEPHANT, Julian remembered Pooky mentioning the place. *They would eat you alive.* Pooky's words rang in his mind. Looking at the strange mix, Julian wondered how much was idle threat and how much was actual truth.

"I know it's been a while since I've been to a club, but is this normal?" Julian spoke directly into Callie's ear to be heard above the loud music blaring from inside the club.

"For my friends?" Callie laughed. "Yes." Once they were on the fringe of the crowd, she began bouncing up and down and waving frantically over her head.

"What are you doing?" Julian asked. "Getting into the spirit of things?" He let his attention be drawn from the interesting assortment surrounding him, long enough to note her strange behavior.

"Stan! Stan!" she called loudly, trying to be heard above the noise of people and music.

The large security guard's stern face broke into a happy smile. "Hey, Callie, come on up."

She turned to Julian and quirked an eyebrow as if to say, "See?"

Stan removed the velvet rope that separated him from the mob and gently pushed some people aside to allow them through. "Hey, little bit," he said, taking Callie into a bear hug. "Your crowd is already here. I bought Pooky a drink earlier. I have to admit, his getting a regular nine-to-five shocked the mess out of me. I never thought I'd see the day. I mean the man was going on interviews in dresses. *Dresses!*" He shook his head, still stunned by the news. "But I'm happy for him. He deserves a break." Just then he noticed her companion.

"Stan, this is my boyfriend, Julian. Julian, Stan the Man. Mild-mannered caterer by day, and by night—superhero," Callie teased, referring to his job controlling the masses that struggled to obtain entry into one of the hottest gay clubs in the Detroit area.

"I wish I did have some superpower. I'd tie half of these freaks up in web and toss them into the Detroit River."

Julian shook the man's hand as the two quickly sized each other up. Then Callie led the way into the club and through the thicket of dancing bodies to her group's usual table in the back.

The closer they came to the table, the more Julian began questioning his sanity in choosing to go there that night. Two drag queens sat together talking, and as Julian would discover, their personalities were as different as their appearance.

One was wearing a conservative, pastel pink satin jumpsuit and long blond wig that strangely enough looked natural with his olive coloring. Two tiny diamond stud earrings and a small gold cross hanging from his neck were his only pieces of jewelry.

His companion, on the other hand, was dressed up like a pine tree on Christmas morning. The man had so many pieces of colorful glass jewelry dangling from every part of him it was a wonder he didn't tip over. He was wearing a burgundy wig that looked suspiciously like the one Pooky had been wearing the night they met. His dark skin was in stunning contrast to the fire-engine red pantsuit he wore, complete with two rows of large brass buttons down the center.

When it came time to make the introductions, Callie, of

course, went right for the Christmas tree. "Julian Cruise, meet Dory. Dory, Julian."

"That's *Ms.* Dory, as in mys-te-ry." The man extended his hand to Julian with ladylike decorum that seemed to come straight out of an etiquette book. "Exotic dancer, *extraordinaire*."

Julian looked at the extended hand. "What's up." He nodded and looked to the next man, awaiting introductions.

Callie stifled a laugh and continued. "This is Tanya."

The man smiled, taking in Julian's elegantly dressed form with one glance. He noted the neat cocoa-brown collarless sweater and chocolate slacks. His graying short hair and full mustache were both freshly trimmed. There was absolutely nothing unique or unusual about him. The man was as out of place as a bride at a funeral. This had to be the one, the man Pooky had told them all about. "Are you the bulldog?"

Julian glanced at Callie, who quickly looked away. "Bulldog, huh?" He turned back to the man in the pink jumper. "That sounds about right."

"Where's Pooky?" Callie asked, after letting her eyes scan the whole large room.

"He left over an hour ago," Ms. Dory said with a wave of his bejeweled hand.

"What?!" Callie's head snapped around.

"Um-hum." Tanya nodded in agreement, taking a sip of his fruit drink. "He met some guy at the bar, and twenty minutes later, they were out of here."

"That cow!" Callie hissed.

Julian folded his arms across his chest, feeling smug and arrogant. He knew that the one and only reason Callie had for keeping him there, or remaining there herself, no longer existed. And by being the understanding, agreeable boyfriend, he felt he must've surely won bonus points.

"Oh, don't worry, Pooky squeezed plenty of partying into the hour he was here," Ms. Tanya said.

"Can you believe someone actually hired that fool?" Ms. Dory added.

Julian found it amazing that any of them were able to find employment in accepted society, but he was smart enough to keep the comment to himself.

"He didn't say anything about coming back later?" Callie was struggling to find an excuse to stay. She really wasn't that upset that Pooky had crept out on his own celebration. In truth, she should've expected it. This wasn't the first time he'd abandoned her in a crowded club for the possibility of getting some action.

But this was the first—and she knew only—time she would ever get Julian inside one of her usual haunts. She'd hoped maybe if he had a good enough time, it might end some of his prejudices against her unusual friends. But with his only reason for being there not being there, she had no plausible reason to ask him to stay.

"Do you work out?" she heard Ms. Dory ask Julian, taking in his long, hard body. "Or is it just good genes?" Dory winked, and Julian cringed.

Callie shook her head, knowing the battle was already lost. Especially with Dory constantly flirting with him and nosy Tanya drilling him for personal information.

"Well, I guess we have no reason to stay," she said to Julian, and was just a touch hurt by the relief she saw flash through his dark eyes.

Julian had never once said anything derogatory about her friends, but she knew how he felt. The evidence was written in his eyes every time he looked at one of them.

Quiet disdain.

She'd hoped spending time in a social setting would allow him to see Pooky's artistic, creative side. Or maybe he'd come to understand that the reason Tanya was so nosy was because by day he was a scientist; it was his natural inclination to study things and even people. And, in time, he would eventually understand that Ms. Dory's bizarre dress and behavior was in direct relation to the abuse he suffered as a child. His hopeless attempt to erase that part of his life.

These things she knew because she had spent years of her life living with and loving these people. A love that had been returned tenfold. A love she'd hoped Julian could come to understand.

She'd brought him here tonight with the high hopes that maybe some kind of common ground could be found, and instead he was leaving believing his first assessment of the situation was accurate and on point. That they were all just a bunch of flaky fruits.

As they crossed the empty lot headed back to Julian's car, Callie kept her head down to avoid making eye contact with Julian. She occupied herself by mentally playing out all the things she planned to say to Pooky once she cornered him.

"Sorry about that," Callie finally spoke, gently swinging her purse by the strap. "I know you didn't want to come with me."

"If I remember correctly, I kinda invited myself," he said with a side glance.

"Yeah, you did, didn't you?" She smiled, relieved that he apparently wasn't going to throw the whole situation in her face.

When they reached the car, Julian took her hand and pulled her against his chest. "Okay, I've been thinking."

Callie went eagerly into his arms. "Oh, no."

"I think I deserve something special for being such a good sport about tonight."

He nibbled at her neck, and Callie moaned. The man really did have the most incredible lips, she thought. "What would that be?" she asked, less interested in that than in what his large hand was doing to her breast.

"An IOU of sorts."

"An IOU?"

"You owe me…one session of sweet, passionate love-making—"

"Agreed," she answered eagerly.

He chuckled. "Wait, I'm not finished. A sweet, passionate session of love-making…in the place of my choice, at the time of my choice."

"Ooh," she purred, "sounds intriguing."

"Do you agree?"

"Hmm." She tapped her bottom lip thoughtfully. "Agreed."

Callie wrapped her arms around his neck and pulled him close, thinking this was going to be one promise that she would enjoy as much as Julian.

Chapter 21

Callie bit nervously at her nails and paced the floor of her small back room office while Julian quietly sifted through her bills and financial statements.

Unable to stifle her curiosity any longer, she turned to him. "Well?"

Julian continued to tap at the calculator; his face revealed nothing of what he thought. "Well, what?"

"Is my business bankrupt or not?"

"Not sure," he mumbled, still using the eraser of his pencil to push the keys on the calculator.

Finally, exhausted with worry, she slumped down in the beanbag chair in the corner. "Some financial genius you turned out to be."

A small smile curved in the corner of his mouth. "Baby, as soon as I understand what you are dealing with here, I'll tell you. But this takes time. You have five years worth of documents and receipts." He frowned at her. "And you were keeping them in shoe boxes—not exactly the most efficient way to organize your business documents."

"But you have my tax records right there. Isn't that enough?"

"No. Your tax records only show your recordable income. I want to know about all the other stuff. The things you probably spend money on and never even record. We all do it, especially proprietary businesses. *That's* what will tell me about how you conduct business, what's waste and what's not."

"Fine," she said with exaggeration. "I'll be under that car." She nodded toward the damaged car sitting in the middle of her garage floor. "Call me if you need me."

She turned to leave.

"Callie."

She spun back around. "Find something?"

He smiled devilishly. "No, but you said to call you if I need you." He stood from the desk and crossed the room, taking her in his arms. "And I definitely *need* you."

Callie pushed back from him. "Oh no you don't, you big sex fiend. Get back to work." She turned and strutted out of the room with a sashay to her walk that said she knew she had an audience.

Julian shook his head and laughed, returning to his calculations.

Two hours later, from her prone position, Callie saw familiar brown loafers approaching the vehicle. "Find something?" she said while struggling to remove a stripped bolt.

Julian took a deep breath to try to hide the concern in his voice. "You could say that." He squatted down beside the car. "Callie, you've spent almost twice as much in parts as you have had in repairs. Where are all these parts going?"

Callie used her heels to push herself from beneath the car. "Well, sometimes I do courtesy work." She sat up on the rack.

"Courtesy work? What is that?"

"Sometimes my friends need work done and they can't afford it, so I give them a freebie. They usually pay me back when they can."

Julian's mouth twisted in disgust. "I thought you would say something like that. You've been giving away parts and service for the past five years, and it's killing your business." Callie eyes widened in alarm, and Julian instantly regretted his words. "What I mean is, it's really put a hurt on your profits."

"Cut to the chase, Julian. Can my garage be saved?"

Not if you keep letting your friends walk all over you. "Yes, but you will have to make some drastic changes." His eyebrow quirked in thought. "Come to think of it, whose car is this?"

Callie smiled guiltily.

"Damn, Callie!" Julian shot to his feet. "This is exactly what I'm talking about! You've just spent most of the day working on this car, and I have no idea how many parts you've used, and you probably won't receive a dime for it, will you?"

Callie stood as well. "Diva Dale is my friend! When I had nothing, nowhere to go, he and the others helped me. Now I'm helping him. It's what friends do, Julian."

"Baby, I understand your loyalty, and I think it's wonderful that you want to help your friends. But you've got a business to run here, and it can't be run on kindness alone. You are going to have to start charging them. We'll set up a finance plan, so if they don't have the money, they can take out a line of credit. How does that sound?" He smiled, believing he'd found the perfect solution.

"And if they can't make the finance payments? Then what?"

"What do you mean?"

"If they don't make the payments, do I bring collection actions against them? Maybe take them to court?"

Julian shook his head. "It won't come to that."

"How would you know! We don't all live in Sherwood Forest, Julian! We're not all spoiled, wealthy businessmen! If my friends could afford to pay me, they would!"

Julian choked on his temper. She was baiting him, and he knew it. "I'm going to *try* and ignore everything you just said." He took a deep breath. "You asked me to review your financial situation and I have. I'm sorry if you don't like the conclusions that I've drawn, but I can't change the truth. Your precious friends are running this garage into the ground, and if you don't develop some backbone soon, you won't have a business!"

"Hello?"

They both paused, hearing a soft voice calling from the front area of the garage. With the hood of the car up, neither of them could see the visitor, but Callie recognized the voice.

"I'm back here, Dee-Dee."

A tall man dressed in a hot-pink jumper and matching sling-back heels came stepping into view. His blond wig was wrapped up in an elaborate pompadour, and his make-up was flawless against his cocoa-brown skin.

Julian's mouth fell open in surprise, and he silently wondered if he would ever get used to seeing men dressed like this.

As soon as Diva Dale came around the car, he stopped in his tracks. The pair was glaring so hard at each other, he feared he'd walked into the middle of a dogfight. "Am I interrupting something?"

"No," Callie said. "Julian, I would like you to meet my *friend*, Diva Dale. Dee-Dee, this is Julian Cruise."

Dee-Dee extended his hand to the handsome stranger. "Hello," he said with a pleasant smile.

Julian was so angry he considered ignoring the hand, but he knew Callie would never forgive him. "Hello." He accepted the handshake and was surprised to find it was strong and solid. Completely different from shaking hands with Pooky.

Despite the cordial greeting, Dee-Dee knew something wasn't right. "Um, I just came to see if my car was ready, but I can come back at a better time."

Julian was so wrapped up in his anger, he had missed the connection between the person standing in front of him and the car repairs in question. "Do you mind my asking what exactly is wrong with your car?" Julian knew he was about to risk his relationship with Callie, but he had to make her see she was only hurting herself.

"Julian," Callie said in a warning tone.

Diva Dale looked from one to the other. "My muffler fell off. The stupid car was so loud I couldn't sneak up on my boyfriend."

Julian frowned in confusion. "What?"

"My boyfriend, I thought he was cheating on me, and I tried to sneak up to his apartment building to see for myself, but he heard my car ten blocks away. When I got to his apartment, he was sitting in the middle of the couch pretending to watch TV, but I knew he was up to something. I could see the tag of his underwear sticking up out of the front of his pants. Now, you tell me—" Diva Dale relaxed with his hand on his hip, warming to his topic "—if he wasn't up to no good, why was his underwear on *backward*?"

"We're getting off the subject." Julian shook his head trying frantically to remove the vivid image that had just been painted on his brain. "You needed a new muffler?"

Diva Dale nodded in agreement.

"By my calculations, with parts for this particular make of vehicle and service, your bill would be approximately eight-five dollars, but of course that does not include tax."

"My bill?"

"Ignore him, Dee-Dee. He doesn't run this garage, I do."

"Yes, your bill," Julian continued. "You see, Callie had to buy the parts for your repair, and if she doesn't get the reimbursement from you—the customer. How can she buy more parts or pay for the expense of running this garage?"

"Julian, stop this!"

Diva Dale looked at Callie thoughtfully. "I guess I never really thought about it."

"No, I'm sure you never did," Julian added sarcastically.

Diva Dale started to reach into his hot-pink handbag, but Callie put her hand over his to stop him. "No! Dee-Dee, you don't owe me anything. Your car will be ready by seven." She gave a hard look at Julian. "You can come back and pick it up then."

Diva Dale smiled sympathetically. "No, sugar bear, he's right. You shouldn't have to pay for my muffler." He reached into his purse and pulled out his pink wallet. He rifled through the bill section and came out with two twenties, one five, and four singles. "All I have on me is forty-nine. I'll bring the rest back with me later."

Callie pushed the money back to him. "Don't worry—"

Julian moved around her and grabbed the money quick as a flash of lightning. "Thank you. I'll post it in her ledger with a outstanding balance of thirty-six dollars to be paid at a later time."

Callie turned on Julian like a wild woman. "You give that back right now!"

Julian just glanced at her like she'd lost her mind, and turning, he headed back to the office.

Callie started to follow, determined to take the money back—by force if necessary—but Diva Dale grabbed her arm.

"No, Callie, leave him alone; he's right." Dee-Dee nodded in the direction of the office. "He's only looking out for you, and it's about time you had someone looking out for you."

"But you're my friend. I can't charge my friends."

"Why not?" Dee-Dee said. "I've often wondered why, with your skills, this garage wasn't doing better than it is. It just never occurred to me that I was part of the problem." He pulled his friend against his false bosom. "Callie, I make a good living. I can afford to pay for my car repairs. I was taking advantage of our friendship and didn't even realize it. I owe you an apology."

"No, you don't. You and the others took care of me when I had nothing."

"And you don't have to spend the rest of your life paying us back for it. That's not what friendship is about."

The two friends kept company for a while, exchanging the latest gossip about their shared circle of friends and trying to acclimate their minds to the new way of thinking they had just been introduced to.

Meanwhile in the office, Julian was doing just as he promised, recording the payments and placing the money in Callie's cash box. He settled back into the small desk chair and folded his arms in front of him, wondering if in his effort to protect her, he had just risked losing the very thing he was trying to protect.

Later that night, Julian stood watching Callie sleep from his bedroom doorway. He'd been spending so much time at her garage lately, his own business matters were being neglected. After a light dinner, he'd sent her to bed ahead of him, wanting to get some of his own work done. That was three hours ago, and now she was sleeping soundly.

Shortly after Diva Dale departed from the garage, Callie had stormed into the office. "I'm a grown woman, Julian! You can't just come in here and take over!"

"I told you, I'm not trying to take over, just help."

"When I want your help, I'll ask!"

"You did, remember?" He held up a stack of her unpaid bills.

"And that was obviously a mistake." She leaned forward over the desktop. "I'm independent, Julian. Always have been, always will be. *I* make *my* decisions. Not you or anyone else. If you are one of those men who can't handle that, just say so now."

Julian sealed his lips in a tight line to keep from responding. Eventually she would have to accept that he was not the type of man to sit by and watch his woman struggle, especially when he had the means to help her. But apparently, that time was not now. Now, she was spoiling for a fight, and he refused to give her one.

"You got that?" She glared up at him with her hands on her hips.

Julian held his peace, refusing to pick up the gauntlet she'd tossed down. Finally, she turned and charged back out of the office, slamming the door in her wake.

Recently they'd begun an evening routine of sharing the task of cooking a meal in his kitchen and cleaning the dishes, followed by a movie or a game of checkers, completing the evening with a dessert of sweet, sensuous lovemaking.

So, it was to his amazement when at the end of the day as he prepared to head home, she'd climbed into his car as she had been doing for the past few weeks. As if the explosive argument had never happened. The only indication of any animosity was the deafening silence between them on the short ride.

Tonight they'd arrived back at his place so late, all they'd had time for was dinner. And given the way he'd treated her friend, Julian wondered if there would be any dessert tonight.

He crossed the room and crawled into the bed behind her, and she immediately stirred, twisting her body until she was nestled comfortably against his side. Julian breathed a long sigh of relief and pulled her closer to him. She was exhausted, and considering the kind of heavy, tiring work she did all day, it was no surprise. But the subconscious body language told him what he needed to know: She was still his.

"Did you get everything done?" She yawned sleepily and reached up to touch his face.

He straightened the covers over both their bodies. "Most of it."

"Good." She strained her neck to kiss his mouth.

Julian accepted the kiss, pulling her back down into his body. "Go back to sleep," he mumbled against the top of her head. "It's late."

"Like that matters to your horny body."

He had to smile at the comment. She was right—he was honed and hungry for her at that very moment. She constantly made jokes that he was some kind of sex machine that never turned off. What he'd never told her was that she was the only woman who'd ever incited that kind of reaction in him. No matter how many times they made love, it just never seemed to be enough.

But not tonight, he decided. She needed to rest, more than he needed her body. And besides, what he really needed she was giving him at that very moment—her warmth and forgiveness. Maybe she understood more than he realized.

"Callie," Julian whispered into the night, "I love you." His confession was met by a soft snoring.

Chapter 22

"Hello, you must be Callie." The older man smiled, and Callie caught her breath.

So this was the model upon which James, Julian, and Jonathan Cruise were designed. When she met Julian's brothers, she'd recognized the strong resemblance the men all held to one another. But, now, looking into the eyes of the father, she could see where that line of handsome, intelligent men began.

She smiled nervously, wondering if Julian's father showing up at her garage unannounced, first thing in the morning, could be considered a good thing or not. Callie wiped her hands on her oilcloth and extended a hand in greeting. "And *you* must be Julian's father."

"That obvious, huh?" James Cruise Sr. chuckled heartily. "Guilty as charged."

"What brings you to this side of town, Mr. Cruise?" She tried to keep her voice casual.

"Please, call me James." He glanced around the garage. "I was hoping you could help me. I have a seventy-five Lincoln that needs some work. Not sure exactly what's wrong with it, but I was hoping you could stop by the house this afternoon and take a look at it."

Callie sensed that this was about more than a car. "Sure, what time would be convenient for you?"

James hunched his shoulders. "I don't know, maybe around noon, if you have the time."

"No problem," she called back over her shoulder as she went to get a pen and paper off the countertop. "I just need to get your address."

He gave her the house address, a phone number, and brief directions on how to get there.

"And don't worry about lunch." He smiled. "My wife loves to cook for company."

"All right, I'll see you later." Callie watched him leave, returning to her work. *Does Julian know about this little visit?* she wondered. Callie knew that whatever was going on was about more than just an old car, and the only thing she could do now was play it out.

Julian paused in his work to answer his ringing desk phone.

"Julian Cruise," he answered in his most professional voice.

"Hey, man." His little brother Jonathan's voice came from the other end of the receiver. "Don't be mad at me, okay?"

Julian sat back in his chair. "What did you do?"

"If you want to blame someone, it should be James. He's the one who told them, first. I just gave Dad the address."

"What did you do, Jonathan?"

"James told Dad about Callie, so of course, being Dad—"

"Damn." Julian knew it was only a matter of time before

his meddlesome parents would want to meet his new love interest. He'd just hoped that it would be at his discretion.

He should've known better. His father felt he owned the lives of each and every one of his boys. He wasn't going to be stopped by a little thing like a formal introduction. "Tell me exactly what happened."

"I'm not really sure. Dad called wanting Callie's address. When I asked why, he gave me some bogus story about the Lincoln."

"You mean the one that's been sitting in the garage for the past twenty years?"

"I told him to call you, but he said he didn't have time, that he was in a hurry."

"So, you caved."

"Sorry, man, you know how it is when you don't give him what he wants. He puts Mom on the phone, and she starts throwing that guilt trip about the trials and tribulations of raising three rambunctious boys."

"It's all right. It had to happen."

"I'm not sure, but knowing Dad, he will probably try to find some way to lure Callie to the house so he and Mom can give her a thorough examination on their own turf."

"Probably."

"What are you going to do?"

Julian braced the phone against his shoulder and continued his typing. "Nothing."

"Nothing?"

"Nope. If she's going to be a member of this family, she will have to learn to deal with those two eventually. Might as well be now."

"A member of the family, huh? It's like that?"

Julian smiled. "It's like that."

"Congratulations."

"Not yet. She doesn't know anything about it. Not to mention she is about to face the Cruise family version of the Spanish Inquisition. After Mom and Dad get through with her, she may never speak to me again."

"That's true," Jonathan concurred without the least bit of sympathy.

"Do they know about Keisha?"

"Don't even think about it!"

The last thing Jonathan heard was Julian's wicked laugh as the line went dead.

"Hello?" Maya Cruise had rushed into the kitchen to answer the telephone.

"Hi, Maya," Julian spoke from the other end. "Is James home?"

Just then, James Jr. came into view of his wife, shaking his head frantically and waving his hands wildly.

"Uh, no, Julian. I think he stepped out for a moment."

James's motions became even more frantic.

"Um, I mean he stepped out for an…hour, a day?" she said, more to her husband than to the person on the other end of the phone. She smiled at her husband, realizing she'd gotten it right. "Yes, he left town for a few days."

"You're lousy at this, Maya. Just put him on the phone."

Maya handed the phone over to her husband and mouthed the word *sorry*. James kissed her quickly and took the receiver. He couldn't avoid his little brother forever, especially since they were business partners.

"You know I'm going to get you back for this, right?"

James smiled. "If I recall correctly, you were the little

birdie who told them Maya and I were living together before we got married."

"I told you a hundred times that was an accident. Dad tricked me—he pretended like he already knew."

"After thirty-two years, you should know not to trust him. He's sneaky, especially when it comes to us."

"So, what did you tell him?"

"Just that you were seeing a very lovely lady mechanic and that it looked to me like things were getting serious. Was I right?"

"Yes, you're right. But the dynamic duo may bring that to a swift halt."

"They are not so bad, really. They mean well."

"No, they don't. They're just nosy."

"That, too, but Mom or Dad would never do anything to hurt any one of our relationships, and they know you care about this woman. They just want to get to know her for themselves."

"Why can't they do things like normal people—invite their children and their significant others to dinner to get to know them? Not creep around behind our backs trying to get information."

"If they asked, would you tell?"

"Hell, no!"

"Which is exactly why they creep around behind our backs."

"Do you know what they have planned?" Julian was getting more worried by the minute.

"No, but they will probably stick with a proven winner."

"What's that supposed to mean?"

"When they wanted to interrogate Maya, Mom went to the store Maya works at pretending she needed a consultant to make over the house, even though we all know she would never allow anyone else to decorate her house. She invited

Maya over, loaded her up with a good meal. By late afternoon, Maya had voluntarily given them everything but the names of our future children."

"Humph," Julian grumbled. "Jonathan said something about Dad's old Lincoln."

"You mean the one that's been in the garage since we were kids?"

"Yep."

"Sounds about right." James nodded as if his brother could see him through the telephone line. "After all, Callie is a mechanic. The Lincoln would be the perfect lure."

"Do you think we will ever be free of their meddling?"

"You know, man, I used to think that once we started having children of our own they would back off. But seeing how possessive they are of Olivia, I've lost all hope."

"How did you get into your line of work, Callie?" Pam Cruise asked between forkfuls of salad. "Most little girls don't grow up playing with wrenches and ratchets." She smiled playfully. "After all, we have to leave the boys something to do, right?"

"Well, actually, it was my dad who got me started working with cars. He was a mechanic, and he let me help him with his pet projects."

"Sounds like your dad's a Renaissance man." She cast a loving glance at her husband.

"He was," Callie said thoughtfully. "He died when I was fifteen."

"I'm sorry to hear that." Pam reached over and touched her hand sympathetically.

Callie smiled. "It was a long time ago."

"So you continued on in the family tradition, huh?" James

Cruise Sr. offered his contribution to the conversation, although most of his attention was on the porterhouse steak he'd grilled for lunch. His wife always marinated the meat in her special spices, and combined with his grilling skills, they could create paradise in a pan.

"I guess you could say that," Callie said as she sliced her steak.

"But isn't auto repair heavy work?" Pam asked between bites. "I mean, it's mostly dealing with metals and glass, right? And you are so petite."

Callie shrugged. "You get used to it."

She was desperately trying not to be overwhelmed by the friendly couple. The moment the front door opened and she was greeted by two pairs of curious eyes, Callie knew it was an ambush. She'd mistakenly dressed in clean bib overalls and a white T-shirt, believing she would actually get to see the seventy-five Lincoln she'd been brought here to repair. But two hours later, she realized that was probably not going to happen.

"Is there any special training involved? Mechanic college or maybe a trade school you were required to attend?"

"Pam, give the girl a chance to eat her food." James Sr. quirked an irritated eyebrow. His wife was practically bubbling with joy at the young woman sitting between them at the table. She was such a drastic change from the carbon-copy dolls Julian usually dealt with. Pam felt certain that this woman would be her next daughter-in-law. And after thirty-five years and three sons, his wife had accepted that daughters-in-law were the only kind of daughters she would ever have.

"It's okay." Callie smiled and took a sip of the homemade lemonade. "Actually both. There is a formal program I attended for a year, and I did an apprenticeship under Sam Fremont for four years. Also, I took numerous certificate programs to learn specific repair techniques and industry updates. Sometimes it seems as if I'm always attending one class or another."

"Wow, it's a lot more in-depth than I would've thought." Pam Cruise couldn't help beaming with joy at the young lady sitting to her right. *This is the woman who has my straight-laced son kissing drag queens.* She already liked the girl long before she'd met her, and nothing had changed in the two hours since she'd opened her front door and found a tomboy standing on her porch.

Pam had had many conversations—all right, arguments— with her son regarding the type of superficial women he'd chosen to spend his time with. The truth was they all looked, sounded, and acted so much alike she had a hard time telling them apart.

But sitting in front of her was the cycle breaker. With one look, Pam took in the bib overalls and T-shirt, work boots, and shiny, thick cornrows that fell past her shoulders and knew the tide had changed. She also understood that there was only one reason her stubborn-as-a-mule, elitist son would throw out his Barbie mold; Julian was finally in love.

Callie spent the afternoon responding to question after question, and although they were all asked politely, she couldn't help feeling as if she were being given the third degree. Finally, the plates were removed, and James Sr. offered to show Callie the Lincoln that needed work.

Callie couldn't help the surprised expression that came across her face at the mention of the car. After the way they'd spent the afternoon, she was convinced there was no Lincoln to be repaired. But once she entered the garage, that opinion changed quickly. The car looked as if it had been up on blocks for years.

"When was the last time you drove this?" Callie asked, slowly circling the dust-encrusted vehicle.

James scratched at his chin. "It's been a few years," he mumbled.

A few? "I see." Callie sat her toolbox down next to the car and pulled out her work gloves. "What's the problem?"

"Not sure, exactly."

Callie couldn't help thinking how much he looked like his middle son when he made that guilty expression. "Well, I'm going to start at the bottom and work my way up." She glanced at the heap of white metal. "This may take a while."

"Take your time." James Sr. smiled. "I'll get out of your way, just come inside when you are ready."

Callie watched the man go, turning her attention back to the vehicle. She ran her gloved hand along the long body of the old car, taking in the special chrome rims and spoiler kit. The interior was tricked out as well, all leather and fully loaded. Like people, each car had its own story, its own history. And like people, some lives were far more exciting and eventful than others. She smiled to herself. This was once a gangsta mobile. Probably a relic from his player days. Oh well, whatever it had once been, it was now a hunk of junk.

She released the lever, lifted the hood, and discovered the engine was the only part of the vehicle not covered in dust. Time to get to work, she thought, bending forward to check the fluids. Her mind brushed briefly over the luncheon. All in all, they were nice people. Although, she still wasn't exactly sure as to the purpose of their little inquisition.

Surprisingly, there were very few questions asked regarding her relationship with their son. And once again, she was left wondering if that was a good thing or not. Callie knew that Julian's family was important to him, and he had become very important to her. Now she could only hope for the sake of her heart that she passed whatever test she'd just been given by his parents.

* * *

Almost thirty minutes later, Callie was focusing her attention on removing a resistant oil cap when she became aware of another presence in the garage with her. She lifted her head to find Olivia standing in the doorway entrance that led into the house.

"Hello." Callie smiled, wiping her hands on her oilcloth.

Olivia just stared at the woman in silence for several seconds. "I'm sorry I spoke to you so nasty."

Callie's heart went out to the teenage girl, seeing the pain in her eyes. "It's okay. I know how you feel."

Olivia's eyes flashed with anger for a brief second, and Callie realized her mistake. How many times had the child probably heard people make that statement with false sentiment? *Your mom's in rehab for a cocaine addiction and you are forced to live with a father you'd never met, but I know how you feel.* No one knew how she felt.

Callie leaned against the car. "Olivia, I'm sorry. *I don't know* how you feel, and I shouldn't have said it."

"It's okay, everyone says it."

"No, it's not okay. My mom died when I was nine and I can remember at the funeral all these people hugging me and telling me they knew how I felt. And I kept thinking, Do you really?"

Callie felt something like connection in those brown eyes as Olivia crossed the room to stand beside her.

"Your mom died when you were nine?"

Callie nodded. "And to make matters worse, my dad remarried within a year."

Olivia turned her attention to the car. "Wow, that's messed up."

"He thought he was doing the right thing for me, and really, as stepmoms go, mine was wonderful. She was kind and caring, and I think she really loved me."

"What was it like? Having your mom your whole life and then suddenly…she's gone."

Callie took Olivia's hand and pressed it against her breast. "I had a big, gaping hole right here."

Olivia nodded in understanding. "When does it stop hurting?"

Callie smiled to try and cover the tears she felt forming in her eyes. "It doesn't."

"I know it's not the same because my mom's still alive, but sometimes I hate her for doing this to me. Leaving me here like this," Olivia whispered.

"Don't. Don't blame her, and definitely do not blame yourself." Callie took a deep breath, realizing this was no naïve little girl she was dealing with. This girl understood a lot more than anyone was giving her credit for. She spoke candidly and deserved to be dealt with in a like manner. She wondered only briefly how Julian would feel about what she was about to say to his daughter.

"Okay." Callie nodded in understanding. "You are right. What she did was wrong. She made a mistake, but she's trying to make it right." She turned the girl until they were face-to-face. "Olivia, I've never met your mother, but the fact that she brought you to your father, the fact that she checked herself into a place where she could get help tells me a lot about her. She loves you, probably more than you realize. And I am certain that love is the only thing keeping her on her feet right now."

"I remember." Olivia glanced back toward the entryway. She lowered her voice. "I remember a lot more than anyone thinks I do. I knew something was wrong long before we came here."

Callie took the girl's hand and walked around the vehicle,

realizing she was hesitant to speak frankly with her grandparents so close by. "Would you like to take a walk?"

Olivia nodded, and Callie tossed her oilcloth on the hood of the car, leading the way out of the garage.

A short while later, Pam and James Cruise Sr. stood shielded behind the peach-colored curtains watching the pair walk down the street.

"I don't know about this, Pam." James Sr. was having second thoughts. From the snippet of conversation he'd heard in the garage, he had a fair idea of the kind of straightforward talk being conducted outside the window. A conversation he was almost certain his son would not approve of. "What will Julian say?"

"I don't care what Julian says," his wife answered bluntly, bending sideways to watch as the twosome disappeared around the corner. She turned to her husband. "That child needs someone to talk to, and if she can talk freely to Callie, then all the better. You heard the conversation in the garage as well as I did. They have a lot more in common than anyone realized."

"But you know how Julian feels about Olivia—"

"Are you going to tell him about this?"

After forty years of marriage, James had his answer down to an art form. "Of course not, sweetheart."

"All right then; he can't *feel* anything about something he doesn't know about." She turned. "And if he does somehow find out and have a problem with it"—her eyes flashed with determination and fire—"send him to me."

Chapter 23

Julian surveyed the small, crowded lobby of the busy bank, which represented one in only five hundred federally funded banks owned and operated by African Americans. If there was an endangered species list for businesses, Julian thought, black banks would be at the top of the list.

"Julian, good to see you." Fredrick Hart, a rotund, middle-aged man took long strides crossing the lobby, his round, cherub face smiling in recognition.

He was the fourth generation in a long line of bankers, and through no fault of his own, the one on watch when a poor economy caused his bank to take a drastic nosedive several years ago.

When the Northern First board of directors commissioned Cruise Corporation to create a workable plan for survival, Fredrick Hart was the one designated to work closely with the financial consultants. Over the intervening months, he'd witnessed the faltering bank recover from a situation many said was critical. And although the board of directors had been suitably appreciative for his part, Fred never forgot the man who'd actually made it happen.

Northern First Bank had asked Cruise Corporation for a miracle, and Julian Cruise had given them one. The end result had left Fred Hart with an impression that bordered on idol worship. An opinion that Julian was fully aware of and had every intention of exploiting today.

Fred led the way to his back office and gestured to the chair across the desk from him. "Please, have a seat."

"Thanks, Fred." Julian lowered his large frame into one of the small wood chairs.

"I know Cruise Corp is not looking for a loan." Fred chuckled. "So this must be a social call."

"I wish it was, but actually I am here to discuss business, of a sort."

"Oh?"

"I have kind of an unorthodox proposal."

Fred leaned forward, his eyes twinkling with mischief. "That's the best kind. What is it?"

Julian glanced around to be sure they'd closed the door. "I want to discuss a customer of yours. I understand you have received—and rejected—three small business loan applications for Tyler Garage."

Fred Hart twisted his face. "Not ringing any bells. Let's see what the computer has to say." He turned to the monitor screen and began typing. "Ah, here it is. Callie Tyler. Tyler Garage." He paused, realizing he was giving out confidential information with no hesitation or explanations. But this was Julian, his friend. It was hard remembering to keep his professional guard up. "What's this about, Julian?"

"I know this is a strange request, but the next time Callie

Tyler comes in here to apply for a loan, I would like you to approve it, and I will underwrite it."

Fred leaned back in his chair. "Wow, when you said unorthodox, you weren't kidding." He scratched at the area above his right ear, a nervous habit he'd had since he was a child. "Julian, I don't think we can do that. She had no real collateral, no security whatsoever. And quite frankly, her business forecast was not good."

"All that's changing. I'm consulting her now. And with a few basic changes, her business will turn a profit in a matter of weeks."

"I'm sure if you're helping her, she will succeed, but I can't give out loans on future forecast. She has to be able to prove it now."

"Fred, hear me out. I'm not actually asking you to finance the loan. I'll provide the funding, but I need you to facilitate it. I need it to look like your bank gave her the loan—not me."

"Why the charade?"

"She desperately needs the money but would never accept it from me. I know from our conversations that she has been here, and seeing a recent application on her office desk, I know she will try again soon."

Fred sat quietly for a moment soaking up the information, and Julian waited patiently. What he was asking of this man was no small favor, and he wouldn't have been surprised if Fred had rejected the idea immediately. But Callie desperately needed an infusion of cash, money her pride would never allow her to accept from him personally. And unless he could convince her to accept thirty thousand dollars for repairing his car, this was the only way to get it to her without throwing up any red flags. Now all he could do was hope this man felt obligated enough to help.

Fred scratched his ear again. "I take it you have more than a professional interest in Ms. Tyler?"

Julian smiled. "Let's just say this is an investment in my future."

Fred sat back in his chair studying his friend. "I don't know, Julian. On the surface it seems like a simple plan, but so many things could go wrong. If I write up the loan on our forms, they would hold up in court, and I would not have the documentation to back it up. This is too risky."

"Fred, most people have no understanding of the interior workings of banks. You could say the loan came through a third-party company. How would she know?"

"But what if my staff sees the documents?"

"What documents? The only copy of the so-called contract walks out of here with her. All they will see is a customer enter and leave your office. How many times a day does that happen?"

"I don't know, Julian."

"Fred, I've thought this through. You won't be in any danger with the FCC; this plan is solid. All I need from you is a place to conduct the transaction."

Fred twisted his mouth in thought. He had no doubt regarding the debt owed to this man. He considered all the people who would've been unemployed years ago, including himself, if it were not for just this type of twisted thinking. For an accountant, Julian Cruise could bend the law like it was rubber and never break it. But more importantly, Fred trusted him. He knew Julian would never put the bank in any financial danger.

Fred's eyes narrowed. "And you are sure you have no qualms about me misleading your lady?"

"Not so long as you are leading her to me."

* * *

An hour later, Julian crept across the concrete floor trying to make as little noise as possible as he approached the red toolbox sitting open on the floor. He opened his hand, and the class schedule for the local community college that was clutched inside slid down, falling on top of the open case.

He quickly stood straight and finished crossing the room to Callie, who was sitting on the bench with her back to him. He covered her eyes and whispered against her neck. "Hey, baby, I'm here, but we better hurry before your *man* gets back."

Callie smiled wickedly. "Take me, my love, here and now," she said with pure seduction.

Julian spun the stool around; his dark eyes burning bright like a raven's wings in the sunlight. With one fluid motion, he parted her thighs and stepped between them, his large hands wrapped around her waist, pressing her against his chest.

Callie was caught completely off guard by his sudden passion. "Whoa, cowboy, I was kidding."

"Coward." He leaned in to kiss her.

"No, just busy." She wiggled free of his hold and slid down off the stool. "You see, my man has this *crazy* idea that I should be making money off this little enterprise," she said with exaggerated annoyance.

"Sounds like a smart guy."

Callie's eyes softened. "He has his moments." She paused for several moments. "I can admit when I'm wrong, Julian. And I was wrong about the favor thing. Since I started charging my friends for the parts, I've actually managed to turn a profit this week. In fact, if this keeps up, I may try for another loan."

"Go for it."

Callie shrugged her shoulders. "I don't know. I've been

turned down three times already. I know you designed that great-looking business plan for me, but what if it's not enough?"

"It will be." Julian came up behind her and wrapped her in his arms. "Trust me, it will be."

"You've been so terrific about all this. So supportive and helpful." She turned in his arms, reaching up to hug him tightly. "Thank you for keeping your promise to not interfere with me and Paul, and thank you…for believing in me."

Julian went completely still. At that very moment, there was a paid detective searching for Paul DeLeroy. And sitting in a desk drawer at the Northern First Bank was a guaranteed loan with her name on it.

She was so full of pride and independence. If she ever found out what he'd done, she would probably hate him. He hugged her tighter. What alternative did he have? What was he supposed to do? Wait until this Paul guy came looking for her? Or stand by and watch her business fail because of her ridiculous pride? *No, it's my job to do what's best for her— for us—whether she realizes it or not.*

"Want to go grab some lunch?" Julian asked, desperately needing to change the subject.

"Love to, but can't. I've got to go to the auto parts store and pick up some parts to finish this car. I was just waiting for Pooky to return so I wouldn't have to lock up the garage."

"I'll watch the garage for you." Julian said, taking up her former position on the stool. He tried not to think about the two piles of work he had on his own desk at home. Lately, all he wanted to do was be in Callie's company.

"Would you? Great. The store is just up the street. I'll be right back." With that, Callie darted toward the front entrance.

Julian sat silently replaying all of the possible scenarios over and over again in his head. Wondering if there was anything he should've done differently, but he kept coming back to the same decision. Protecting Callie was more important than any promise he would ever make.

After ten minutes of boredom, Julian stood up and began circling the garage looking at the various tools scattered about. Callie bought tools the way some women bought shoes. Many of which she would never need and could never use, but she couldn't pass up a good sale to save her life.

He picked up a shiny, black-handled ratchet, one of a hundred in all shapes and sizes. Yes, he thought, tools were definitely her candy.

He circled the room, picking up this and that, looking it over and moving on to the next item. *I have so much work to do. What am I doing here?* He circled around to the large drafting table on the far side of the room. A large portfolio rested on the slanted surface. Out of curiosity, he lifted the cover and was instantly stunned by what he saw.

The drawing of a tall, nondescript female form draped in a bright, colorful tunic. The vibrant orange and blue coloring jumped off the page. The tunic was trimmed in gold sequins that matched the pants part of the outfit.

Soon, he found himself turning page after page of the portfolio, drawn into the rich colors and fluid lines. Julian had never considered himself a fashion expert but felt he had acceptably good taste. And what he was looking at would appeal to anyone. He could almost see the fabric in motion, rich hues of green and yellow.

He turned one more page and stopped dead cold when he found himself looking at the beautiful turquoise dress Callie had worn the first time they went out.

"What the hell do you think you are doing?"

Chapter 24

A high-pitched screech came from the doorway. Pooky stood clutching his purse to his false bosom. He looked so scared and vulnerable Julian almost felt sorry for him. "Those are my personal things! You have no right to go through my personal things!"

"You shouldn't leave your personal things out for people to find."

Pooky crossed the room quickly and grabbed his portfolio off the table, slamming it shut in the process. "How would you like it if I came into your house and started rummaging through your things?"

Pooky was fuming with both anger and embarrassment. His portfolio was very personal, and *he* decided who got to see it. Not everyone appreciated his use of colors and fabrics. How many times had he shown it to potential employers and been laughed out of their offices? Now he would have to contend with ridicule from Callie's snobby, homophobic boyfriend.

"What's your problem anyway?"

Pooky froze with his large foot on the bottom step leading up into the apartment. He turned slowly. "What did you say?"

"I said what's your problem? Every time I come over here, I try to be civil to you for Callie's sake and all I ever get back is this bitchy attitude of yours."

"Civil? Is that what you call it? A complete disregard for the privacy of others and an absolute disrespect for anything or anyone different from yourself? That's your idea of civilized behavior?"

"You want to talk about respect? Okay, let's talk about your respect for Callie," Julian said, his deep baritone hiding the anger that bubbled just beneath the surface.

"What's that supposed to mean?" Pooky crossed half the distance between them.

"When I invite her someplace, I have enough *respect* for her to actually *be there* to greet her."

Pooky glared at the man. "My relationship with Callie is none of your damn business!"

Julian closed the gap until he was standing toe-to-toe with the shorter man. "Well, I guess it's time you learned that everything that has to do with Callie is my business, including your sorry ass. Do you even care that she was hurt the other night? She dragged me halfway across town just to celebrate with you and you don't even care enough to bother to stick around!"

Pooky put his hand on his narrow hip. "That's what this is really about, isn't it?" He narrowed his eyes. "That you had to *demean* yourself by entering a gay bar. Poor baby. That must've really been hard on you."

Julian took in the man's sun-yellow skirt and matching silk

blouse, the single strand of pearls hanging around his neck, and pale yellow high-heeled sandals. Who was this man to criticize him?

"Not as hard as it's going to be for you when Callie moves out." Julian's mouth twisted in triumph at the flash of fear he saw go through Pooky's eyes. Finally, something managed to cut through that impenetrable arrogance.

"What are you talking about?"

"I'm going to marry Callie, and when I do, your free ride will be over."

Pooky laughed. "Callie won't marry you."

Julian was so sure of himself he was able to accept the laughter without flinching. "Don't be too sure of that. She loves me, and eventually she *will* marry me. Then who is going to carry your dead weight?"

Pooky's full-bodied laughter continued. "Yes, Mr. Man, I do believe you are right. Unfortunately, she *does* love you. But she would never marry a bigot."

"Who are you calling a bigot?" Julian's fist balled and released at his sides. Hitting this man would be the worst mistake he could make right now. Callie would never forgive him, and it would make Pooky look like the victim.

"You think I don't know how you feel about me? It's in your eyes every time you look at me or one of my friends. And Callie sees it, too."

"What is going on here?" Callie was standing in the middle of the open bay doors with two large bags, one in each arm.

Julian quickly worked to relax his face and stepped away from Pooky. Instinctively, he knew he would suffer the most from this little confrontation. By the way Callie was glaring at him, he would've thought she'd walked in and caught him kicking her cat.

Callie moved into the center of the room, her head swinging back and forth between the two men who were so incredibly different. "I said, what is going on here?"

Pooky glanced in Julian's direction. "Ask your man," he said, then turned and rushed up the stairs to the apartment.

Damn, Julian thought, *I should've left first.*

"Julian?" Callie dropped her bags on the counter and crossed her arms over her chest.

He turned his back to Callie, running his hand through his hair. "Callie, I can't take this. This relationship between you and your cousin, it's not normal!" He started pacing the width of the concrete floor.

"Pooky is a part of me, and if you want me in your life, you are going to have to accept that."

"Baby, I'm not trying to tell you who your friends should be. I—"

"Aren't you?"

"No. I'm just saying that…" He paused in the middle of the room. "You are a businesswoman. Surely you realize that your relationship with him could hurt your business." Placing his hand against his heart, he rose up to his full height of six feet. "Not everyone is as open-minded as me."

"Open-minded?"

"Yes, open-minded. I have been extremely patient and understanding about this whole living together thing."

Callie took several deep breaths. "Julian, I think you should leave now."

"So that's the way it is?" His lips set in a firm line. "Callie, eventually you are going to have to decide what you want. There is no place in our future for that…that person. Baby, can't you see? He's just using you."

"Using me?"

"Of course." He crossed to her and took her arms in his. "Where would he go if he didn't have you and this garage? He needs you more than you need him, and he knows I'm a threat to that relationship."

"Julian, what are you talking about? Pooky and I don't use each other. We help and support each other. But I guess if anyone *was* being used, it would be Pooky." She broke free of his hold. "His parents left him over a million dollars when they died. He's used a large portion of that money to help me."

Julian felt his lips separate in surprise. Why hadn't she ever said anything about this before? "You're just saying that to protect him. You told me yourself that he just found a job. If he has all that money, why does he need to work?"

"I just told you! Because over the years he's *used* most of that money to take care of me and this garage!"

"But I thought—"

"No, Julian, you didn't *think*. You took one look at him, then judged and condemned him." Callie turned and raced up the stairs as her cousin had done only moments before.

When Julian reached the top landing, he realized it was the first time he'd been in Callie's apartment. Usually they spent their time together at his house. He heard a soft buzzing sound of a machine as he turned the corner and knocked on the open door leading into the rest of the apartment.

"Hello?" He knocked again. When he peeked his head around the corner, he saw Pooky sitting at a large sewing machine in the middle of the room.

Pooky spotted him at the same instant and shot to his feet. "What are you doing here? You don't belong up here." He glanced over his shoulder toward another doorway, and Julian thought it was possibly Callie's bedroom.

Julian came into the room and swallowed hard. "I owe you an apology."

Pooky was not going to be swayed that easily. "Really? Exactly how does one apologize for who they are?"

Julian looked around the walls, taking in the framed pictures that lined them. The room was small, and the furniture was draped in red and white coverings. The wood tables were short and coated in black lacquer giving the room an overall oriental feel. *Oriental?* Julian thought. Not a taste he would've ever associated with Callie.

His eyes were drawn back to the only other person in the room as he realized there was more than one person's taste to consider. "You're not going to make this easy, are you?" Julian moved into the room, but paused to study a small Buddha figurine protected inside a decorative glass case.

"You think I don't know what this is about? You think apologizing to me will get you back into Callie's good graces."

Julian began walking again, taking in the assortments of knickknacks that composed the combined memories of the small apartment's occupants. "I'm hoping." He stopped and turned to face Pooky. "But that's not the only reason."

He crossed the room to stand beside the sewing table. "Look, I won't pretend to understand why you—" Julian gestured to his yellow outfit "—why you do this. Although I've never thought of myself as a bigot, I have to admit, I did treat you unfairly, and it was because of some poor assumptions I made about you based on your appearance."

Pooky relaxed his posture, realizing the man really was trying to make this right. He could meet him halfway. "It's okay. I'm used to people making wrong assumptions about me. And in all fairness, I haven't exactly been accommodating to you. But we've got to find some sort of accord, Jules. For Callie."

Julian held up his hand. "And the first step in that would be for you to stop calling me Jules."

Pooky smiled. "Sorry, didn't realize it bothered you."

A quiet fell over the pair, and Julian realized it was his turn to offer an olive branch. "You do have talent, you know. That's what I was thinking when you came in downstairs. That gown you designed for Callie was amazing."

"Thank you, I don't usually show my designs to just anyone. But since you are going to be family…"

Julian looked away, feeling very uncomfortable when he realized the man was blushing.

The silence returned and stretched into several long, uncomfortable seconds before Pooky sat back down behind his machine. "I don't mean to be rude, but I have a deadline to meet."

Julian put up both hands and backed away. "Don't let me stop you." He gestured toward another open doorway. "Is she…?"

Pooky nodded and continued his sewing. He paused before Julian disappeared through the doorway. "Julian."

"Yes?"

"It takes a big man to admit he's wrong. Just wanted you to know I appreciate the effort it took for you to come up here."

Julian crossed the floor and extended his hand. "And I want to thank you for taking care of Callie when she couldn't take care of herself."

Seeing the truth of his words in his eyes, Pooky smiled and accepted the handshake. "Callie coming into my life was more my blessing than hers."

Across the room, Julian knocked on the bedroom door before cracking it open. He stuck his head inside the small, neat bedroom decorated in neutral colors and spotted the blanket-covered lump in the middle of the bed.

He silently crossed the room, trying to decide how best to approach her. He sank down on the side of the bed and found he was more interested in studying her face than making peace. She was so beautiful with her small, fine features and golden skin.

He shifted to kiss her forehead, deciding to let her sleep. But when he bent forward, his lips honed in on her mouth instead, and her lips parted under his in recognition.

She shifted onto her back, and Julian, unable to stop himself, went with her.

"What are you doing here?" she whispered, pulling at his cotton sweater, trying to pull it up over his torso.

"Trying to say I'm sorry," he managed between kisses, feeling her need take them over.

"I was just dreaming about you. When you kissed me I thought it was part of the dream." Callie's bated breath and pounding heart were evidence of just what type of dream she'd been experiencing.

"Baby, I'm sorry," Julian whispered, releasing his belt buckle and removing his pants. He quickly donned a condom and with practiced ease parted her thighs.

Callie gave herself over without reservation, reaching up to guide him inside her. When his heat met hers, she sighed with both relief and anticipation.

As Julian shifted his body seeking her rhythm, he heard the small sound as she whispered, "You're forgiven," against his shoulder, right before sinking her small teeth into it.

Chapter 25

"Okay, you see that?" Callie pointed at the torn black rubber hose.

Olivia bent her head to see the hose Callie was pointing to. "Yes."

"That's our culprit. That's the reason the tank won't fill up."

"That little tear?"

Callie shrugged her shoulders. "You'd be surprised what one little tear can do. I can't patch that; I'll have to replace the entire hose."

Olivia stood straight and glanced at the length of her grandfather's car. "I don't know why Grandpa is having this fixed anyway. He never drives it."

"It's a beautiful car. It's worth fixing even if just to sell it. The body still looks good," Callie spoke while twisting her wrench to release the clamp holding the hose in place. "And it has only forty thousand miles on it. There's a lot of life left in this beauty."

"I'm never selling this car," James Sr. spoke from the garage entry. He crossed the room and draped his arm over his granddaughter's shoulders. "Your dad was conceived in this car."

Olivia scrunched up her nose in disgust and moved back from the car. "Grandpa! That's disgusting!"

"What's so disgusting about life being created? Most natural thing in the world."

Since the initial luncheon, Callie had dedicated one afternoon a week to working on the ancient Lincoln—more a labor of love than anything else.

Julian's parents had used the car to get Callie into their home that first afternoon. After that, the Lincoln had once again been forgotten. But Callie couldn't forget it. Her relationship to damaged cars was like doctor to patient. She couldn't stand by and watch a car in need and not help it. And if ever there was a car that needed her help, it was the Lincoln.

But Callie knew it wasn't just the car that drew her to the house again and again. It was her budding friendship with Julian's teenage daughter. That first day, they had taken a long walk together, and Callie had shared her whole life with the girl. Callie spoke of the death of first her mother, then her father and stepmother, then the betrayal by her stepbrother. She wanted Olivia to understand that what seemed hopeless today could turn into something completely different the next day. The key was sticking it out until *the next day* showed up.

Olivia had shared her own story, giving Callie the intimate details of life with a cocaine addict. She found herself telling Callie things she'd never shared with her father. Callie knew it was a risky relationship, and she kept the girl's confessions a secret. Julian was paying a therapist sixty dollars an hour to discover what Olivia would give her for free. But Callie feared if she betrayed her, Olivia would never trust her, Julian, or anyone else ever again.

James Sr. was running his hand along the sleek fender of the car. "Olivia, when you turn sixteen, this baby will be all yours. What do you think of that?" he boasted.

"Lucky me," Olivia muttered, just loud enough for Callie to hear. The two laughed.

"What was that?" James Sr. called from the rear of the vehicle.

"I said, thanks, Grandpa."

James Sr. cast a side-glance at the two females. He doubted very seriously that Olivia had said anything resembling "thank you." But James Sr. was so pleased with the budding relationship between Callie and Olivia that he found it hard to scold either of them.

Both he and his wife had taken to Callie right off, believing that Julian's drastic deviation from his usual pattern meant something significant. Her growing relationship with their granddaughter only confirmed what they believed. Now they could only hope their stubborn son realized it as well and made it a permanent arrangement.

Callie finally managed to get the hose off the car and dropped it into her box. "I'm going to have to buy this part and bring it back with me next week," she said to no one in particular. James Sr. had given her complete authority over the vehicle long ago.

Pam appeared in the house entry. "Callie, aren't you staying for dinner?"

"Thanks, Pam, but I've got too much work waiting for me back at the garage," Callie called back.

"Okay, I'll let you off the hook this time, but I expect you to come over this weekend for the barbecue. Remind Julian; he tends to get so wrapped up in his work he forgets."

"Tell me about it." Callie chuckled.

"It's a surprise birthday party for James Jr., so don't say anything to him if you see him before then."

Callie smiled. "I won't."

As she began packing up her toolbox, she had to remind herself not to get too addicted to the feeling of warmth and kindness that surrounded her whenever she was in the company of the Cruise family. As much as she loved Julian, Callie still could not see what life would be like with him beyond the next few months.

"Will I see you Saturday?" Olivia asked, poorly hiding the eagerness in her voice.

Callie smiled at the girl. "Wouldn't miss it for the world."

James Sr. grabbed his granddaughter's hand and started toward the backyard. "Since you won't be needing your assistant anymore, I think I'll steal her for a game of hoops."

"Poor Grandpa," Olivia said with heartfelt sympathy. "Just a glutton for punishment."

"We'll see about that," he called grumpily, remembering the last three games of one-on-one in which his only grandchild had thoroughly thrashed him. And yet for the happy, laughing trash-talking she did when they played, he would willingly take a hundred more beatings.

"See you later, Callie," Olivia called, as the pair disappeared around the corner of the garage. As Callie picked up her heavy box and headed for her car, she heard the sound of Olivia's laughter coming from the backyard.

When she'd first met the girl, she'd seemed incapable of laughing, but now, a few weeks later, Callie had seen her smiling, making jokes, and starting to enjoy life again. Callie wanted to believe that she had been a small part of making that happen.

Callie rounded the corner, entering the kitchen, and found two men squatting and rolling dice across the floor as they played Bones. She recognized the game right away. "Hey, fellas," she said to Julian's brothers as she went to lean against the counter to watch.

After both men spoke, James looked over his shoulder at the woman. "By the way, if Julian didn't have a chance to say it, I want to apologize."

He rolled the dice and all six went sliding across the floor.

"For what?" Callie asked.

"My parents," James answered with complete sincerity. "They can be a bit…"

"Overbearing," Jonathan supplied.

"What are you talking about? Your parents are great." She reached back and took a handful of the snack mix Pam always kept on the counter.

Both men turned and looked at her, their dark eyes wide with disbelief.

"If you say so." James chuckled.

"No, really. I liked them right off."

"They're easy to like—for crazy people," Jonathan offered.

"Hey, that's a bit disrespectful." Callie wasn't sure why she felt the need to defend these people from the people who'd known them all their lives.

"No, it's the truth," Jonathan continued. "Take today for instance." He sat back on his haunches. "Mom calls us both up and asks us to make ourselves available to help her with her spring cleaning. So we made the time available and came over here prepared to work like dogs. Why? Because Mom needs us. Then we get here and she tells us to just relax for a while and she'll let us know when she needs us." He glanced at his watch. "That was four hours ago. Where's Mom, you might ask? In the attic, spring cleaning. When we tried to go up there, she shooed us away, but if we try to leave, then…"

James filled in the blanks with a high-pitched imitation of his mother. "You worthless, trifling, ungrateful, etc., etc."

"See what we mean?" Jonathan said. "Crazy."

Callie grabbed another handful of the snack mix and munched, deep in thought, while the men returned to their game.

"How often do you guys come by to visit her?"

Both men stilled.

"I don't know. A few times a month," Jonathan offered.

"So the only way she gets you here is to tell you she needs help with something? Being the good sons that you are, you rush right over. Is that what I'm understanding?"

They looked at each other. Neither was willing to comment, and both were too afraid Callie may have hit on something.

James rolled the dice, and Callie jumped up eagerly. "A run of six! Way to go, James."

He looked back at the little woman in coveralls, with her face slightly smeared with black grease, still amazed that this was Julian's latest love interest.

"What do you know about Bones, little girl?" he asked in the most taunting tone he could muster.

In that instant, Callie decided the Cavalier she had waiting for her up on the rack in her shop could wait another hour. These men needed to be taught a lesson about underestimating women—and about parental respect.

"Not much." She hunched her shoulders. "Something

about scoring and sequences, but I haven't played in years." She took comfort in knowing that last statement was true.

"Tell you what—" she stood from the counter, dusting snack mix residue from her hands "—I'll play you a game, and if I win, you two have to take your parents out for a nice dinner," Callie offered.

"What about Julian?" Jonathan asked. "Why is he left off the hook? Because he's your man?"

"No, because he's not here. This is between you and me."

"And if we win?" James asked.

Callie made a hand gesture. "Name your price."

The two men put their heads together; they were snickering before they parted. James was the chosen spokesperson.

"If we win, we each get a free oil change and tune-up for *each* of our cars."

Callie had to hide the confident smile that crept to her lips. "Sounds like a bit much, but I'm game."

She used her hip to push Jonathan out of the way so that she could squat down between the two. Soon, the threesome were heavily engaged in a lively game of Bones.

Thanks to a set of three twos and five fives, Callie was ahead by twelve hundred points. At one point, Jonathan, refusing to believe he was being so badly beaten by a girl, took the dice and closely examined them. Much to his dismay, they were still the dice they'd begun with.

So engrossed in their game, not one of them heard Julian enter the kitchen an hour later. He stood not believing his eyes for a moment. Okay, she was a bit tomboyish, and yes, she had lousy taste in clothes, but he could accept that. Even her strange assortment of friends could be tolerated from a distance. But shooting dice with his brothers? Hell, no!

"Callie?!"

"Hey, baby," she called back over her shoulder, shaking her dice cup for the next roll.

"What do you think you are doing?" His brothers heard the steel in his tone, even if she missed it.

"Winning!" She laughed happily. "And..." she tossed the dice out and watched the precession of one, two, three, four, five, six roll across the vinyl floor. Both arms shot straight up into the air. "A run of six!" She scooped them up again. "Teaching your brothers a lesson," she said with all the arrogance of a peacock, and then began shaking the cup once more.

Both her play partners had lost interest in the game; they were too busy staring up into the face of their brother, who looked about ready to kill.

Instead of following on his instinct to drag her up off the floor by her collar, Julian turned and stormed out of the kitchen. As much as he cared for Callie, she was just too uncouth, too vulgar, too *street* to ever be an acceptable social partner, and that was just a reality he was going to have to face.

Julian leaned against the wall. No clothes could change who she was. He loved the elf like nothing he'd ever felt before, but it would never work. They were just too different. His analytical mind couldn't make sense of it. How could he have ever considered being with this woman for the rest of his life? Julian walked out of the house without saying another word to her. He was too upset to be reasonable.

He did not call her that night, nor visit her garage, unsure of what he would say when he did. He wanted to tell her that she would have to change or it was over. But his brain was a lot braver than his heart. His greatest fear was, what if she decided she wouldn't change?

The next day, Julian went to Callie's garage, and her affectionate greeting told him she was completely unaware of his internal struggle. He said nothing, hoping his confused mind would resolve itself. *At this point, a sign from God would be nice*, he thought. Some reminder of why this woman moved him, body and spirit. What was it about her—other than great sex—that made her so irresistible?

Several hours later, seated behind Callie's desk, which had somehow become Cruise Corporation headquarters over the past few weeks, Julian watched a hesitant young boy about ten or twelve enter the garage.

He looked in both directions with wide, curious eyes, taking in all there was to see. Out of sight, Julian heard Callie's voice call to the young visitor.

"Hello? Can I help you?"

The boy moved forward just enough to stand directly in front of the office door, never noticing the man a few feet away. "You the lady with the bikes?"

"Yes, that's me," Callie answered, now moving into view.

She crossed the room to the stack of damaged bike parts Julian had wondered about since his first visit to the garage. She reached up and yanked on the white sheet behind the pile and revealed three completely repaired bikes. Julian could smell the fresh paint all the way across the room. *So that's what she does with those parts.*

The boy's eyes widened even more, and his small face spread into a huge grin.

Callie folded her arms across her chest and stood over the boy, who was just under an inch shorter than her. "You know these are not free bikes. You have to pay for them," she said sternly. "Whoever told you about them should've told you that."

"I've got money." The boy dug deep into his front blue jean pocket. His curled fist opened to reveal a ball of crumpled bills and a few coins. "See?"

Julian's attention was engaged enough that he moved from the desk to stand in the door, and the movement caught the attention of the boy. His fist clenched as he eyed the newcomer.

Callie's hands slid down to her hip bone. "That's an awful lot of money for a kid. How did you make all that money?"

The boy's chest pushed forward with pride, and Julian fought the smile that edged his lips.

"I find bottles people toss out and turn them in."

Callie moved closer to the boy. "How much do you have there?"

"Eight dollars and twenty-seven cents," he said quietly, refusing to look up. "Is it enough?"

"Actually, more than enough. The bike only costs five dollars. You save three dollars and twenty-seven cents."

"Really?" His young face shone with excitement and gratitude.

"Really." Callie went around the pile of parts. "Which one?"

He pointed to one, bright red with black trim. "That one."

Callie tried to pull the bike from its resting place, but when it snagged on the pile of parts, Julian moved forward to help, lifting the bike over the pile and handing it off to its new owner.

The boy ran his hand over the smooth metal, his eyes filled with an emotion that looked a lot like new love. "Thanks," he said offhandedly, rolling his new bike toward the entrance.

"Hey! What about my money?" Callie stood with her hands braced on her hips, trying not to laugh at how easily she'd been discarded.

"Oh." He used his foot to knock down the kickstand. Carefully straightening every wrinkled bill, he counted it off twice before handing it over.

"Wait while I write out your receipt," Callie said, moving behind the counter.

"That's okay," he said, his attention returning to his bike.

"No, it's *not* okay. You always get a receipt." She quickly scribbled off a note. Moving back to the boy, she squatted down in front of him. "You worked very hard for your money and bought your bike fair and square. If you don't have a receipt, anyone could say you stole it." She looked meaningfully into his young eyes. "You understand?"

The boy nodded with true understanding.

"Okay." She offered her small hand to his even smaller one. "Nice doing business with you."

He smiled and shook. "Yeah." He glanced at Julian once before turning and rolling his new bike out of the garage.

Callie's eyes met Julian's, thinking she recognized the soft, dreamy expression on his face. "Oh no, there won't be any of that this afternoon. We both have too much work to do."

Julian just chuckled lightly. "The drag queen with a purse full of money you let off scot-free, but the kid with eight dollars in bottle returns has to pay?" He tried to sound serious but could not hide the laughter lurking in his eyes.

"It's the principle of the thing. I'm trying to teach them that nothing in life is free; you have to work for what you want. What's wrong with that?"

She frowned and Julian could hold back no longer. His hearty laughter rang out across the hollow building as he turned and walked back into the office.

Julian finally accepted the truth for what it was. His heart was already hers, and his mind would just have to learn to live with it. How could he have ever considered *not* being with this woman for even a moment?

Chapter 26

Julian reached across the desk and grabbed the ringing telephone from its base. "Hello?"

"I found your guy, Mr. Cruise," Chris Mathers, the private investigator Julian had hired, spoke from the other end.

Julian paused. "You found Paul DeLeroy."

"Yes, sir. He lives in a nearby suburb."

"Are you sure it's the Paul DeLeroy I'm looking for?"

"Mr. Cruise, if I made mistakes like that, I wouldn't be in business very long."

"No, I suppose not. Did you speak with him?"

"No, sir. You told me to just locate him, not to contact him directly."

"I know." Julian rubbed his thick mustache thoughtfully. "I know. I just wondered what approach I should take with this guy."

"Well, from what I observed, he seems like a pretty normal guy. He has a wife, a nice home."

"Well, despite appearances, if this guy is who I think he is, he's anything but normal."

"Would you like me to approach him? Make contact?"

He'd promised Callie he wouldn't look for her stepbrother, *not* that he wouldn't contact him if someone else did the locating. What he needed to say to Paul DeLeroy, he needed to say to him directly.

"No, I'll take it from here. Just let me grab a pen so I can write down the information." Julian found a pen in his desk drawer and scribbled the address and a few general directions, completing his call with the private investigator.

He slumped down in his chair in deep thought. Julian knew he was playing with fire, using wordplay and technicalities to justify his behavior. Regardless of the exact words, he knew the implication of his promise to Callie and what she believed.

What would she say if she found out that he had not abandoned the investigation as she thought? She'd probably be angry. Maybe hurt. But more importantly, with Paul DeLeroy properly warned off, she would be safe. In the end, that was all that really mattered.

He did a quick mental calculation. Picking up the phone again, he dialed Jonathan's number. He considered James for all of a second and decided against it; his elder brother was even more straitlaced than he was. He already knew what James would say about the way in which he bent Callie's promise. James would not approve. Jonathan, on the other hand, could be easily bought with a pair of tickets to the next Pistons home game. He smiled as he dialed the seven digits. *Thank God for sports fanatics.*

"Hello?" Jonathan answered the other end.

"Hey, man, I need a favor." Julian decided to cut straight to the chase.

"What's up?"

"I found Paul DeLeroy."

"What!"

"I plan to confront him and tell him to stay the hell away from Callie."

"Whoa, man. I don't know if that is such a good idea. I mean, you don't know anything about this guy. He could be a nutcase for all you know."

"All the more reason why he needs the warning."

"What does Callie have to say about this?"

"She doesn't get a say in this."

"Come on, Julian. That's not right."

"I'm just a man trying to protect what's mine. What's not right about that? Now, will you help me or not?"

"You're my brother. You already know the answer to that."

Julian hid his relief well. He would've faced the unknown threat alone if he had to, but it never hurt to have someone he trusted watching his back. "I thought we'd do it this weekend."

"Can't. James's surprise party, remember?"

"Oh, yeah. Okay, next weekend."

"All right. I just hope you know what you're doing."

"Jonathan." Julian paused, deciding to hold back on all the heavy emotions running through his mind. "Thanks."

"Don't thank me for this…I have a bad feeling about it."

Mona DeLeroy paced the hospital lobby, ringing her hands nervously and silently scolding herself. She'd known for some time that something wasn't right with Paul. She felt he might have gotten into something way over his head. She should've said something, should've confronted him. But instead she'd stuck her head in the sand and pretended everything was okay.

And now he lay on the operating table in a hospital with several broken bones, multiple contusions, and internal bleeding. And still, she was unsure exactly what was going on.

"Hello, Mona."

The coarse, unfamiliar voice startled her, and she spun around to find herself staring into cold, gray eyes. She studied the man for several seconds without speaking. She was normally a friendly, open person who typically responded pleasantly to everyone, friends and strangers alike. But there was something about the man standing in front of her that felt evil.

"How's Paul doing?" he asked.

"Do I know you?"

The stranger's face spread into a smile that could never be called pleasant. "I'm a friend of Paul's."

I doubt that. She didn't know who this man was, but she was certain he was not a friend.

Suddenly he produced a bouquet of flowers. "I just wanted to drop these off and offer my condolences."

Mona almost didn't take the flowers, but some survival instinct deep inside told her that offending this man would be a greater mistake.

"Thank you," she said, taking the elegant bouquet. "Who should I say came by?"

The man's face sobered instantly. "He won't have any doubts about who I am."

As she watched the stranger leave through the automated doors, Mona felt a cold chill slide down her spine.

Chapter 27

Callie twisted and twisted the wrench until the bolt felt secure. She scooted across the floor and started on the next one, until she realized she needed another washer. She reached for her red toolbox and tugged it close. Without needing to see, her small hand felt around inside; she knew exactly where everything was inside her box. Which was why it was such a surprise when her fingers skimmed across what felt like paper. There was nothing paper in her box, only metals and rubbers.

She pushed herself out from under the vehicle and sat up. It was an unusually warm spring day, and the large bay doors were standing open, letting in the bright sunlight. A cool breeze rushed over her sweaty skin, feeling like heaven, and Callie leaned into it, loving the sensation. She rubbed the back of her hand across her forehead, only then remembering it was covered in grease. She shook her head in disgust. Not the first time that had happened, and it wouldn't be the last.

She dug into her back pocket for her oilcloth and wiped her hands as clean as possible and continued her search. Opening her red box wider, she spotted the college catalog sitting on top of her washers and screws. She picked it up and began browsing through it. The more she read, the angrier she became. Callie jumped to her feet and rushed across the room.

"Julian!" She stormed into her small office, which over the past several weeks had somehow become his. She paused in the doorway for a moment, noting for the first time the stacks of Cruise Corporation files that now sat on the end of the wood desk. Callie's ancient desktop computer had been pushed aside, and Julian's little laptop sat in its place.

Julian was talking to seemingly no one, but Callie knew from experience that a tiny cord ran from the cell phone at his waist and tucked behind his ear out of sight. Seeing her in the doorway, Julian lifted his finger to indicate a pause. Callie was angry but not enough to tarnish his professional image by screaming at him like a crazy woman while he was on a business call. She folded her arms across her chest, fighting to hold back her rage.

"No, I hadn't heard anything about a takeover. Of course, I'll look into it," Julian said, and then listened silently to the person on the other end.

Meanwhile, Callie stood by his side, counting backward from one hundred, trying to calm her throbbing brain.

"No problem, Bob." Julian waited again. "Um-hmm." He frowned thoughtfully, listening for several more seconds.

Callie forced her tight fist to loosen when she felt her nails digging into her palms.

"Well, don't worry about it. That's why you have me."

Callie fantasized about taking the paper catalog and beating him senseless with it and silently congratulated herself on the amount of restraint she was showing in not doing so.

Finally, after another brief interlude, Julian concluded the call. "All right, I'll give you a call as soon as I know something." He pressed a button at his waist and turned to face Callie, noting for the first time the very unhappy expression that clouded her normally clear brown eyes. "What's wrong?"

Callie extended her arm to show him the crumpled magazine, then realized she'd almost crushed it beyond recognition in her palm. "What it this?"

Julian took a casual glance at the catalog before turning back to his laptop. He was working hard at appearing less worried than he was while trying to come up with an answer to her question that would not end in his death. Never had he expected her to become so angry over something so small. Irritated maybe; definitely not incensed.

"It's a college catalog. I got it in the mail and thought you might be interested, so I left it on top of your toolbox."

"And why did you think I would be interested?"

"I thought you might like to take some business courses."

Callie tossed the catalog at his chest and placed her hands on her hips. "This is just like the *clothes* thing!"

"What are you talking about?"

"You keep trying to change me to fit what you think I should be."

"Don't be silly, Callie. Why would I want to change you?"

"I don't know, Julian. All I know is that in one breath you say you care about me, then in the next you are trying to change my wardrobe." She gestured to the magazine that now lay crumpled on the floor. "That's not about a few business courses. You've had a problem with my job ever since you met me—now you are trying to change that, too."

Julian stood to face her. "You're blowing this completely out of proportion." He bent and picked up the catalog, tossing it into the trash. "Okay, I get it. Not interested. Now you can get back to your work, and I can get back to mine." He sat back down and resumed his typing.

Callie stood staring at his bent head for several seconds. She knew she was in love with Julian, but what kind of future could they have if he kept trying to cast her into some kind of neat, little mold every few days? And how could they deal with the problem if he would not even acknowledge there was a problem? "Why can't you admit it?"

"Admit what? If you don't want the catalog, fine. Now, can we let it go?"

Feeling defeated and not knowing how to change it, she turned to leave but got as far as the door. The need to speak her mind overcame her. She turned to face the man whose full attention was now focused on the computer screen. She stretched out her arms like angel wings.

"If the woman standing in front of you right now, right this minute, is not good enough, Julian, no amount of expensive clothes or education is going to change that."

Julian's heart broke at the battered look in her eyes, realizing his gesture had been completely mistaken. This was never what he intended. He was only trying to make a subtle suggestion, not cause her to question their whole relationship. "I'm not trying to change you, baby. I just want what's best for you."

"What's best for me is your complete acceptance of who I am today. If in time I choose to go back to school, it has to be because it is something I feel I want for myself. Not something I have to do to satisfy you or live up to your expectations."

Julian ran both hands over his short-cropped hair. "I just don't get it." He shook his head sadly. "I don't understand how wanting you to improve yourself is wrong."

"The thought itself is not wrong; it's your reasons behind it that I find offensive."

"What reasons do you think those are, Callie?" His full lips twisted in exasperation.

She blew out a long breath, realizing just how much of her life Julian would never accept. What kind of future could they possibly have? "We can't fix what's wrong between us if you won't even acknowledge something is wrong."

Julian was thinking about all the work he had waiting for him, the many calls he had left to make, and the day wasting while they stood arguing over what he felt was a nonexistent problem. "Acknowledge *what?*" He threw up his hands in frustration. "I can't believe all this started over some damn college catalog I wish I had never given you in the first place. Okay, I'm sorry about the catalog, and I'm sorry about the clothes. But I love you, and I'm never going to stop wanting to give you more than you have and trying to help you be the best person you can be."

"I am the best person I can be right now, Julian," Callie said with resignation. "That's what you don't understand."

He sighed. She was determined to turn this into a major argument, Julian thought. The only way to end this with any semblance of peace was just to leave and return when her good sense did—after he'd gotten some work done. He quickly packed his laptop in the leather case and shoved piles of papers down into the side pockets.

Callie watched him in silence. His jerky movements and tightly sealed lips revealed more than he realized. He was as fearful of their future as she was.

With a few long strides, he reached her standing in the doorway. He bent his head for what he intended to be a gentle, intimate see-you-later kiss, but in the heat of anger it became a fiery collision that quickly turned into a battle of wills. Julian using his tongue to try and pry her lips apart, and Callie holding her lips tightly sealed refusing him entry. She finally jerked her head away, and the battle ended in a tie.

Julian's dark eyes flashed. "You need to understand something, Callie. I'm a conservative man. I believe men should wear men's clothes. And I believe that God made a woman to love a man. And I believe a man should help his woman when and however he can. And that will never change. And if we have any chance of being together, you're just going to have to accept that that is who I am."

She lifted her chin, and even with the additional inch that movement gave her, she was still a dwarf in comparison to him. "Well, here's something you're going to have to accept about me. I like my job. I like spending most of my day underneath cars, my hands covered in grease. It's my identity; it's who I am. As far back as I can remember, my hands have looked like this." She held up her greasy palms. "I love getting to know the history of a car, unraveling the problem and fixing it—it's important to me. And that's never going to chan—" She broke off, ashamed of the pleading sound of her voice. "That is who *I am*, Julian." She poked at his chest with her index finger. "That is who I want to be. And that is who I will *always* be."

The pair stood locked in a stare, neither willing to give an inch. Julian could feel the heat coming off her body. He knew it was generated by anger, but it didn't matter. His whole body was responding in a completely different way.

Callie sensed the change in his posture immediately. She turned her head just as he reached to cup her chin. "Just go."

Julian turned to look toward the open bay door, which now seemed like a walk down death row. He had no illusion about his dependence on Callie. He was certain he needed her a lot more than she needed him. And instinctively he knew if he walked out of the garage at that moment in anger, it would end their relationship.

He shook his head slowly. "No," he whispered.

Her head snapped back, and her eyes blazed with fire. "You've packed your bags, now get out."

He met her anger with quiet defiance. "No," he said again.

Callie stood trapped between the man she loved and the small doorway. Her head was pounding; she was so sure her relationship with Julian was about to end, and it terrified her. There were so many major differences between them. How were they ever going to find an acceptable medium? She'd watched him pack his bag and prepared her heart for the very worst: losing Julian. And now he was *refusing* to leave.

Julian bent his head toward her until their faces were within an inch of each other. "No, sweetheart. I'm not letting you toss us away that easily."

Callie fought the tears forming in her eyes. She had never been so torn in her life. One part of her desperately wanted to return to the numb state of being she'd existed in prior to Julian coming into her life and setting it on fire. She hadn't know what she was missing and therefore led a happy and contented life in ignorant bliss. But now, another part of her could not even imagine a world without him in it. He had done this to her, and some small part of her resented him for it.

"We're so different, Julian. We always will be. Can you accept that?"

Julian moved forward, pressing his body against hers. "I can accept whatever I have to, to be with you." With one motion, he wrapped his arm around her waist and lifted her small body from the ground, pressing his lips to hers. This time when he used his tongue to demand entrance, she easily surrendered, opening her mouth to let him inside. Julian's kiss became more demanding, telling her with his tongue everything he felt, everything he wanted from her, everything he planned to do to her.

With a backward kick, the door slammed shut, and he dropped his computer case on the floor near the desk, laying Callie out on the almost empty surface. Their lips never lost contact.

Callie's heart was pounding. Just the way he touched her had her hormones in a raging storm. She felt his warm breath skim her dirty coveralls; her nipples rose up, pressing against the cotton fabric, demanding release so they could rush out to meet the promise of pleasure. She heard the snaps on her coveralls coming undone, and suddenly she remembered her filthy hands and smeared face.

"Julian, we can't do this now. I need to—" The rest of the statement was cut off as the feel of his warm mouth on her flesh overrode her senses.

Julian pressed his mouth against her exposed skin, his tongue sliding gracefully over the contours of her flat stomach, following the trail his hands were leaving. He pushed the coveralls off her shoulders and lifted the thin T-shirt she wore beneath. He was a starving man, and the only thing that could feed his need was beneath the shirt.

Callie wanted to touch him, hold on to him, and press his body against her own. But with her hands being covered in grease, all she could do was lie there in sensory overload while he tortured every part of her.

Julian pushed both T-shirt and bra up and out of his way; his eyes completely focused on what lay beneath. He paused only long enough to wrap his large hands around each of her small breasts, still marveling at how well they fit into his palms. Squeezing the pliable flesh between his fingers, he was mesmerized by her flawless, golden skin. He had no words to describe what she did to him, what seeing her like this did to him. But he didn't need words. He could tell her with his actions.

Callie was unable to stop the cry of pleasure that exploded from her throat. Her whole body lifted from the desktop as Julian sucked the whole of one breast into his mouth. The powerful suction of his mouth closing around her left breast stunned her, but not so much as the ferocious nature of the onslaught.

Julian took the opportunity her arched body presented, wrapping his arms around her back to keep her pressed tightly against his mouth.

Working his tongue around her areola, lapping back and forth, he feasted like the starving man he was. Using his teeth, he tugged gently at the nipple, watching the expression of both pain and pleasure rush across her face. He switched to the other breast with the same wild abandon.

Covering her with his mouth, holding her inside, remembering how close he'd come to losing this. The smell of her skin, warm and familiar. The taste of her—all soap, lotion, and Callie. The feel of her, hot and supple and incredible.

Julian rained small, wet kisses over her torso, torn between his frantic need to be inside her body and his inability to let her go long enough to remove their clothing. He forced his hands to release her long enough to unbuckle his belt. But the compulsion to touch her again overcame him and he found his head pressed between her legs, kissing her through the material of her coveralls, soaking up her essence.

"Oh, Julian!" Callie cried out, careless of whoever may hear.

"You're going to have to help me, baby," he whispered

against her thigh. His throbbing erection made standing almost unbearable.

Callie sat up, and heedless of her messy hands began tearing at his belt buckle. She unzipped his slacks and watched in fascination as the result of his desire appeared. Julian was removing her clothes, pulling her coveralls down off her torso. Then with one arm, he lifted her small body and pulled them completely off along with the terry cloth shorts she always wore beneath. As soon as her mound was revealed to his eyes, Julian felt his whole body begin to tremble. But still, he patiently bent to remove her work boots. Then he stood again to completely remove her shirt and bra.

The brief reprieve had given Callie some time to gain control of herself, and she realized she was lying completely naked on her desktop. "Julian, look at me. I'm filthy." She held up her hands again. "We can't do this now. I need a shower."

Julian quirked an eyebrow as if she spoke a foreign language. He pulled a condom from his wallet, pushing his slacks down. Although typically meticulous in his appearance, he completely disregarded the grease on the leather belt and linen slacks.

"Baby, you could be covered in leeches right now and it wouldn't matter," he spoke offhandedly while donning the condom. He kissed her again, his tongue immediately searching for hers. He needed to prove to her how much he desired her. He kissed a path along her cheek, up behind her ear. Using his body to push her back, he positioned himself at her entrance and was immediately engulfed by moist heat. Julian buried his head against her neck as he slowly drove into her.

Callie reached over her head and gripped the edges of the desk, reveling in the feel of her body stretching and accepting the invasion. Her mouth opened as a soft sigh escaped, and Julian paused in his own pursuit of pleasure to experience hers.

He took her small earlobe between his teeth, and she squirmed just as he knew she would. "How can you question us?" he whispered in her ear. "How can you question anything when we make each other feel like this?"

He reached beneath her, lifting her hips to him, and his hands slid up her back, pressing her against his body. He pulled back and drove forward again. Callie gasped, and he was certain he had reached her core and touched the center of her being. All his considerable willpower, all of his self-discipline meant nothing as he lost control of his body. His hips bucked of their own accord. With an inborn knowledge, his body sought out the treasure hidden in the depth of hers. Soon, Julian felt the pressure building inside his aching organ, and he knew he was reaching the end, and if Callie's sensual moans were any indication, so was she. He tried to regain control, to still his body. This was too soon. He needed to stay with her as long as possible. This was just *too soon*.

His fingers dug into her fleshy cheeks, sweat formed on his brow as he tried to slow his insatiable body. What was it about this woman? Why couldn't he ever seem to get enough of her?

Julian held her hips tightly in his palms, certain he'd bought himself another thirty seconds at least. Then Callie began to move on her own. She pushed and rubbed against him, purring like a happy kitten. The slippery, wet connection of their bodies created a uniquely erotic music all its own. Julian felt the pressure building in the head of his penis and knew how close he was to coming. He didn't want to. He just wanted this moment to last forever. This single space of time when there was no doubt, no disagreements, and no differences between them—when two parts of one soul came together and formed the perfect union and time stood still.

Callie's eyelids parted, revealing glimmering, brown eyes

filled with lust and desire for him. Her soft lips parted. She called his name. And Julian literally felt himself come undone.

His body took control of his mind and began thrashing uncontrollably, slamming into her small body again and again until he felt the nuclear explosion that passed for an orgasm. His whole body stiffened, spasmed, and stiffened again until finally there was no more. Julian fell forward on top of her, exhausted and confused. Wondering how one small fender bender could change a man's world so completely.

Chapter 28

Julian sat in the medical building parking lot typing away on his laptop, which was positioned on the passenger seat. He waited for Olivia to come out of the doctor's office. These twice-a-week visits were costly and time-consuming, but Julian definitely felt he was seeing an improvement in his daughter's behavior and attitude toward him. And according to the school, Olivia's visits to the rehab center had ceased as well, although Julian thought that might have more to do with her now knowing she was under surveillance than any real internal change.

Soon, the glass doors opened, and his daughter appeared. Julian quickly unplugged his computer and tossed it into the backseat to make room for her as she slid inside.

Olivia buckled her seat belt and took her usual position, staring out the window at whatever happened to be there.

"So, how was your session?" Julian asked while pulling out into traffic.

"Okay, I guess."

Julian knew that was probably the extent of her conversation, so he contented himself with driving.

After several minutes, Olivia spoke. "Is it okay if I come back home?" she asked.

Julian clutched the wheel tighter but refused to show any other reaction to this news he'd been waiting to hear, these words he'd feared he would never hear. And she'd said *home*, not *his house*, but *home*.

"Anytime you're ready."

Callie sat stunned into silence. "What do you mean I'm approved?"

Fred Hart almost laughed at the comical expression on the young woman's face. "Just what I said, Ms. Tyler. You have been approved for thirty thousand. Now, if you would just take a few minutes to read over the terms and agreements and then sign here and here—" he gestured to the legal sized document on the desk between them "—we can wrap this up."

"But I don't understand. I was denied three times."

Fred Hart sat back in his chair, scratching painfully behind his ear. "Well, your new business plan was very impressive. Cruise Corporation is a very reputable company. The plan seemed solid, and we believe if implemented, it will work to turn your business around."

"So, just like that—" she snapped her fingers "—I'm approved?"

Fred Hart stared at the woman across the desk from him, not exactly sure what to say. Julian had run through the loan process with him in detail. Trying to cover any possible obstacles that might come up, any questions she might ask. But he'd said nothing about what to do if she could not accept that she'd been approved. Fred scratched his ear once more. "Look, do you want the money or not?"

Something in his eyes told Callie she was about to lose the loan. She sat forward and began reading over the document. Everything looked in order; it looked like a standard contract: the amount of the loan, compounded interest, payment schedule.

Not one to look a gift horse in the mouth, she signed the documents and accepted the check, immediately depositing it into her business account.

When she'd left his house early that morning, Julian had assured her that with his plan in hand, she would have no trouble getting the loan. She had wanted to believe him, but after three denials it was hard. Now here she was, five hours later, walking out of the bank with money for repairs and advertising, and a whole new take on what seemed like a bleak future for Tyler Garage. Julian was picking her up in an hour for James's surprise birthday party. She couldn't wait to share her good news.

"Who is that man, Paul? What does he want from us?" Mona pleaded with her husband as she watched him run from room to room, searching for his recently purchased box of bullets.

"Stay out of this, Mona. This has nothing to do with you." Paul glanced out the window as he passed just to assure himself that the man leaning against a mailbox across the street was still there. Once that curiosity had been satisfied, he returned to the search.

"It's the man from the hospital, isn't it?" Her eyes widened as the pieces began to click into place. "That man works for him, doesn't he?" She grabbed her husband's sleeve as he sped by. "Doesn't he?"

Paul easily shook her free. "Leave me alone. I told you I'll handle it."

Mona sank down on the floor beside her husband's favorite recliner. The tears flowed freely down her face as she contemplated a future without him. "Oh, Paul, what have you done?"

He came to stand over her. "What did you do with my bullets, Mona?" The empty gun dangled from his right hand. His left arm was still in a sling, healing from where it had been broken in two places.

She glared up at this man she'd once bet her future on, taking in his partially healed black eye and swollen jaw. The hospital had patched him up as best modern medicine could. The rest was up to the human body's natural healing process.

"I told you when we first married I would not tolerate guns in my house."

"Will you tolerate my dead body, Mona? Because that's what you are going to end up with if you don't hand over those bullets."

She stared up into his resolved face wondering how she could've been so wrong about a person. Wiping at her tear-stained face, she crossed the room to the fireplace mantle. She picked up a crème-colored ceramic vase and turned it bottom up; the heavy box slid down into her hand.

Paul snatched the box out of her hand, and using a nearby side table as a left hand, he quickly loaded the gun. He went back to the window once more, and the man was still there. Taking a deep breath, he turned to his wife.

"I'm going to go out there and try to talk to him. If I'm alive after the next five minutes, I'm taking you to your sister up in Lansing." He peeked out the window again, silently hoping the man would magically disappear. He was still there, looking directly at Paul behind the curtain.

"And if you're not?" Mona asked quietly. She wanted to

tell him that what he was planning to do was suicide, but she knew he would never listen to her.

He turned and looked at her with his heart in his eyes, and for one shining moment, she saw the Paul of her youth. The Paul who'd charmed her with sweet words and talk of all his big dreams, elaborate plans that never came to fruition.

"If I don't make it—" he swallowed hard "—I want you to haul ass out the back door and don't stop until you reach a police station. You got that?"

She came around the chair and clutched him to her chest. "If that's the case, why don't we go to the police together?"

Paul looked down into her hopeful eyes, realizing how much she loved him and hating that he had to hit her with the cold, hard truth; but she needed to hear it to understand the seriousness of his dilemma. "Mona, the police can't protect me from this man. He could get me anywhere if he wanted to. But you…you haven't done anything to him; you don't owe him anything. If what I've heard about him is true, he won't come after you."

"Oh, Paul." Mona squeezed him tightly, disregarding whatever pain it might cause and wishing she could hold on to him and keep him safe.

He kissed the top of her head before prying himself free of her strong hold. Paul took a deep breath and stepped out onto the front porch. The usually bustling avenue was strangely deserted, as if the whole neighborhood had sensed the impending trouble. "I ain't got your money," he called across the wide street.

He waited for a response from the man still resting comfortably against the mailbox as if the gun dangling from the other man's fingers was of no concern.

"Tell Silver that when I have it, I'll pay him with *two hun-*

dred percent interest. Tell Silver that killing me won't get him his money back. He needs me alive to pay, right?"

The other man just watched him in complete silence.

"Just tell him for me." Paul began backing away, knowing this was the biggest gamble he'd ever taken in his life. Once he was safely inside the house, he closed the door and instantly felt Mona's arms come around his waist. He returned the hug and kissed her passionately, feeling luckier than ever before.

He circled the couch and went to the window. In the few seconds that had passed, the man across the street had disappeared just as Paul had hoped. He sighed in relief, lifting his lucky rabbit's foot hanging on a chain around his neck and kissing it.

His mind was suddenly clear. He would get Mona out of town as quickly as possible and then find a good card game to sit in on tonight. Lady Luck was smiling on him, and he had to strike while the fire was hot.

Chapter 29

"Stop," Callie whispered in the dark closet, trying desperately to keep her mind off Julian's quickly rising erection pressing against her behind.

"Stop what?" Julian whispered seductively in her ear, tugging at her lobe.

Callie felt his large hand sliding around her waist, seeking her own heat, and she quickly stopped it in its path. "Look, we are going to have to jump out and yell 'surprise' in a minute, and if you don't stop this right now, that's going to be an embarrassing moment for more than just James."

"Come on." Julian nipped at her neck. "I'll be quick. We've never done it in a closet."

"And we won't today. Now cut it out. James and Maya will be coming through the door any second."

The house was completely quiet, which was why it was so easy to hear the people fumbling around on the front porch.

"They're at the door," Callie whispered, ignoring the feel of warm hands kneading her bottom.

Large, heavy feet trod over wooden stairs, a bump against the front door, the sound of keys. They heard someone, who Callie assumed was Pam, making a shushing sound to indicate the guest of honor had finally arrived.

"Get ready," Callie called over her shoulder, and the reality of the situation finally sunk into Julian's brain.

What had started out as playful teasing had turned to genuine lust very quickly, and now his whole body was wired for action. How was he supposed to jump out and say "surprise" when he had a little surprise of his own pushing out the front of his pants? His brothers would never let him live it down, not to mention all the other guests who would witness his humiliation.

"Callie, wait, I can't go out there like this," he whispered frantically. He took her hand and ran it over his bulge. "Look at what you've done to me."

"Me? You did that to yourself," she hissed. "I told you to stop."

The front door swung open, and chaos erupted. Callie swung the closet door open and jumped out screaming "surprise" along with everyone else.

Confetti filled the air; laughter and noisemakers galore created a cacophony of high-pitched sounds. And Julian was nowhere to be found.

James stood in the doorway surrounded by friends and family, a stunned expression in his wide eyes. Maya stood by, beaming with satisfaction. Pam was already coordinating the efforts of trying to move the crowd into the backyard and out of her house.

Luckily, the crowd was large enough that no one noticed Callie standing off to the side by herself. She waited until after the gathering had moved out of the room. The closet door stood ajar, but she could still see the large, shadowed outline inside.

"Everyone's gone. You can come out now."

When she received no answer, she leaned into the closet. "Julian?" Callie felt an arm grab her around the waist and pull her inside; the door closed behind her.

"What do you think you are doing?" she whispered in the dark.

"Cashing in my IOU." Julian gently backed her up against the wall, his throbbing manhood pressing against the front of her blue jean shorts. "What are you doing to me, Callie?" he whispered against her skin. His mouth skimmed her orange tank top, seeking the shape of her. He was desperate for her, and it terrified him that he could need anyone so much. "I feel like I'm losing my mind."

Callie's heart sped up as she realized the extent of his desire. Julian had passed want and went straight into need. Callie threw her arms around his neck and returned the kiss. Julian needed no further encouragement.

He pressed her into the closet wall, needing to feel the whole of her form pressed against his. "You're like some witch who's cast a spell over me." He took her hand and rubbed it over his throbbing erection. "See what you do to me?"

Callie's topaz eyes sparkled mischievously in the dark room as she slowly slid down the length of his body to kneel before him. Julian felt his insides melting like butter when he realized her intent. He said a silent thank you and braced his arms against the wall, knowing it was the only way he would remain standing once she touched him. He closed his eyes as he felt the zipper slide down. Soon his painful erection was exposed to the air, and he sighed in relief. But that lasted only a moment. The feel of a small hand closing around his length sent him into another painful fit.

Callie slid her hand down the length of him, enjoying the feel of silk on steel that always amazed her. The thick rod thumped against her palm and jumped as she ran her fingers over each of the individual veins. Using her other hand, she cupped both testicles, gently squeezing until Julian was seeing stars.

"Callie." He swallowed hard. "Baby, please…" That's as far as he got. He felt himself being surrounded in heat. Julian fought the urge to pound the wall and instead cupped her head in his palm. Fighting the instinct to pull her closer; fighting the urge to take control of the situation.

Callie lapped and suckled with a slow precision that was no accident. She loved the feeling of power and control she had over this strong man when he was like this. It was a reality that she could bring him to this state, and only she could give him relief. It was a heady sensation, and she took her time and reveled in every drop of it. Slow, long strokes, at times taking the full length of him into her mouth, then at others barely touching him with just the tip of her tongue.

Julian felt his temples throbbing, felt the volcanic pressure building in the head of his penis and knew he could not wait another second. He grabbed her under her arms and lifted, turning her to face the wall.

"I wasn't finished," she teased.

Julian pulled a condom from the pocket of his linen slacks and donned it quickly, releasing the clasp on Callie's blue jean shorts and sliding them down her legs along with the bright orange panties that matched her orange T-shirt and bra. "If I hadn't stopped you, *I* would've been," he whispered close to her ear, sliding into her from behind.

Callie purred in satisfaction as Julian pulled back and pushed forward again and again. He paused, needing to bring her to where he was quickly, He reached around and found her moist opening with his fingers. He took her clitoris between his fingers, and when Callie's head fell back against his chest in surrender; he knew he'd reached his mark. He pulled back and pushed forward, again and again and again until he was absolutely certain they were there together, standing on the edge of heaven. Julian reached around to cover Callie's mouth as he drove home the final thrust, and she cried out against his palm in sweet ecstasy.

Callie stepped into the backyard feeling like a guilty child. She quickly scanned the crowd for any suspicious glimpses or questioning glances. All she saw were children running back and forth across the lawn with large balls and Frisbees; most of the adults were broken off into small sitting groups, talking and laughing, some holding pop and beer cans. A few grouped around the grill, waiting for their pick of ribs and burgers to finish cooking. She sighed in relief, deciding that everyone was too caught up in their own activities to notice her and Julian's absence.

Julian appeared by her side with a paper plate containing a few barbecue bones, dripping with sauce. "Here." Julian offered her one of the bones. "You've got to taste this. My mother's meat seasonings are out of this world."

Callie turned to look at his relaxed, smiling face. Apparently, Julian was feeling no remorse whatsoever about what they'd done in his parents' closet. He lifted the bone to Callie's lips, and she took a bite. He was right—the meat was delicious.

"Do you think anyone missed us?"

Julian hunched his shoulders. "What if they did?"

Callie tilted her head to the side. "Aren't you feeling even the slightest bit ashamed for missing your brother's surprise?"

"What? You think this is the first surprise birthday party he's ever had? Baby, James has been my brother for thirty-two years. Trust me, I've jumped out of more than my fair share of closets and other hiding spots." He shook his head. "No, there's no shame." His mustached mouth spread into a devilish smile. "Just satisfaction." He bent his head and pecked her lips quickly.

"Callie!" Pam called from the back-door entry. "Callie! Can you give me a hand here?"

Callie rushed to the door and took the large aluminum foil pan from the woman.

"Just place it on that picnic table over there." She waved her hand airily. "Anywhere is fine," Pam called over her shoulder, rushing back into the house for more.

Callie crossed the field and put the tray on the table, and she found herself temporarily distracted by the wonderful smell coming from the grill. "Ummm, what is that?" she asked James Sr., who was coming up beside her at the grill.

"Cedar," James boasted proudly. "I always grill my meat on cedar chips. Some people say it doesn't make a difference, but you'll see; it gives the meat more flavor."

"I can't wa—" That's as far as Callie got. James Sr. shoved a small piece of meat into her mouth. Her eyes widened in surprise as she struggled not to choke.

"See what I mean?" James was still smiling proudly.

Callie chewed until she could maneuver the meat in her mouth and then smiled in response. Smart enough not to open her mouth again, she gave him a thumbs-up.

"Between Pam's seasonings and my cedar chips, we could put Tony Roma's out of business if we wanted to."

Callie looked around the yard for Julian and found him standing with his brothers. The three handsome men together drew more than their fair share of attention. She surveyed the crowd of partygoers, taking in all the unfamiliar faces of

Julian's family and friends, many of whom she'd just met that afternoon. Just then, she realized someone was missing. "Where's Olivia?"

James Sr.'s smile faltered briefly. "She doesn't like crowds. Usually stays in her room when we have gatherings like this." He hunched his shoulders. "We've tried to draw her outside, but over time we've learned to just accept it."

That seemed so unfair, for her not to share in the festivities. To be up in her room all alone. Callie glanced up at the second-story window.

"Last Fourth of July, she and Julian got into a terrible battle right in front of all our friends and neighbors. After that we all decided to just leave the situation alone."

Callie glanced over her shoulder at Julian, wondering why he was out here having a good time when his daughter was inside, sad and alone and needing him.

Callie turned and stormed into the house. She had no control over Julian's behavior or that of his family. *But I'll be damned if I just let that child sit in her lonely room all day by herself.* She blew past Pam, who was so caught up in mixing her pasta salad, she never noticed the gust of wind at her back.

Callie climbed the stairs, two at a time, and did not stop until she was standing outside Olivia's room. She paused, trying to find the right words of encouragement. What did you say to a depressed teenager? She took a deep breath and prepared to knock, and that's when she heard the noise coming from inside the room—laughter and music.

Without knocking, Callie cracked the door and found Olivia and two other girls sitting in the middle of the bed. Olivia's long legs were crunched up as she bent over her knee, polishing her toenails in a bright red. The other two girls were still working on their fingernails with equally bright colors of orange and blue.

"Yeah, girl," one of the other girls spoke loudly, "I told him, if you are just going to believe whatever Shawntae tells you without so much as asking me if it's true, then fine, let Shawntae be your girlfriend."

"No better for him," Olivia said with a twisted mouth.

"That's what I said," the third girl concurred.

Callie stood in the door, gaping at the activity in the room. The television was blaring as Fantasia leaned forward into the screen singing "Be Free." Callie was so certain of what she would find that it took a minute for the actual truth of the situation to register on her brain. Olivia was not sitting alone and depressed in her room; she was having a party of her own.

All three girls noticed her at the same time. Olivia's face widened into a bright smile. "Hi, Callie." She turned back to her friends. "That's who I was telling you about."

"Oh," one of the girls said slowly. "That's your dad's girlfriend?"

"Um-hum." Olivia nodded.

"That's the mechanic?" the other said.

"She knows all about cars," Olivia said with a touch of pride. "She says that every woman should at the very least know how to change a tire. She says a woman should never have to depend on a man to take care of her."

Although Callie was flattered that Olivia felt her important enough to share her words with her friends, she found herself becoming annoyed by how easily they ignored her. They were speaking as if she was not there and could not answer for herself.

"Hello," Callie spoke up, and moved forward into the room, refusing to remain a ghost in the hall. "Olivia, aren't you going to introduce me to your friends?"

"Oh. This is Michelle." She pointed to the thin girl with rich, dark skin and a short fade sitting closest to her. She was the one with the boyfriend problems. "And that's Becca. Well, actually it's *Re*becca, but everyone calls her Becca." She gestured to a medium-brown-skinned chubby girl with a sweet, round face, her hair curled in ringlets that cascaded down her back. "They are my friends from Murray Wright. My old school."

Both girls had been taking the time to look Callie over from head to toe, and Callie was left wondering what else had been said about her.

"Nice to meet you," the girls said almost simultaneously.

"Well, I just wanted to say hello and see how you were doing." Callie turned her head and noticed the tray of burgers, chips, and drinks sitting on the dresser. Apparently, someone had taken the precaution of making sure the girls had plenty of food and drink to sustain them during their makeover party. *Nothing wears you out like polishing toenails*, Callie thought sarcastically.

She'd climbed the stairs prepared to do whatever it took to help her new friend and was feeling foolish realizing her friend didn't need her help. Her friend *had* friends. She should've known that Julian would never have abandoned his daughter to loneliness. And she silently scolded herself for not having more faith in him.

Olivia smiled and Callie felt instant justification, seeing the understanding in the girl's eyes. "I'm fine. Sometimes on the weekends, Daddy goes and gets my friends, and we spend the whole weekend getting caught up."

"It's rough being without my girl," Becca pouted. "The three of us used to be inseparable. Now all I have is Michelle."

"Hey!" Michelle said with a frown, feeling like three-week-old bologna.

"You know what I mean."

Michelle twisted her mouth playfully. "Yeah, I miss her, too."

Olivia smiled. "Group hug!"

The three friends fell forward in what was supposed to be a hug but turned into a heap of bodies. Their laughter was the last thing Callie heard as she pulled the door closed and found Julian leaning against the wall outside the bedroom door.

"I wondered where you disappeared to," he whispered. "When I realized where you were, I decided to wait out here. I avoid that nest of hens as much as possible." He hunched his shoulders. "When it comes to teenage girls, I'm basically a coward."

Callie crossed the short distance between them and reached up, wrapping her arms around his neck. She pressed her body against his and pried his lips apart with her tongue. She wormed her way into his mouth, tasting and exploring.

Julian took her hips between his hands and sat her back from him. "Please don't do this to me again."

Callie just laughed and turned to head down the stairs.

Julian grabbed her arm just as her foot touched the top stair. "Hey, what was that for anyway?"

She smiled sweetly. "For *not* living up to my expectations."

With that statement she began descending the stairs. Julian glanced back at his daughter's bedroom door, feeling confused. He shook his head and followed Callie back down the stairs.

Chapter 30

Paul DeLeroy had hated Callie Tyler from the moment he laid eyes on her. He knew, he just *knew* that she would be able to have the love his mother had never given to him. So cute in her pretty little girl clothes; he despised her. Just as he despised the baby his parents had brought into their home when he was four years old.

He could still see his mother and father cooing like idiots over every little thing she did. They'd even tried to draw him into the fun, encouraging him to hold his little sister. But he'd never liked her, not even a little. So it had been no great loss to him when three months later she was gone. Although the memories of that morning would haunt him forever.

He could still hear the ear-piercing screams when his mother went in to wake the baby for her feeding. By the time he reached the doorway, she was just a heap on the floor, clutching the baby to her chest and wailing to God.

His father was working midnights, and Paul felt he needed to step up and be the man of the house in his absence. But when he tried to approach her, she flailed at him, screaming like a madwoman. He scooted across the floor to a corner, trying to get as far from the lunatic as possible. He never again saw the woman his mother had been before then. And soon after, his father left as well. When the stress of his wife's depression and the memory of his infant daughter's lifeless body became too much, John DeLeroy began spending more and more nights away from home until finally he did not return at all. Four months after he left for the last time, Sarah received the divorce papers. She signed them without complaint. In less than a year, her entire life had caved in on itself.

And then she met Max and Callie Tyler, and some semblance of the woman he remembered returned. But by then, Paul was a man. In Max and Callie, his mother felt she'd been given a second chance. A second chance that Paul felt had come too late.

For that, Paul hated the Tylers, and as punishment, he did everything in his power to make Callie suffer after the death of their parents. Pampered little brat that she was, she never knew what hit her. Last he'd heard she was living with one of her cousins, that dress-wearing freak Max was always taking up for.

He now studied the two men on his front lawn, wondering how she had gone from devastating poverty to becoming a rich man's whore.

Julian was staring at the man with intense scrutiny, while Jonathan hung back taking in the surroundings. "Do we understand each other, Paul?"

Paul glared at the man. He was thinking about the loaded gun he had hidden right inside the door and calculating how long it would take to reach it. "Yeah, we understand each other. But this wasn't even necessary, man. I haven't seen Callie in years."

"Keep it that way," Julian said, and turned on his heels. Jonathan fell into step beside him.

Paul watched the two men climb into the little red Stingray and pull out of his driveway.

Ten minutes later on I-75, Julian felt his testosterone finally subsiding. He felt his fingers loosen their hold on the steering wheel and his heartbeat slowing down. His urge to kill was fading.

Sensing the change in him, his brother glanced in his direction. "You all right?"

"Yeah, I'm all right. Although, I'm not sure how much more I could've taken of him insulting her."

"You did the right thing. You sent your message, and that was all we went there to do. He understands what time of day it is," Jonathan said with a definitive shake of the head. "If you had attacked him on his lawn, we'd be dealing with the police right now."

"I still wish there was some way to get rid of him for good."

Jonathan laughed. "Not legally. Besides, we'd have to dispose of the body, and this is my best Sean Jean." He tugged at his leisure suit.

Julian felt the smile on his lips, and at that moment he was very happy to have brought his little brother. He only hoped their meeting had served its purpose.

"Hello?" Callie peeked her head around the door to Julian's office. "Anyone home?" Certain that the coast was clear, Callie crept around the door and crossed the room on silent feet. She sat the small bag from the lingerie store down in the middle of the desk and, turning, started back out of the room. Then, realizing she should leave a note explaining the unusual gift, she crossed back to the desk and picked up the pen and Post-it pad and scribbled:

Still disapprove of my taste in clothes? Happy anniversary, my love, and I'll see you tonight.

She smiled, remembering the tiny black negligee she'd picked up that afternoon while she was shopping for their six-month anniversary gift. She had planned to fix a small, romantic dinner, and when he arrived, answer the door wearing it. But later she decided leaving him with the gown and his own imagination for a few hours would be far better.

She started to add a footnote telling him what time to arrive for dinner, but the pen ran out of ink. Callie opened the top drawer and rummaged around but found no writing utensils. *What kind of accountant doesn't have a drawer full of pencils?*

She checked the other drawers and was about to give up when something in the bottom drawer caught her eye. She pulled the page out and realized that it was indeed *her* name she'd read across the top.

Lifting it out of the drawer, she quickly scanned the information and realized she was looking at the contract she'd signed at Northern First Bank. What would Julian be doing with a copy?

Her eyes widened as she took in the deep, blue ink of her signature and realized that what she was looking at was no copy—it was the original contract!

"What would Julian be doing with my contract?" she whispered, as if asking the question aloud would somehow make the answer clearer.

She glanced around the empty room, finding no signs that Julian would be returning soon. In fact, the reason she'd brought her surprise when she did was because of the message he'd left on her machine earlier saying that he would be out with clients until late afternoon. She folded the contract to take with her. She would confront him tonight.

Then another thought occurred to her. How easy could it be for a person to walk in and walk out of a secured bank with important legally binding documents?

No. Someone had to have given it to him, but who and why?

She was halfway to the door when it occurred to her that maybe she should take her gift back and leave no signs of her being there. At least until she found out what was going on. Her mind felt scrambled into a hundred tiny pieces, and her hands began to shake. *What is going on here? How could Julian have ever ended up with this document? Why would he want it?* She scooped up her small bag but forgot the note that had begun her search.

She left the house as quietly as she'd entered it, still completely baffled. Even as she drove across town to Northern First Bank, her mind was playing out every possible scenario and still came up with nothing. As she entered the bank and stood waiting in the office of the bank manager, still nothing.

By the time Fred Hart entered his office and noticed the angry woman standing in the middle of the room, Callie had already decided to say as little as possible. Hoping that if she did not show her lack of information, maybe the man would assume she knew more than she did and tell her something relevant.

"Ms. Tyler." Fred crossed the room. "Is something wrong?" he asked, hoping against hope that what he feared was wrong was not the case, but as the small packet of papers landed on the desk in front of him, he knew that hope was lost.

Looking up into the face of the woman, he froze in fear, realizing he'd been party to the manipulation of a person he knew very little about. With this legally binding document, the woman could make things very ugly for his struggling bank. She could sue and quite possibly win, and the bank's reputation would be ruined. What was he thinking allowing Julian to use his bank to play out his little games?

Fred hunched his shoulders. "I'm sorry, Ms. Tyler. Julian is an old friend, and he said he wanted to do this to help you. Since I couldn't actually give you a loan based on your current circumstances and he could, I didn't see what harm would be done. I considered it like a third-party loan. You'd get your money and he'd get to remain anonymous."

Callie sank down in the chair. She hadn't known what to expect when she arrived here today, but certainly this was not it. "Julian gave me the loan? Thirty grand of his own money?" Callie's eyes widened in amazement.

"Well…yes."

"How long? How long had he been planning to do this? *How* did he do this? How could he know which bank I would apply to? How much I would need?" Her mind was working frantically; she didn't really expect an answer, but Fred Hart answered anyway.

"He saw the application for the loan on your desk in your shop office. You have to understand; Julian and I have an old relationship. I daresay, we would not even be in business today if it had not been for him. I know firsthand, what he can do for a struggling business. I just wanted to help you."

"Julian's money. Thirty thousand dollars of Julian's money." Callie kept repeating the refrain as a song, hoping the words would sink into her malfunctioning brain. "*Julian's* money?" She covered her mouth in horror. "Oh my God, my garage! I used my garage as collateral!"

"He said he was doing it for you. Believe me, Ms. Tyler, if I thought for one moment that I could've given you the loan,

I would've. But I couldn't, and Julian was offering a winning situation for everyone."

"So I'm indebted to Julian Cruise?" Callie felt her knees go weak, even though she was already seated. "My collateral? My garage? It belongs to Julian?"

Fred Hart felt the knife cutting his heart. What had he done? "Technically. But I assure you he never intended to collect; that was not his goal. That was part of his explanation for why he wanted to be the one to give you the money. So, if you are ever unable to make your payments, the debt would be to him, not to an outside company."

Callie shook her head in confusion. This was too much information to assimilate at one time. "What have I done?"

Fred was frantically scratching at his ear. "Ms. Tyler, please...I don't think you understand. Julian was just trying to help you. He would never collect on your garage if you could not make the payments. *That's* why he wanted to do it this way."

Callie simply rose from the chair and, without another word, turned and walked out of the bank.

Fred began flipping through his Rolodex looking for Julian's cell phone number. When he found it, he dialed three times before finally getting it right, only to receive a recorded message that the caller was unavailable.

He sat down in his own chair, now as concerned as Callie. Julian never turned his cell phone off; he lived by it. What kind of mess had he gotten his bank involved in?

Julian was standing in his foyer, thumbing through his large stack of mail, when it occurred to him to turn his cellular phone back on. He'd wanted no interruptions during his conversation with Paul DeLeroy.

His mind was still racing with his recent confrontation. After dropping Jonathan off at home, he'd spent the remainder of his time in the car replaying the conversation. Still, he had no regret. Callie's safety was his only concern.

The *plat-plat* sound that he recognized as his flat-footed child walking barefoot on their wood floors became louder and louder until Olivia rounded a corner and appeared.

"Daddy! Daddy!" Olivia looked like a Callie clone in her green coveralls and backward baseball cap. Her brown eyes were lit with excitement, giving her face the look of a four-year-old, instead of the fourteen-year-old she was.

"Hello, sweetheart. How was your day?" He gave her a quick peck on the cheek and returned his attention to the stack of mail.

"You are never going to guess who's here!"

"Who would that be?" he mumbled, his attention fully focused on the letter in his hand. He tucked the letter back into the envelope and tore open the next.

"Hello, Julian."

Julian's head shot up as the voice registered on his brain. She stood before him in faded jeans and a white button-up shirt, clean and neatly pressed, looking a lot like the teenage girl he'd known so many years before. All except the tired eyes and hesitant smile—they revealed a woman who'd spent some time in hell.

"Rachel."

Chapter 31

Julian absently tossed the stack of mail onto a nearby table, moving farther into the foyer. "Rachel, what a surprise." Julian tried to hold a blank expression while his insides were warring between fear and stupefaction.

She smiled. And Julian was just amazed that she could. When last he'd seen her, she was barely coherent.

"I'm sure it is." She glanced at her daughter. "Olivia let me in. I hope you don't mind."

"No, no, not at all." He gestured to the living room. Rachel entered the larger room with Olivia close on her heels.

Olivia paused long enough to beam at her father. "Isn't this great, Daddy?"

Julian tried to curve his lips to form a small smile that he wasn't certain had appeared. Olivia's happy expression remained firmly in place, which meant she was none the wiser regarding his emotions in turmoil.

"Can I get you something to eat or drink?" he asked Rachel, not really knowing what else to say.

"No, I'm fine." She paused, seeming as lost for words as he. "But thanks for offering. She sat down on the couch, slid her hands over the leg of her blue jeans, and Julian realized she was as nervous as he was.

Somehow, that knowledge instantly put him at ease, and he was able to take the reins of the situation in his typical controlling manner.

Olivia was seated by her mother's side on the couch with her long legs pulled up to her chest, and Julian hesitated to speak in front of her. But he needed to know the truth of the matter; he needed to understand where he stood in all this. And he knew there was no chance of prying his daughter away from her mother's side.

He sat down in a large chair across from the sofa and leaned forward. "Please don't take this the wrong way, Rachel, but were you released or…did you walk out on the program?"

Rachel glanced down at her daughter by her side. apparently having the same hesitations as Julian. "I was released. I completed the entire program."

Julian did not miss the touch of pride in her voice, and he knew it was well deserved. Rachel would undoubtedly spend the rest of her life fighting this particular demon, and only God knew who'd win the battle in the end. But she'd taken the first step, the most important step. And for that she deserved her moment in the sun.

He sat back, hating to put her on the spot. "Now what?"

Rachel could see the unspoken question lurking in his dark eyes. "I've been out of the center for about a week, but I didn't want to come here until I had a job."

"You've found a job already?"

"Yes." She laughed. "I may be a junkie, but I'm a damn fine programmer." Her breath caught when she sensed her daughter tense up beside her. For one terrible moment, she'd forgotten Olivia's presence and had spoken freely. "I'm contracting with a company, at least until I can get on my feet again. Then I thought I would try to go it alone."

"Sounds like a plan," Julian said softly.

Rachel shifted on the couch until she was facing her daughter. "Livie, I found a place for us. It's just a small two bedroom, but it's nice; you'll like it."

Olivia smiled reassuringly. "I'm sure I will."

Julian felt his lips tightening and his temper flare. "So just like that you walk in here and take her away?"

Rachel's soft smile disappeared. "Julian, you knew this wasn't permanent."

"But I did expect some kind of warning. Not for you to just show up like this."

Olivia looked from one to the other, sensing the increasing tension in the room.

"Mama, guess what?" Olivia asked, trying to turn the tide of this conversation. "I can bust a tire in under five minutes." She beamed with pride.

"Bust a tire?" Rachel asked in confusion.

"You know," Olivia said in slight exasperation, as if this was such a common term anyone should know it, "when you get a flat tire, you take off the hubcap, the bolts, and remove it."

"Oh?" Rachel looked to Julian in confusion.

"Callie taught me."

"Who's Callie?" Her attention shifted back to her daughter before Julian could offer any type of explanation.

"Daddy's girlfriend. She's an auto mechanic. Cool, huh?"

"Very cool," Rachel said with one quick glance in Julian's direction.

Julian sat mesmerized, watching his daughter chatter on to her mother about his girlfriend as if it wasn't the slightest bit inappropriate. And when had she learned to bust a tire or anything else for that matter? How much time had she spent with Callie while living in his parents' house? He was going to have to talk with his tomboyish woman about the things she was teaching his daughter.

Rachel turned back to face Julian again and took a deep breath. "I appreciate everything you've done for Olivia—and me. But you knew when I went into rehab that I eventually planned to come back for her." She squeezed her daughter's hand. "She was my motivation...my guiding star."

Julian looked at the two hands, almost the same, securely entwined. This was where Olivia had received love for the first thirteen years of her life. This was the person who represented her true home. How could he even consider trying to keep them apart? He couldn't.

But, by that same token, how was he supposed to just let Rachel waltz in and take Olivia away from him, as if the past year had never happened? They were only now beginning to come to some kind of accord, find the father-and-daughter relationship that they both desperately wanted.

"I understand how you feel, Rachel. But I've waited fourteen years to have Olivia in my life. I'm not going to just let you take her away again."

"I'm not trying to take her out of her life. Just out of your home. She belongs with me; she always has."

"How do I—"

"I've got an idea." Olivia's soft voice interrupted the rising voices. She turned to her mother. "Mama, why don't you stay here with us for a while, just a few days? That way we can all be together. The house is more than big enough for the three of us." She looked to her father. Hopeful expectation shone from her eyes. "Right, Daddy?"

Julian glanced at Rachel, who looked as if she was holding her breath. "Right," he answered, wondering how wise a decision this was. How was he going to explain to Callie that he was shacking up with his baby's mama?

"Julian, really—" Rachel shook her head "—I couldn't ask you to inconvenience yourself like that.

"No inconvenience," he lied.

"See?" Olivia was grinning from ear to ear. "Now we can all get to know each other again."

Uh-oh.

Julian suddenly had a bad feeling in the pit of his stomach. Exactly what was his little girl thinking was going to happen here?

Olivia bounced up off the couch with enough exuberance for all three of them. "Come on, I want to show you my room." She took her mother's arm and pulled her up off the couch. "You can sleep in the room right next to mine." She led the way toward the stairs.

As Julian just watched them leave, Rachel glanced back over her shoulder just once, right before disappearing into the hallway. Julian had only caught a glimpse of her face but was certain her lips had silently formed the words "thank you."

Lady Luck had failed him once again, Paul thought, lying curled in a ball on the cold ground of a dark alleyway. The gang of men who stood by watching his death occur were completely silent in deference to their leader.

Silver circled the prone figure, prowling like a hungry cat

wondering where to strike the final blow. "I did some checking on you, Paul, and you know what I found?"

Paul lay quietly, certain this was a rhetorical question; but even if it wasn't, he was not feeling charitable enough to answer. He was too busy trying to breathe through his broken ribs.

"Apparently, a few years back, you were like a millionaire or something. Inherited a bunch of money from some dead relatives." This information was more for the crowd around them than for Paul.

"What happened, yo?" Silver chuckled evilly, and his cohorts joined in. "I understand." He shook his head sympathetically. "It's hard making ends meet on a few mill?" The crowd laughed again, and Paul closed his eyes, hoping death would take him over. It did not.

"Oh, well." Silver sighed, with exaggerated exasperation. "That was then and this is now, right?" Paul had been so quiet that Silver nudged him with his foot. Paul's painful groan was satisfaction enough that he was not talking to a dead man.

He came around to stand in front of the crumpled body. "I tell you what, Paul. Since it's my mother's birthday and I'm feeling generous, I'm going to give you one last chance to save your worthless life." Through the slit of his swollen eye, Paul watched Silver remove the clip and empty the gun. He shoved the clip back into the handle and squatted down beside Paul.

"There is only one bullet left in this gun." Silver pressed it to Paul's temple. "If you can give me one, just *one* reason why I shouldn't kill you before that bullet fires, you get to live."

Paul searched his frantic mind, but all thoughts were erased as the gun was fired next to his temple. Paul cracked his one good eye and realized he was still alive. But for how much longer?

"Paul, way to go!" Silver laughed. "You survived round

one, but without a reason, I will be forced to go to round two." He pressed the gun back against Paul's head.

"Wait," Paul whispered through his swollen lip. "I have something to offer you. It's worth more than what you loaned to me."

Silver leaned closer, his sterling-silver eyes twinkling with anticipation. "I'm listening."

Paul only hesitated for a moment before telling Silver everything he knew about the only piece of property he'd been unable to liquidate after the death of Max Tyler. The property in question had been placed in a trust as a gift to Max's only child.

Of course, Paul had to alter ownership of the garage to himself in the version of the story he offered to Silver. To ease his conscience, he told Silver that as far as he knew, no one presently inhabited the place. Then he worked hard to convince himself that he did not know for sure.

He let his scrambled mind consider for one moment what would happen to Callie if Silver found her there. Then he erased the image from his brain. He told himself that either way, someone had to die tonight, so why did it have to be him?

Meanwhile, Silver squatted by his side, considering this information and how best to utilize it. Finally, he stood and returned the gun to his hidden holster. "Congratulations, Paul, you just bought yourself a reprieve." He signaled to the men behind him, who came forward to lift the heap of pain-filled flesh and broken bones.

"My boys here are going to keep you company until I can check this out," Silver said, turning to his second in command. He laid out his plans and his orders, and his soldiers accepted their instructions without question.

* * *

Julian stood staring down at the empty desk drawer, his mind in a tailspin. *How did she find out? There was no way she could've known!*

He picked up the phone to call Fred Hart, knowing that would've been Callie's first stop. Just then, he heard arguing coming from the kitchen. He recognized the voices of the only other two residents in his home. Olivia and Rachel. Julian returned the cordless phone to its base and went to investigate.

"That's a lie! Stop lying to me, Mama." Olivia's brown eyes were sad and weary well beyond her years. "The lying has got to end now."

Rachel was shaking her head frantically and rubbing her hands together nervously. "No, sweetheart. You remember it wrong."

Olivia moved across the room closer to her mother. "Mama, it's okay." Olivia put her hands around her mother's shoulders. "I understand you couldn't help yourself, but please don't lie to me about it. I was there. I remember you selling my things—my bike, my jewelry. So don't tell me I'm remembering it wrong." She bent her head to look directly into her mother's eyes. "Just say you're sorry and let's move on from here."

Rachel noticed the movement near the door. When her eyes met Julian's, his heart broke.

What was going on here? He moved into the room.

Olivia completely ignored him, continuing to focus completely on her mother. "A friend of mine once told me that you can't blame a person for doing the best they know how. You were doing the best you knew how. I understand that. But don't lie to me about it and pretend it never happened!"

Julian froze, thinking that those words of wisdom sounded a lot like something Callie would say. In fact…

Rachel swung away from her daughter's embrace, still wringing her hands. "I…" She crossed the room to the window facing the pool area. Julian and Olivia waited. "I…it's just…"

That was all she managed to say before the dam broke. Rachel fell to her knees and wailed like a wounded tigress.

Olivia rushed across the room and closed her arms around her mother. "Shh," she cooed, and set their bodies to rocking gently. "It's okay, Mama. I forgive you. It's okay."

Julian still stood across the room, watching in wonder as the child comforted the parent. When had his little girl grown up? He considered how many times he'd heard the words "Callie said" and "Callie did" and "Callie thinks" over the past few weeks. And he wondered again just how much time they'd spent together while Olivia lived with his mother and father.

He considered the empty desk drawer in his office and the best way to move forward. He knew Callie would be angry. Julian huffed, realizing that was the understatement of the year. Actually, she would be furious and possibly want his head on a platter. But he was certain that once he could talk to her, he could convince her of the prudence of his actions. He just needed to find her. He'd tried calling the garage since his return earlier that day, but no one had answered.

He looked again to the two females curled in a human ball on his kitchen floor and decided that his inevitable confrontation with Callie would have to wait a day. Although his role in this reunion so far seemed to be only that of an outside observer, he felt he couldn't leave them to face this alone. Even if he did nothing but stand by the door with open arms for whomever may need them, he had to be here. For his new-found relationship with his daughter. For his past relationship with Rachel. He could not abandon them to this fight.

Then he could face his own ordeal, which took the form of a four-foot-eleven-inch, tawny-eyed elf.

Chapter 32

The attack came before dawn. All Callie remembered were hands covering her face and being flipped onto her stomach. Something tight was being wrapped around her wrist. She lay on her bed with a gag tied tightly around her mouth, struggling to hear the quiet conversation in the hall.

"He said the place would be empty! But instead I find two women sleeping soundly," a coarse voice whispered. "The SOB dies tonight!"

The other voice chuckled. "I got news for you, Silver. That second one is not a woman."

"What?"

"The one in the pajamas is, but the one in the negligee is a dude."

"Aww, hell." Silver sighed, not all that interested in the bit of information. Man or woman, he still had a decision to make. Paul DeLeroy told him he would find an empty garage.

He hadn't completely believed the man but was curious enough to check it out.

When he entered the empty garage, he'd thought it was too good to be true. The many tools that lined the walls, the expensive restoration equipment, a veritable treasure chest of potential wealth. And that was the problem.

Silver had not survived as long as he had without trusting his intuition. This was no abandoned garage. The place felt like someone's home, and when he'd crept up the back stairs, he'd discovered he was right.

Had he been thinking soundly, he would've ordered his men out and returned to deal with Paul DeLeroy, who he was sure was trying to set him up. But his greed had momentarily overridden his good sense and he'd ordered the two hostages bound and gagged.

Now he had to decide what to do with them. If he killed them, it was certain to be all over the newspapers and television the next day. "Business Owners Found Dead" or something like that. And the problem with the media was that they tended to draw more police interest than normal. Silver didn't need any more problems with the police. His inside man had recently been busted. He knew he was already on their radar.

He had two hostages, and he really wasn't sure what to do with them. He rubbed his forehead. "Bring them both into the living room," he said, and moved back into the front part of the apartment.

Soon, Callie's small form landed at his feet. She blinked once, flipping over onto her back to stare up at her captor.

Silver squatted down beside her bound-and-gagged figure, taking in her shapely body and golden skin. When he got closer, he noticed the large topaz-colored eyes glaring at him.

"Damn, you're fine," he whispered to the prone woman, and her deadly stare intensified. *If looks could kill*, Silver thought.

Soon, the other hostage was tossed onto the floor with a minimum of gentleness. Silver looked at the tall bald man clad in a white negligee, his eyes widening in amazement. Up until that moment, the hardened criminal had thought he'd seen it all.

"What the…" He looked to his lieutenant, and the other man shook his head in confusion. "What the hell are *you* supposed to be?" he asked Pooky, knowing the man could not answer with his mouth gagged.

"All right." He turned back to the three men who'd accompanied him. "This is what we are going to do…" He proceeded to lay out the plan he'd concocted in a matter of minutes, and his underlings were once again left in awe of the devious mind of their leader.

Standing just inside the sliding glass doors, Julian watched Rachel dangle her feet in the pool, and his mind wandered back over the years as he considered what could've been. This was the woman he'd once believed he would spend his future with. The mother of his only child. Now he couldn't imagine a life with anyone but Callie.

Growing up in the same neighborhood, going to school together, he'd felt he and Rachel knew each other as well as any two people could. That belief had been completely wiped away. Now all that was left was this stranger, and he realized for the sake of his daughter that he needed to get to know her.

He opened the doors and stepped out onto the patio. Rachel turned at the sound and offered a small smile. He came to stand beside her.

"What are you doing out here so early?" He gestured to where the sun was just clearing the horizon.

"I haven't been to sleep." She chuckled. "Olivia and I spent the whole night talking. She just fell asleep a little while ago."

Julian sat down beside her but folded his legs beneath his body to keep his feet dry. "Are you okay?"

She smiled again. "Better than ever." She glanced at his profile. "Julian, I want to thank you again for all you've done for both of us. I don't know what I would've done this past year without you."

"She's my daughter, too, Rachel." He looked down into the water. "I just wish…"

"I know," she said quietly. "I'm sorry for all the years I cheated you by hiding her away. First it was my family keeping me away, and then by the time I finished school and got out on my own, she was almost seven, so I thought…what's the point in opening old wounds now? I wasn't really sure how you would react. By the time I was ready for rehab, I was desperate. I felt I had no choice."

Julian reached over and squeezed her hand. "It's okay. What's done is done. We can't change that." He looked out across the expanse of deep blue water. "Let's just make the most of our second chance."

She nodded in agreement. After a while, Rachel looked at him with a confused expression. "I have the excuse of not having been to bed, but why are you up so early?"

His thick brows crinkled. "I don't know. I couldn't sleep. I tossed and turned all night. Ever have the feeling something is wrong, but you don't know what?"

She chuckled softly. "Oh, yes, I've had that feeling many times."

He hopped up from the poolside with ease and rubbed his hands together. "Well, since we're both up, I'll go make breakfast." He turned to leave and heard Rachel call his name.

"I've been thinking that maybe—" she gently kicked her feet in the water "—if it's okay with you, I think that Olivia should stay here with you for a while longer. You know, just until I'm…sure."

Julian bent over and kissed the top of her head. "You're both welcome here as long as you like."

"No, I'm leaving today. I've already spoken to Olivia about it. I think I need some time by myself." She lifted solemn eyes to his. "Living alone on the outside."

He nodded. "Okay, whatever you think is best."

She turned back to the water, and Julian stood staring down at her for a few moments, his mind racing in a thousand different directions before he finally turned and entered the house.

When Rachel entered the house a few minutes later, she found Julian standing over the stove with an solid egg suspended over a heated skillet. His eyes were on the skillet, but she could tell he was not seeing it.

"What's wrong?"

Startled out of his reverie, Julian turned at the sound of her voice. "I've got to run out for a while." He turned the skillet off and returned the egg to the carton.

"Is everything okay?" she asked as he hurried by her.

"I don't know," was his only answer as he rushed up the stairs to change clothes and race across town.

During the night, Julian had thought his sleeplessness had to do with Rachel's return, but Callie had also been heavy on his mind. Standing at the stove, he realized he'd never reached her the day before. He'd called several times, and neither she nor Pooky had answered the telephone. That situation in itself was unusual but not alarming; there were many different reasons why they might not have been available to answer the phone. But when combined with the dread that was creeping into his heart, he knew it was more than coincidence.

Pooky looked at Callie, who was still bound and gagged on the floor. He was standing on the other side of the room, just inside the living room, with a gun still trained on his head by one of the henchmen. But at least he'd been given a temporary reprieve from the restraints.

Silver turned at the sound of them returning. "That's more like it." He shook his head in approval of the blue jeans and button-up shirt Pooky had been forced to don. Apparently, a man dressed in a negligee was too much for his criminal mind to handle.

Pooky only pursed his lips in annoyance and glanced back at Callie, wondering if there was any way he could convince their captor to release her from her bonds. The problem fixed itself.

Silver squatted down beside Callie's slumped form again. "Okay, pretty girl, I'm going to take the ropes and gag off you…don't make me regret it." He began untying the restraints.

Callie's eyes met Pooky's, and he silently signaled her to behave. He knew his cousin's temper and feared where it would take them. When they'd been so abruptly awakened, Pooky had heard one of the underling's call to their leader, "Silver."

Pooky had heard of the criminal but was almost certain Callie had not. Quite frankly, given what he'd been told about the man, he was amazed they were still alive. But if Callie let her ferocious fire get the better of her brain, this could end very quickly.

Callie heeded the warning, realizing she was dealing with an unknown factor. She had no idea what these men wanted. Whether this was a random robbery or if they had something far more insidious planned. For all she knew, they could've just landed in the wrong place. Until she had the answer to that question, she knew she could not risk any action that would further jeopardize Pooky or herself. The way that Silver kept leering at her, Callie knew she was already in enough danger as it was.

The knock on the downstairs door surprised them all.

Silver's icy gaze swung from Callie to Pooky and back. "Who is that?"

"How would I know? I'm up here with you." Pooky's flippant remark earned him a punch in the side.

Callie gasped as she watched her cousin bend forward. "It's probably a customer," she added quickly, mostly to distract Silver's attention from Pooky. The look in his eyes was akin to a tiger tasting blood, and she feared he'd want more. "We start very early."

"Go answer it." Silver gestured toward the front entrance.

Callie rose to leave.

"No, wait." Silver stopped her, and she knew something in her demeanor gave her away. Maybe too much eagerness in her rising or hope in her eyes. Whatever the reason, he no longer trusted her to answer the door.

"You." He gestured to Pooky. "Answer the door and send them away. If you try anything, I'll kill her." His gun was pointed directly at Callie's head.

Pooky had regained his composure and moved forward with his armed shadow right behind him. He took the moment to glance back at Callie, wondering how safe it was to leave her alone with these men. He, too, had seen the sultry looks Silver had been giving her off and on. Then deciding he had little choice, he turned and headed down the stairs, hoping against hope that who ever was at the door would save them.

The knocking came again, and Pooky picked up his pace, fearing their savior would give up and leave. He cracked the pedestrian entrance and felt his heart soar when he realized who it was. This was not a man who gave up or went away easily. This was a bulldog.

"Morning, Julian." Pooky had to force himself not to look back over his shoulder, although he tried to gesture with his eyes to the man standing behind him. He was depending on Julian's intelligence, his unique ability to assimilate information quickly.

Julian took in the blue jeans and shirt, realizing in all the time he'd known him, he'd never once seen Pooky in men's clothes. He saw the worried look in Pooky's eyes and knew the anxiety that had only increased on the ride over was grounded in reality. Something was very, very wrong here.

"Hey, Pooky, is Callie here?" Julian tried to keep his voice neutral, his questions simple. He needed to gather information.

"No," Pooky said without inflection. "She spent the night at her man's house."

"Oh." Julian took a deep breath. His sweet love was in more danger than he realized. He had to get inside. "I was supposed to pick up some parts she ordered for me. She probably left them on the counter. Can I just grab them?"

Pooky felt the gun dig into his side. "Uh, no, your parts haven't come in yet, but I'll tell Callie you stopped by. Okay? Bye now." He slammed the door shut in Julian's face, knowing his life and Callie's was now in very capable hands. His only fear was that Julian wouldn't act quickly enough.

As he returned to the upstairs apartment, he struggled to hide the encouraged light he knew Silver would see reflected in his eyes. The man saw way too much.

"Who was it?" Silver asked as the pair returned.

"Just a customer." Pooky took a seat beside Callie on the couch.

One of those three words triggered something in Silver's sharp mind. "What did they want?"

Pooky realized he would have to be very careful with his answer. He looked to Callie; he needed her help to convince this criminal that nothing out of the ordinary had happened downstairs. "Julian came by to pick up those parts you ordered for him."

As smooth as silk, Callie's mouth twisted in frustration. "That man! I *told* him those wouldn't be in until next week."

"You know how pushy he can be sometimes," Pooky said with a shake of his head.

Callie successfully hid the smile that almost formed on her lips. "Yeah, I know."

Silver watched the exchange with a keen eye and accepted the answer. He turned to his lieutenant and gave his instructions for the next phase of their plan.

Chapter 33

With every roll of the Corvette's tires, Julian felt his heart sink a little further. But he had to drive away. Whoever was inside the garage holding Callie and Pooky would expect him to drive away.

He turned the corner and pulled to the side. He needed to think. His first instinct was the same as anyone's: to pick up his cellular phone and dial 911. But what if the patrol cars showed up with sirens blaring and deafening bullhorns ready to storm the place? Callie and Pooky could be killed just to make a point.

No, that would never do. He didn't know who was in the building, why they were there, or what they wanted. All he knew for certain was that Callie and Pooky were there against their will.

He needed stealth. He needed cunning. He needed SWAT. But how to make sure his call was routed to that department of the police force and not relegated to a lesser division?

When he got right down to it, he didn't really have positive knowledge of a crime being committed. What was he going to say? *My girlfriend's cross-dressing cousin answered the door in men's clothes and seemed a bit nervous.* Julian knew he would be laughed out of the building.

His mind searched and searched for anything useful, and it finally came to him. Julian had discovered early on in his career that the thing about saving people from financial devastation was that they tended to be exceedingly grateful. Not only them, but the people who would've been affected by their financial woes. People like spouses.

A few years ago, Julian had pulled a small architectural firm called Hirsch Development out of the clutches of impending bankruptcy. Peter Hirsch had been one of those exceedingly grateful people, and so had his wife, Police Chief Candice Hirsch.

He picked up his phone and quickly obtained the correct phone number from information. As he dialed the number, he said a silent prayer that Candice Hirsch would remember what he'd done for her family and would still be suitably grateful.

She did. She was. His prayer was answered.

"You want me to what?" Callie was staring up at the gang lord as if he was completely insane. To her way of thinking, he was. "I'm not signing that," she huffed loudly and with an arrogance that completely defied the gun pointed at her chest.

"I think you will." Silver sneered and leaned forward to whisper in her ear, "Baby, you don't know how bad I want to get with you. *Not* signing this will be all the excuse I need." His silver eyes were practically sparkling with a perverted combination of lust and anger. "Sign the papers and I'll have my boys escort you and your freak out of the building unharmed. *Don't* sign the papers—" he smiled evilly "—and it will be my pleasure to change your mind."

Callie was fighting to hold her temper in check, knowing it would only end in her death or Pooky's. But what he was asking was impossible. He actually expected her to sign over ownership of the garage to him, neat and tidy. Then pack her stuff and walk away from the only legacy she had left from her father.

She glanced at Pooky and instantly regretted that move. Silver's sharp eyes honed in on the deep emotion she let show for only a second. But it was one second too long.

He grabbed Pooky by the collar and hauled him to his feet. Even though he was the shorter man, Silver's strong arms closed around Pooky's neck like a vise. He pressed the gun to his temple. "On the count of ten, sign or I'll blow his freaking head off!"

Callie felt the shaking start in her feet and come up through her body like a tidal wave, until she was shaking uncontrollably. Her temper erupted like an inferno, and she launched herself across the room at the man holding her dearest friend like a bag of potatoes.

"Let him go!" She felt herself get swept up by a pair of strong arms and held back. She kicked and scratched but it got her nowhere. The man holding her was the equivalent of three of her. When sanity returned and she realized what she'd done, she could only hope Silver didn't kill Pooky just for spite, knowing he was fully capable of it.

"One." he pressed the gun harder, and Pooky flinched. "Two."

"Okay," Callie surrendered in defeat.

Ten years ago, when Callie came to learn of the stipulation in her father's will that gave the garage to her when she turned eighteen, she thought of it as a miracle. Having lost so much, she would have one small part of him to hold on to.

The garage had come to symbolize renewed hope in her life, and she loved it dearly. But she loved Pooky more.

"All right, I'll sign."

During the whole interaction, Pooky had been silent. But the hurt, defeated look that passed through his eyes in that instant spoke volumes to Callie. He expected her to hold out. He knew how important the garage was to her and fully accepted dying in exchange for it. Callie realized that until that moment, he had no idea how much he meant to her.

Bahh-dummp, bump

Everyone froze in place and looked at one another.

"What was that?" one of the henchmen called to no one in particular.

Silver's stony gaze locked on Callie, then went to the ceiling, then to Pooky. He pressed the gun even harder against the side of Pooky's head. "Who was at the door, yo?! And don't give me that crap about a customer!"

"I told you! It was just a customer!" Pooky pleaded.

Silver pushed the man away from him. "Watch them!" He gestured to one of his men, then signaled for his lieutenant to follow him out of the room.

Callie and Pooky both fought the urge to share a knowing look. They were being too closely watched. But they had a fairly good idea of who was on the roof of the garage. If not the man himself, then certainly someone working on his behalf. In other words, help was on the way.

The prone figure clad in the black that made it so easy for him to disappear lay still as a stone in the shadow of the rooftop fan. He heard the footsteps on the stairwell leading to the roof and knew he would have company soon.

He silently cursed, realizing that this visit was the result of that blunder earlier when he first landed on the roof. He'd pulled his slight weight up by his arms and thrown his form over the edge of the roof in his usual manner, but for some reason he'd lost his footing. He'd slipped. A small miscalculation that could cost him his life.

The door leading to the rooftop creaked open but no form appeared. The man in black continued to lie still. He'd been trained to lie that way for hours if necessary.

A man appeared on the roof, his small pistol shifting in every direction. The man was young, thuggish…and from the way he swaggered forward, arrogant. This was the man who needed to be removed first. He was obviously the leader.

Soon another man appeared, a little less confident; his main priority was protecting the first man. The figure in black felt assured the first man was his target.

The second man spoke first. "Silver, there's no one up here; probably just a squirrel or something. Come on, man, let's just get this over with."

The first man's light eyes scanned the entire rooftop. "What do you think of that little honey with the braids?" he asked without ever turning to face the other.

"She all right," the second man said with little interest.

Something about his tone told the man in black he was lying. Apparently, the man with the light eyes heard it as well. He turned to look at his partner with a disbelieving look.

The second man chuckled. "Okay, she's fine as hell, and we both know it. You keeping her?"

The man with the light eyes returned his attention to scanning the rooftop. "I'm thinking about it." Seemingly satisfied, he turned and gestured to the other. "Let's go."

The man in black lay still another five minutes after their departure, having too much experience to fall for that trap.

Within three minutes, the door swung open, and the one called Silver reappeared, took one confident look around, then turned and headed back down the stairs.

"Man, you're getting paranoid in your old age," the man in black heard the partner say with a laugh.

"My paranoia is why I've made it this long," the other said.

Then both their voices and footsteps faded into nothing. The man in black had recognized the name Silver immediately. Most of the department had some knowledge of him. Vice, narcotics, homicide. Silver was an equal-opportunity criminal who dabbled in a little of everything.

The man in black slithered along the rooftop. This particular criminal had been a menace to society for far too long. As best he knew, the young man was approximately twenty-five, and in his business, that did indeed qualify as a long life. Too long. It was time for his reign to end.

Crouching like a small black leopard, the man in black cracked the rooftop door open, went through, and silently closed it behind him. He'd managed to gain entry to the building, and no one was the wiser. He felt his adrenaline pounding in his veins as he moved down the stairwell into the main apartment.

He moved along the walls like a wraith until he came to the voices. He looked behind him and saw his backup slinking through the shadows. Together the two men moved forward until they were right outside the room where the prisoners were being held. Both were confident others from their department were closing in from the opposite direction.

Silver was pacing the room, trying to decide what to do next. He didn't care what his best friend and partner in crime said. That was no squirrel on the roof.

"Okay, both of you on your feet." He came across to stand

in front of their hostages. He stared from one to the other, considering, deciding.

Callie dared to speak. "You said once I signed those papers giving you the garage you'd let us go." Her eyes narrowed. "I should've known not to trust you."

Silver smiled. "Tell you what. Get your friend there—" he gestured to Pooky "—to tell me who was at the door earlier and maybe I'll keep my promise. Otherwise, I'll just have to pop you both."

Silver was the only one who heard the cracking of the floor, but even that small warning came too late.

Before he could give the order to have the noise inspected, the room was flooded with SWAT team members. Callie remembered someone grabbing her by the neck and pushing her down on the floor.

"Stay down," came the muffled voice. She felt the man pressing his body protectively over her while positioning himself to fire his rifle over her back. She only hoped someone was doing the same for Pooky.

Gunfire ricocheted off the walls, and she briefly worried what her small apartment would look like when all was said and done. She wondered if she would survive this. She sent a mental message to Julian hoping he could sense her love, know how much she truly cared.

After what seemed an eternity, the firing stopped. The room was suddenly so quiet, Callie's first thought was that she and the man over her were the only survivors. But that did not last. Another eruption exploded shortly after. Others rushed into the room to subdue the surviving gangsters. And behind that second wave of cops came the face she needed to see the most.

Julian rushed across the room and scooped her up. Even

before he kissed her, his large hands ran over every inch of her body assuring she was safe and whole.

"I'm fine, really." She laughed for no other reason than that she was alive and in his arms. Then he kissed her with more passion than she'd ever imagined. The kiss told her so much of what he was feeling, and she tried to answer it with her own passion-filled response. When Julian was forced to release her to breathe, Callie took the time to face her greatest fear.

She turned and searched for Pooky. Her eyes scanned the carnage and what she found horrified her. Two lifeless bodies—neither of which was Silver—were lying on the floor covered in feathers from the sofa and chairs. Tables were overturned; the glass case containing Pooky's figurines was lying on its side with the glass completely shattered. Their walls were Swiss cheese.

Silver and his lieutenant had somehow survived the fray and were being hauled out of the room by two officers. That's when she saw him standing outside the door. Pooky had one hand on his narrow hip, the other flaying through the air as he ranted and raved about punitive damages and lawsuits. She even heard Julian's name being tossed about like some kind of secret weapon. Callie smiled. Even in men's clothes, the queen reigned. Feeling much relief, she returned to the safety of Julian's arms.

"I can't believe the police acted so fast," she said against his chest.

"By the time I called, they already knew about it."

"How?"

"Paul. I guess he had second thoughts about what he'd done. He went to the police and confessed everything. Of course, they took him into custody."

In some fit of guilt and remorse Paul had confessed everything about his shady loan and everything he knew about Silver, which made Julian's efforts that much easier. The police had already been made aware of the situation before he'd ever made his call to the chief. But it was his insistent involvement that forced them to act sooner in a situation where time was of the essence.

"Oh," was all she could manage in her present traumatized state. The full weight of the incident was finally coming down on her.

"Are you going to press charges against him?" Julian asked.

Callie sighed with what sounded like years of relief being lifted from her shoulders. "No. What would be the point of that?"

"Well…he did try to have you killed," Julian stated the most obvious reason and wondered if he would have the fortitude to be so forgiving if he were the victim of such a scheme.

"The way I see it, there is nothing the law can do to Paul that is worse than what he does to himself. I never really understood what his problem was with me, but I'm certain it started long before he met me." She snuggled closer to Julian. "I really hope he can find peace one day." *The kind of peace I've found with you.*

Julian placed a gentle kiss on the top of her head and contented himself with just the pleasure of holding her.

Later that night, when they snuggled in for the night, Julian was still holding her tight. He remembered something very important, a conversation he'd had with himself in the car while he waited for the SWAT team to arrive.

"Callie, I'm sorry about the loan incident, but I was just trying to help you. Please understand that."

Callie curled against his side and nodded against his chest. "I know, Julian."

"And I'm sorry I found Paul, even though I said I wouldn't. That was a lie no matter how you slice it, but once again, I was just trying to protect you."

She yawned sleepily. "I know, Julian."

"I'm sorry about the clothes thing as well…and the school thing." He paused. "Did I forget anything?"

She was quiet for a moment in thought. "Nope, that pretty much covers it."

He squeezed her tighter. "Okay. Well, I'm sorry for it all, and I will do everything in my power to make it up to you in the future."

She turned and let his large body spoon around hers. "I know, Julian." She kissed the arm that held her tight.

They lay together in the dark, listening to the night sounds.

"Thanks for letting Pooky stay here until he can find a place," Callie whispered, on the verge of sleep.

"What else would I do?" Julian said quietly. "He's family." Julian sat up on one elbow to look down at her face. "Why are you being so understanding about the loan thing? I thought you would be furious, and the fact that you are not, well…it makes me nervous."

She laughed softly in the night. "Why would I be? Everything you've done, all those things that so annoy me, were done out of love for me. You were listening to your heart—" she touched his face "—and its promise to love and protect me. That's *your* heart promise, Julian. Just as it is mine to you." She lifted her lips to his, and Julian accepted the offering and ended it there. After the day she'd had, he was determined she would get some sleep tonight. Even if it killed him.

Although he still wasn't absolutely certain he understood the whole heart promise thing, he was just happy she accepted his actions for what they were. Tokens of his love.

He pulled her back against him and spooned her body once more and waited to hear the soft sounds of her snoring before allowing himself to drift away.

Chapter 34

"No, no, and no!" Julian stormed across the parquet floor of his foyer heading for the front door with Callie close on his heels.

"But, Julian, listen to reason. Think of the cost savings?" She tried to appeal to his base accounting instinct with no luck.

"I don't care about the cost; spend whatever you like. If you want Pooky to make all the gowns, fine, I'm willing to pay him whatever he wants." His dark eyes flashed. "Since you're only marrying *once,* feel free to go all out. I don't care about the cost, but Pooky is not marching in my wedding as your maid of honor."

He was on the front porch before he realized he did not have his keys. He turned and stormed back into the house. Callie, who apparently knew he did not have his keys, was waiting just inside the door.

"But, Julian, you said you would leave all the decisions regarding the wedding up to me."

That decision was the very reason he was looking for his keys. He'd made that decision in the heat of passion, and after careful consideration realized his mistake. That reality was brought home when Callie began describing her ideal wedding, and Julian was left with the clear image of his business friends and Callie's queens mixing and mingling in the dimly lit White Elephant Club.

He had a two o'clock appointment with a wedding planner. It was time to bring in a professional.

Julian went from tabletop to tabletop looking for the chain of keys and assorted attachments. "That was before I knew you wanted RuPaul in the procession." He stopped abruptly and felt Callie's slight form bump into him. "Where are my damn keys?" He looked in every direction.

"Daddy, Daddy, look!" Olivia came bounding around the corner in a buttercup-yellow gown that perfectly accented her olive skin. "Look at what Pooky made for me!" She spun in a circle; her enthusiasm revealed just how much child was left in this almost-woman.

Julian paused in his ranting to look at this child of his heart, who was so beautiful; he could clearly see the woman she would become and was incredibly grateful that he would now have a chance to see her become that woman.

Rachel came by often, but by mutual consent, Olivia was still residing with him. Julian had seen and recognized the determined light in Rachel's eyes and knew eventually she would be well enough to take her daughter back to the life she was working so hard to create for them. But for now, he was just thankful that he was allowed to experience moments like this.

"Oh, Olivia, that's beautiful." Callie moved forward to touch the gown. She bent forward to examine the intricate detailing around the bottom of the gown, and Julian had to force his eyes away from the tempting sight of her rounded hips and golden thighs being displayed like an offering to the gods. If he spent too much time looking at that, he would forget why he was angry. No, he decided, she'd tricked him like that too many times before.

"You're beautiful, sweetheart," Julian answered his daughter's pleading eyes. "It's perfect."

Satisfied, Olivia disappeared back around the corner into the small guest room that had temporarily become Pooky's bridal shop.

Callie turned her attention back to him and picked up the argument. "Julian, you know there is no one closer to me than Pooky. I don't understand why this is such an issue."

"You know how I feel—" Julian broke off at the sound of laughter coming out of the guest room. Laughter that was not his daughter's or Pooky's.

It almost sounded like…

He moved around the corner and stopped dead in his tracks to find his mother standing atop the pedestal in the middle of the room. When had she arrived?

Pooky was on his knees, pinning the hemline for future sewing. "Well, not really," Pooky was answering some unknown question his mother had asked before he heard them. "But I have been thinking about getting the surgery done. You know, make it official."

"Really?" Pam Cruise answered with genuine interest. "But that's so permanent."

Pooky sat back on his haunches. "Yes, but isn't that the point?"

Julian gripped the doorjamb and braced his body in the entryway, realizing that what he was witnessing was his mild-mannered mother discussing a sex-change operation with Callie's cross-dressing cousin. Not only was she openly discussing this, but apparently she saw nothing wrong with the idea. And when had she decided to let Pooky design her gown?

His conservative mother had completely accepted Callie and all her strange baggage into their lives. The elf was stealing his allies one by one. How was he going to keep any sense of order in his life after they wed if everyone he knew and loved sided with Callie?

Olivia smiled from her seat across the room. "Isn't she pretty, Daddy?" she asked, gesturing to her grandmother's lavender gown. Buttercup and lavender were the colors that Callie had chosen, although Julian strongly suspected Pooky had a say in it.

His mother looked every bit the elegant matriarch she was, standing atop the pedestal in the formal lavender gown with matching jacket. She was beautiful, as always.

"You look great, Mom," Julian said from the entrance. "Has anyone seen my keys?"

Olivia frowned in concentration. "Last I saw them, Callie had them."

Julian's mouth twisted in frustration. No wonder she was so insistent—she knew she had a captive audience. He turned and realized she'd disappeared from behind him.

He was on his way in search of her when he heard his front door opening. *Why don't these people knock?* he thought, watching his two brothers and his father step through the door.

"The cavalry has arrived," James Sr. said, stepping around his sons. He was immediately aware of all the activity in the normally quiet house. "What's going on here?"

"Gown fittings," Julian answered with his arms folded across his chest.

"Uh, yeah, that's kind of why we're here," Jonathan said, smiling.

"We were told to come collect you around twelve and take you for your tuxedo fitting." James Jr. looked at his watch. It was almost 2:00 P.M. "Sorry we're late."

Julian's eyes narrowed. "Told by who?"

The three men looked at one another.

Julian turned in a complete circle. "Callie!"

He went raging through the house. Julian was determined to put his foot down once and for all. He needed to let this woman know at the beginning that he was not going to be one of those punk husbands who were managed and manipulated by their wives. She might be the family mechanic, but he still wore the pants.

Realizing they had failed in their mission, the three men slunk back out the door. James Sr. was very glad his wife never knew he was there.

Julian finally found Callie a few minutes later in his bedroom. He quietly entered and closed the door behind him, clicking the lock in place. He leaned against the door, letting his eyes feast on the ravishing vision before him.

"You like it?" Callie was on her knees in the middle of the bed, dressed in the little black negligee she'd originally bought for their six-month anniversary. Four months later, Julian was seeing it for the first time.

Julian slowly crossed the room and reached for her. "How can I not?" He wrapped his long arm around her waist and pulled her forward, and she went eagerly into his arms.

Pushing her back onto the bed, Julian came down on top of her. His mouth covered hers, and Callie opened her mouth beneath his and welcomed his warm tongue, savoring the rich taste of this man she loved and remembering how close she'd come to losing him. The memory was too scary to focus on for long. As if in response, her body instinctively wrapped around him; her legs came around his waist, and her arms pulled him tighter to her.

Holding her cradled in the palms of his large hands like a precious treasure, he let his lips explore, outlining her jaw bone in tender kisses, erotically flicking his tongue behind her ear. He tasted her with the expertise of a lover who knew his partner well. And in reward for this knowledge, her body opened to his like a flower seeking the sun.

A thought occurred to him. He lifted his head, just enough to look down into her hungry eyes. "This changes nothing. Pooky will *not* be your maid of honor, and that's final." Enough said, he returned his attention to the spot just beneath her chin. And on cue, she began to purr like a contented kitten, and he knew she was ready.

She looked over her head, and Julian followed her eyes. "There's your keys," she whispered seductively, already knowing his response.

"That's okay. I don't need them anymore." Julian reached down between their bodies and found her moist opening. Gently he inserted a finger inside her warm, welcoming body to confirm his suspicions. She was ready and waiting for him. His. Now and forever. He sat up long enough to find a condom in his bedside drawer and remove his clothing.

Callie realized he was more eager than she thought and began pulling the thin straps of the negligee down to remove it when Julian's hand came and closed around one of her small breasts. "No," he whispered, "leave it."

Callie smiled and settled back into her position beneath him, deciding there was no place she would rather be.

He parted her thighs and paused to take in the woman laid

out before him. He thought of how different his life was before her, how different it would be with her. Just goes to show,
you never know what life has in store for you until you open
your heart to the possibilities. Like a drag queen marching in
your wedding, for instance. Julian sighed with resignation. He
moved his body forward, pushing into the warm haven of love
and acceptance, and his breath escaped him again. But this
time it was the sigh of a man satisfied with the life fate had
chosen for him.

Elaine Overton currently resides in the Detroit area where she was raised. She attended a local business college before entering the military and serving in the Gulf War. Currently she is working as an administrative assistant for an automotive industry supplier and is an active member of Romance Writers of America.

She enjoys reading, movies, board games, and traveling. She is the proud mother of one son. Her first novel, *Love's Inferno*, was given four and a half stars by *Romantic Times Magazine*, as was her second novel, *Déjà Vu*.